FORCED
Vacation

The Organization-Book Three
M.K. MANSON

One Night Publishing

FORCED VACATION
Copyright 2024 M.K. Manson

The characters and events portrayed in this book are fictitious. Any similarity to real person, living or dead, or events is coincidental and not intended by the author.

ISBN: 979-8-9993141-4-7
LCCN: 2025921347

Edited by: Editing4Indies
Proofread by: Karen at Barren Acres Editing
Formatted by: Bravia Books
Cover photo by: Ellen Christy Intimate Portraits
Cover Model: Sarah Jones
Cover Design by: Frank Manson and Ellen Christy Intimate Portraits

Printed in the United States of America

Trigger Warnings

Murder
Kidnapping
Incest
Alcohol Abuse
Drug Abuse
Childhood Trauma
Torture
Sensation Play

To all the badass bitches out there who would love to be a cold-hearted killing machine, this one's for you.

Chapter 1
Sasha

"You wanted to see me, Boss?" I ask, letting myself into his office.

"Yeah, have a seat." I sit across from him, ready to take notes. "You don't need to take any notes. I just want to talk to you."

"What about?" I ask, putting down my pen.

"Remember when I took over The Organization and told everyone they'd get a week of paid vacation?"

"Yeah."

"You've organized everyone else's time off, but you never took yours."

"Well, I, um…" I stammer.

"I want you to take it now."

"Now?"

"Yes, now."

"But I don't want to take a vacation," I say a little too loudly. I know better than to raise my voice to my Don. I lower my head in respect.

"Everyone needs time to get away and decompress, and that includes you, Sasha. Get the hell out of here."

"But what the fuck am I supposed to do for an entire week? I've never been on a vacation before."

"Go to the mountains, hike, and camp, or go to the beach, lie in the sun, and read a good book. I. Don't. Care. I don't want to see your face in this office for a whole week."

I open my mouth to argue, but he cuts me off.

"Got it?" His tone is loud and firm.

"Got it," I concede.

I'm sitting behind my desk when the boss's wife, Lola, arrives.

"Hi, Sasha, is Ethan ready for our doctor's appointment?" Lola is seven months pregnant with their second child and is starting to do that waddling thing.

"I think so," I say on a sigh.

"What's wrong?"

"Your *husband* is making me go on vacation." I point my thumb over my shoulder toward his door.

"Making you?" She chuckles.

"Yeah. He says everyone gets a week's vacation, and it's time for me to take mine." I toss my pen on the desk and fold my arms over my chest.

"Why's that so bad? You know most people would give their left nut for a week's vacation, right?" Her voice almost sounds amused at my distress.

"First of all, where the hell am I supposed to go?" I throw my hands in the air.

"I can think of a lot of places I would like to go."

"Second, who am I going to go with?"

"You don't have to go with anyone. Man, what I would give to have a week all to myself. Go to the beach, read a smutty book, sleep." She swoons.

"Third, where would I even go?"

"There's a resort I know in the Caribbean. I can make a call and see if they have a room available." She's bouncing on her heels, waiting for my answer.

"Whatever," I grumble in defeat.

"Listen, I know you don't want to go, but why not turn it into a game?"

"What do you mean, a game?"

"For one week, go to a new place and be someone else. I know you adopt different personas when you *take care of business*. Creating a new identity might make your vacation more fun. And think of all the people you could mess with along the way."

"I'll think about it." My mind floods with thoughts of who I could become for a week.

"Go meet some new people and have some good sex," she says with a wink.

"Lola!"

"Ah, come on. You'll never see them again. Who cares?"

"You make it sound so simple."

"It is simple. Just go relax and have some fun."

"Okay, you've convinced me. Can I have the resort information?"

"I'll text you after my OB appointment. Start packing for the beach," she shouts excitedly, throwing up her arm.

I came to work for The Martinelli Organization a few years ago. Rocco Ethan Martinelli found me overdosing in an alley, and he saved me. He offered me the chance to get clean, and if I put in the work, he would train me to be an assassin. He believed in me when no one else did. I owe him my life.

After my yearlong training was complete, I was planted in his father's office as a spy. My assignment was to keep my eyes open and report back to Ethan about what Antonio was up to. In turn, I would be the one to get to take him out when Ethan gave the word.

Antonio Martinelli was an evil man. He was an expert in manipulation and dealmaking. He did everything he could to pull Ethan into a life of crime, but Ethan didn't want any part of it. He graduated from college and built his reputation as a savvy businessman at the Brandish-Martinelli advertising firm. He stayed away from Antonio for as long as he could.

When Antonio kidnapped his girlfriend, Lola, and threatened to end her life if she didn't leave Ethan, his world fell apart. He gave up his dreams of a normal life and became the person he never wanted to be, all the while planning to take down his father.

When his plan was almost in place, a brother he didn't know had emerged from the shadows and changed everything. Eliseo DeLuca came from Italy to take revenge on his biological father, Antonio Martinelli. He was determined to destroy him for deserting his mother and leaving him a bastard to be raised by an abusive stepfather. Ethan didn't stand in his way.

Of course, I was disappointed because I didn't get to take care of Antonio. Still, Ethan rectified the situation by sending me to take out Eliseo, but not before he signed over all of his holdings to Ethan.

Ethan inherited all of Antonio's and DeLuca's holdings and became the new Don Supreme of The Martinelli Organization.

Ethan sold all of DeLuca's assets to the Mafioso in Italy. He married Lola and cleaned house. He divided everything into legal and illegal businesses.

Antonio was a dictator, but Ethan runs The Organization more like a business. He provides health insurance and rewards good work with a week of paid vacation every year. He shows his men respect, and in return, he expects their unwavering loyalty. He has the final say whenever necessary. He was the enforcer for his father, so he knows how to inflict pain in some of the most horrific ways. Don't ever cross him, or you *will* regret it.

Freddy Acosta runs all the illegal businesses. He's an enormous mountain of a man. Back in the day, he started as a bouncer for The Organization. He's the oldest in the group at the ripe old age of thirty-four. He's a fair man, but he can be a real grump sometimes.

In addition to my work for The Organization as Ethan's personal assistant and assassin, my services can be purchased for the right price. My specialty is taking down men who hurt their women.

My identity has remained a secret because I assume a different persona for each kill. I might be dressed as a whore or a prim and proper schoolteacher. I'm a chameleon who changes my colors to blend in with my surroundings. I don't play around when I'm on a mission. Jerry, my trainer, taught me to conduct thorough research and anticipate all aspects of the job. No one even knows Sasha "The Assassin" exists outside my inner circle.

After work, I go shopping. I buy a suitcase, clothes, make-up, bathing suits, purses, and shoes. As I shop, I'm building the character I want to play in my head. Gone for one week are the black clothes and dark makeup I hide behind as Sasha "The Assassin," the business suits and pumps of Sasha "The Professional," and enter sweet, flirtatious, Sasha "The Vacationer." I take all my purchases home and throw them on the bed. My phone lights up with a call from Lola.

"Hey, Lola. So where am I headed?"

"The Grand Cayman Islands."

"Just the name sounds fancy." *Bougie, more like it.*

"I think you'll love it. Listen, I talked to Ethan, and we agreed we're going to pay for your plane ticket and your room."

"You don't have to do that." I shake my head, even though she can't see me.

"Yes, we do. You've given so much to The Organization and to the shelter, and we want to treat you."

The Organization is where I work Monday through Friday for Ethan. The shelter is Lola's baby. She left her career as a high-powered advertising executive to create the Johnsonville Battered Women's Shelter. They help women in abusive relationships who need a safe place to stay. They help them rebuild their confidence and equip them with the knowledge and skills needed to stand on their own two feet again, without a man. I help whenever my *special* skills are required.

Taking care of business is a nice way of saying *killing people*, if you haven't figured that out by now. I help the women at the shelter eliminate their abusers, but any woman in the city can request my services.

"I don't know," I hesitate.

"Well, I *do* know, and we're paying. Bennie will bring all the trip details when he picks you up at eight in the morning. Make sure you have your passport and have a great time," she singsongs and hangs up the phone before I can say another word.

⁓

I get up early and begin my day as the new, *softer* Sasha. I'm not normally the frou-frou type. I would rather go to the gun range than a tea party any day. I've picked this softer version of Sasha because she's way out of my comfort zone, and I've always wondered how the other half lives.

My long black locks fall in soft waves over my shoulders, and my makeup features soft shades of pink. I feel naked without my black eyeliner and thick mascara. I'm wearing a comfortable dress for the long trip. It's white with pink and red flowers covering it. Straw wedges finish the ensemble. It's cute and fun. *Cute and fun. Who the hell talks like that?* I lock my guns away in my gun safe, and now I really feel naked.

I pull my rolling bag out to the curb and climb into the back of the Escalade. With Bennie behind the wheel, I settle in for the hour-long drive to the airport. Let the forced vacation begin.

Chapter 2
Sasha

I arrive in plenty of time to check in and make my way through security. I flirt with the security officer at the metal detectors and giggle when he searches me. But I wanted to throat punch him for laying his hands on me. *This sweet Sasha is so weak.*

I board the plane and find I'm seated in first class. I get comfortable just before a glass of champagne is thrust into my hand. I could get used to this. I went to rehab for drug addiction. Cocaine was my drug of choice.

I sat through hours and hours of group and private sessions to work through my mommy and daddy issues. I rarely drink anymore, but when in Rome, as they say.

I've been on a plane before, but I had a job to do. I wasn't thinking about taking off and cruising at forty thousand feet. I was thinking about getting the boss's papers signed and killing five men.

I'm not even sure how Lola got me on these flights because the boarding agent said they've been booked for months. Never underestimate the power of a Mafia wife.

When I'm all settled in, watching the crew load bags onto

the conveyor belt into the belly of the plane, I feel the seat beside me dip. Their clean cedar and citrus scent floods my senses, and I turn to look to see who I'll be spending the next hour or so with.

He looks tall, at least six feet. He has wide shoulders, but it's hard to tell what kind of physique is hiding under that dark blue suit of his. His dark hair is styled with an undercut but there are long waves on the top. His face is freshly shaven. I can't evaluate him any further until I see his eyes.

"Hi." I smile sweetly.

He says a quick hi back but doesn't look up from his work. *Don't worry, buddy, I don't want to talk to you any more than you want to talk to me.* His head is buried deep in his computer, and he's tap, tap, tapping away. I reach into my bag under the seat, pull out the romance novel Lola gave me months ago to read, and settle back for the flight instructions.

The flight attendants close the door and give their little speeches while the engines rev up. It's not very long before the attendant comes to our row. I hand her my glass, and she tells Grumpy Guy to stow his computer away for takeoff. I raise my eyes and peer over my book as a disgusted sigh comes from the man.

"When can I turn it back on?" he asks.

"The captain will announce when you can use your electronic devices again," she answers saccharin sweet. He shoots back his champagne in one gulp and hands her the glass. Then he puts his computer in his backpack and scoots it underneath the seat in front of him. He sits back with his arms crossed over his chest, leans his head back, and closes his eyes.

The plane taxis, and the captain announces we're next in line for takeoff. I put my book in my lap and look out the window as the plane begins to barrel down the runway.

My heart begins to thump, and I start to feel queasy. The thought of hurtling down the concrete runway in a tin can is causing me to panic. My hands clamp down on the armrests, and I lean my head back and close my eyes.

"First time flying?" Grumpy Guy asks. Is he talking to me?

Right now? He's decided *this* was the best time to talk to me. I turn my head and stare at him.

"What?"

"Is this your first time on an airplane?"

"Uh. Yes, first-time flier here." I give him a weak smile. It's a lie. But this guy will never know that.

"It'll get better the more you fly. Landing, now that's a whole other experience."

"Great." My voice is filled with sarcasm.

"Take some deep breaths and here, take this." He holds out a piece of gum to me. I know I'm looking at him like he just grew a second head, but I release the death grip on the armrest and take the gum.

"Thank you," I say, before popping it into my mouth. I close my eyes and concentrate on the cool wintergreen taste. After a few minutes, I realize the plane has leveled off, and I'm feeling much better. I go back to reading my book. Lola said it was a romcom, but this book is so *not* a romcom. It's a smutty dark romance, and it's just starting to get good.

A ding goes off in the cabin, and I guess it's the go signal for Grumpy Guy to finally get back on his computer. He digs it back out of his bag, and in a split second, he has his nose stuck in it once again. *Good grief, can he type any louder?*

I look over the top of my book at him and roll my eyes. Glad this is a short flight, or I might have to snap his neck. The flight attendant comes back around for drink orders and asks me if I would like more champagne.

"Do you have anything else?" I ask.

"Of course. What would you like?"

"A Coke, please."

"Of course. And for you, sir?"

He points a finger at me, never lifting his eyes from the computer, and replies, "I'll have what she's having." I smile and duck my head back into my book.

We begin our descent into Chicago O'Hare, and he was right, landing is a whole new experience. I feel like I'm on a roller coaster, and we're plummeting to the ground. *Well, that's what my brain thinks anyway.* When we do a little bank to the left, I think I'm going to be sick. I move to grab the armrests again, but this time, Grumpy Guy's hand is there.

My hand clamps down on his, and I squeal with a jump.

"Oh my God, I'm so sorry."

"It's okay. No problem," he says, just as we land with a thud, and I grab his whole arm instead.

"Oh my gosh, I wasn't expecting that," I chirp.

"Yeah, sometimes landings can be kinda rough. Other times, it's just a little bump. All depends on who the pilot is, I guess."

"Do you fly a lot?"

"I travel for work, occasionally."

"This trip might be my last," I say under my breath.

The plane taxis to our concourse, and they open the door. Grumpy Guy stands, takes his bag from the overhead bin, and exits the plane. Gee, I thought he might be a gentleman and take my bag down for me, but I guess not. I retrieve my bag from the overhead bin and head out to find the gate for my next flight.

I ride on a train, almost get run over by a beeping go-cart, and have to walk a mile to get to my gate. When I reach it, the board shows *Delayed*. Dammit. I speak to the attendant behind the desk and find out the flight has been delayed two hours. *Two hours.* What the hell do you do at an airport for two hours?

I roam all around, stopping when I come across a little bookstore and buy some gum for my next flight. I wander around some expensive-as-hell shops, but I'm bored as fuck. I try to read my book, but I can't concentrate on the characters fucking in the middle of the noisy airport, so I decide to find something to eat. There's a restaurant just a short walk from my gate, so I belly up to the bar.

"What can I get you, hun?" an older redhead asks. Her name tag reads Sue. She has a nasal quality to her voice.

"Coke or Pepsi, please." She brings my drink, and I turn around to people watch.

"Flight delayed?" Sue asks.

"Yeah, two hours."

"Can I get you something to eat while you wait?"

"That would be great. Can I get a burger and fries?"

"Sure can. I'll put the order in for ya. It'll be just a few minutes." She walks into the back, and ten minutes later, she's setting a plate in front of me. "Here you go, hun," she says.

"I love your accent. Are you from here?"

"Born and raised right here in Chicago."

"Thank you."

I scoot my plate closer and take in the huge burger with thick-cut fries. I lift the burger to my mouth, about to take a bite of the greasy goodness, when I hear a familiar grumpy voice from over my shoulder.

"I guess you're stranded too." I swivel my stool to see Grumpy Guy, suitcase in hand, standing behind me. This is the first time I've seen him head-on and Oh. My. God. What a cool drink of water. He's taller than I thought. He must be six foot four. He has muscles for days bursting from his dark suit. His big blue eyes hide behind tortoiseshell-rimmed glasses, and nothing can compare to the clueless look on his face.

"Yeah, I am."

"Can I sit?" He points at the stool beside me.

"Free country," I reply uninterested, and turn back around to my food. He parks his rolling bag between our barstools and tucks his backpack safely on the floor between his feet. I haven't decided whether he's clueless or just a jerk.

He leans over and steals one of my fries. And that would be a jerk.

Chapter 3
Sasha

I want to stick my fingers down his throat and get my french fry back. I get Sue's attention.

"Sue, this gentleman would like to order some food of his own, please," I deadpan, staring at Grumpy Guy.

"What'll it be, bub?"

"Yeah, I'll have what she's having." *Doesn't he ever say anything else? Really? Be a little more original.* Pulling my plate away from the french fry stealer's reach, I proceed to eat *my* food.

"You on a delay too?" he asks.

"Yes. Are you?"

"Yeah. Where are you headed?"

"I'd rather not say. You know, a single female traveling alone and all," I say, waving my hand around.

"Aw, come on. We shared a row in first class together. We're practically friends. You can tell me where you're headed." I just stare at him over my burger. "What are the odds we're going to the same place, anyway?"

"Fine," I let out an exasperated breath. "I'm going to the Grand Cayman Islands."

"Oh," he says more to himself than me, and turns his head away.

"Where are you headed?" There's a long pause.

Quietly, he mumbles, "The Grand Cayman Islands."

You've gotta be shittin' me!

"That's great." My voice lilts with what sounds like glee. *This good-girl shit is hard.*

Sue brings his food, and we sit in silence while we eat.

When he's almost done, he assures gently, "I'm not a stalker... really, I'm not."

"It's okay." I smile awkwardly. *I could snap that pretty neck of yours if I wanted to.*

When he's finished with his food, he pulls that damn laptop out of his backpack and places it on the bar.

"Is that all you do?" I snap.

"What?"

"Type on that thing. Is that all you do?"

"I have work to do," he argues.

"It's just annoying."

"The computer?"

"No. All the tap, tap, tapping you do on it. It's loud and distracting." I make tapping gestures with my fingers and roll my eyes.

"Uh. I'm sorry. Am I annoying you?"

His aggravated tone tells me it's time for me to make my exit.

"No, I'm sorry. I shouldn't have said anything. Just forget it," I say, gathering up my things.

"Where are you going?"

"I'm going to go wait at the gate. See ya around."

I don't see Grumpy Guy again. Not that I'm looking for his tight mountainous body in the crowd, but I don't see him anywhere. *Stop it, he's annoying.*

Sasha "The Assassin" would've fucked his brains out in the lavatory just for fun. But sweet Sasha "The Vacationer" is more polite and demure and would never be caught doing something so risky. The flight attendants begin to load the plane. I scan my boarding pass from my watch and enter the jetway.

I'm greeted by an all-too-perky woman who shows me to my seat in first class and asks me for my drink order. This time, I just go with a bottle of water. I dig deep into my bag for my smutty book and settle into my seat for the flight to Miami.

I don't fucking believe it. Here comes Grumpy Guy. I put my head down. *Don't sit by me. Don't sit by me... Son of a bitch.* He's sitting by me.

"You're kidding me, right?" I hiss.

"What are the odds?" He laughs. His eyes are wide, and he smiles the same crooked smile.

"Not high enough, obviously," I mutter under my breath and turn to look out the window. He puts his rolling bag in the overhead compartment and sits. Same routine as last time. He taps away on his laptop until they tell him to stow it.

I'm prepared for takeoff this time. I pop my gum in my mouth, lean my head back, close my eyes, and try to take deep breaths. When the plane levels out and I open my eyes, he speaks, "See, I told you it would get better the more times you fly."

"Yeah, it wasn't too bad that time."

He drags out his computer when the captain gives the all clear and proceeds to tap away for an hour until the flight attendant brings around snacks and drinks. He takes a break from tapping for sustenance.

"You know, we've been together most of the day, and I don't even know your name."

"It's... Sandra... Sandra Jones. What's yours?" I ask.

"Joe Johnson," he replies, holding out his hand to shake.

"It's nice to meet you, Joe Johnson. Are you traveling to the Grand Caymans for business or pleasure?"

"Business first and then pleasure, if it doesn't kill me."

"I know, right? My boss is *making* me go on vacation. I would rather be sitting at my desk where I'm comfortable, instead of riding in a petri dish full of germs on my way to a vacation I didn't even want to go on in the first place."

"I know what you mean. I have one meeting, and then I'll have to stay for the rest of the week since there's only one flight back to the States left. So my boss says, 'Take some time. Enjoy the sunshine,'" he mimics in a funny voice that makes me laugh.

"So you're being forced to have fun too?"

"Yep. Maybe we can have dinner or do something together while we're there? You know, since we're both being forced to have fun," he suggests.

"Maybe," I say coyly. *Do I want to spend time with the annoying tapper?*

Chapter 4
Joe

This woman sitting beside me is beautiful, but she's not really my type. She seems so soft and dainty, dressed all frilly and proper. I'm used to a good, strong woman. One who can take care of herself. I don't have time for a woman anyway. I have business to take care of on this trip. *If I'm not interested, then why can't I stop sneaking peeks at her legs?*

Her toenails are painted with a soft pink polish that matches her fingernails. Her ankles are round and smooth, and they lead the way to her toned, tanned calves. *Oh my God, I need to stop.* I can't get involved with a woman when I'm on assignment.

"I'm so sorry to bother you, but I need to use the ladies' room," she says, touching my arm.

"Oh, yeah, sure," I stammer like an idiot.

I stand, let her out, and sit back down. I watch as her tight ass sways, making her skirt swish back and forth, almost putting me in a trance. It makes me think about touching every inch of her skin beneath that dress. Kissing my way up those tanned legs of hers, all the way to her...

My thoughts are caught off guard as she exits the bathroom and walks back toward me, and I really get to look at her for the first time. She has the most magnificent doe eyes and soft creamy skin. Her long jet-black hair falls in waves over her shoulders and past her tits. I imagine how good it would feel wrapped around my fist while I fuck her. Those soft pink lips of hers would look incredible sucking my cock too. *Oh my God, I need to stop this shit.* I didn't come here to hook up. I came here to do my job.

Standing, I let her back into her seat.

"Thank you," she says sweetly.

"Sure," I reply, trying my hardest not to stare at said lips.

The rest of the flight I keep my head down and get my research done. I don't know what I would do if this plane didn't have Wi-Fi. When we touch down, I grab my bag from the overhead bin and take off down the jetway, leaving Miss Fancy Pants behind. I have a ship to catch.

Chapter 5
Sasha

I hated lying to Grumpy Guy, I mean Joe, about my name, but I never tell strangers my real name. It's all part of keeping myself safe.

I grab my rolling bag and take off through the Miami Airport, looking for my flight to the Caymans. I had just enough time to get to the gate and board. I take my seat and get organized. I'm a little sad I haven't seen Joe board the plane yet. I thought we were going to the same place, but I must've misunderstood.

An older lady sits beside me. Her name is Mona. She's on her way to visit her son's family for a vacation. She's crocheting an afghan for her granddaughter's new baby boy. The baby will be here any day now, so she's a woman on a mission to get it done. Thankfully, we don't talk for long. I put my earbuds in, listen to a meditation I saved on my phone, and try to think about something other than the french fry stealer.

⌣

I was hoping to see the crystal-blue water when we arrived, but the darkness from the flight delay made it look black. The plane lands with an easy bump this time, and I make my way to the podium for a taxi.

The hotel porter shows me to my room. It's the most beautiful room I've ever seen. It has a seaside view, with a wraparound balcony, a king-sized bed, and a small living room space and kitchenette. The air coming in off the sea is warm, and there's just enough breeze to move the sheer curtains around. The smell of the salt water is fresh and clean.

I put my things away, take a hot shower, and sit on the balcony. Maybe this won't be so bad after all. I send Lola a text.

I made it.

LOLA
How was the trip?

There was a two-hour delay, but it's all good.

Meet anyone interesting?

There was this grumpy guy on the planes.

Planes. More than one?

Yeah, it was the weirdest thing. We sat beside each other on two planes.

Yeah, weird. Was he good-looking?

I guess.

He was delicious, but I'm not telling her that.

You'll find someone.

I'm not looking for someone.

Just one fling won't hurt anything

If you say so. Thank you for the trip.

You don't have to thank me. You deserve it.

No one's ever done something like this for me. Well, other than Ethan saving my life.

Just promise me you'll try to relax and have some fun.

I promise. Night.

I settle into my bed. My big, lonely bed. The warm breeze falls all around me, lulling me into a good night's sleep, I hope.

Chapter 6
Joe

The name on my passport is John Miller. I board the cruise ship and find my room on deck four. I'm in a small interior room. I don't need much space because I won't be here that long. I step inside and lock the door behind me, put my bags on the bed, and go to the bathroom.

I sit down on the floor in front of the sink cabinet. I open the door, reach my hand up into the top of the cabinet, and remove the Glock 26 that was taped there for me. It's a good gun for a job like this. The recoil is small, and it fires accurately. It holds ten rounds, but I'll only need one. I check the weapon, put the safety on, lay it on the bed, and go take a shower.

After a good night's sleep, I take advantage of the breakfast buffet, spend some time reading my book, and get a little sun by the pool. It's time to get back into character and take care of some business.

I put on navy dress pants and a gray collared button-down, put the fake tortoise shell glasses back on, and brush my hair back neatly. I store the gun away in the room safe and head to deck eleven for dinner.

First, I get a drink in my hand to blend in with everyone

else and try to make myself look at home. I don't drink on the job, but it's all part of the act. I casually wander around the expansive dining area searching for my mark.

I spot him sitting with an older woman. Milo Watson owes my boss a shit ton of money, but here he is on a cruise ship having the time of his life. He's no doubt on the hunt for a sugar momma to pay his bills. I watch him shmooze the woman he's sitting beside, and I decide it's time to join them. I slide down the dinner buffet and fill my plate. Then I wander around like I need a place to sit.

"Good evening. Is this seat taken?" I ask, pointing at the one across from the couple.

"No, no. Sit, sit," the lady says with a big smile and Southern drawl. "My name is Miriam, and this is my new friend Milo. What's your name?"

"John Miller." I reach out and shake Milo's hand.

"Nice to meet you, John," she coos.

"You too Miriam," I say with a nod.

"We were just talking about the excursions we signed up to take tomorrow. Are you going to take any on this trip, John?" she asks.

"I'm not sure yet." I smile.

"We're going snorkeling and paddleboarding in the morning. Oh! We could all go together. That would be so much fun," she chirps and claps her hands.

We eat dinner and make small talk. *Where are you from? What do you do? Yada yada.* When we're finished eating, I push my seat back to leave.

"Oh no, you're not leaving already, are you, John? The evening is just getting started," Miriam whines.

"Yeah, I'm beat. It was a long day of traveling," I say as I put my napkin on the table. "Maybe I'll see you both tomorrow at the beach. What are your room numbers, so I can ring you?"

"I'm in 1202," Milo says as his hand shoots up into the air, and I can tell he's tipsy already.

"I'm in 1220." She beams at Milo. "We're right down the

hall from each other." She gives him a little wink. And that's my cue to exit. Older people's sex doesn't do it for me.

"It was nice meeting you," I say. Miriam jumps up, rounds the table, and swallows me up in a hug.

"I'm from the South. We hug, honey." She pulls me in and hugs me like we've known each other for years. "Have a restful sleep, sweetie."

I take her by the shoulders and gently remove her from my space. "You too, Miriam."

I walk past Milo's room, and in one swift movement, I place a tiny camera on the door across the hall and keep walking. I need to be able to tell when he's back in his room. I make my way through the maze of elevators and stairwells to my room on deck four. I stretch across my tiny bed and use the app to keep an eye on the camera.

Around three in the morning, a drunken Miriam and Milo bounce into view of the camera. He's three sheets to the wind and can barely stand. I watch as she leans him against the wall beside his door and digs into his pocket for his key card. She slides it in the slot for a green light, and they stumble inside, closing the door behind them. Dammit. I wanted to take care of this before dawn.

Two minutes later, Miriam exits the room. She leans her head back on the door and lets out an obvious deep breath, rolls her eyes, and turns left toward her room.

Showtime.

I rumple my clothes, mess my hair, and rub my hands over my face. I screw the silencer onto my weapon, tuck it into the back of my pants under my untucked shirt, and exit my room, heading for 1202.

I turn to the right and around the corner stands just the person I'm looking for, a steward. He's helping a young couple with directions to their cabin. I approach them, and when he's done, he turns to me.

"Yes, sir. How can I help you?"

"I'm so embarrassed," I slur, acting drunk off my ass. "I've locked myself out of my room, and I was hoping you could help me."

"Of course, sir. Which room is it?"

"It's that one." I point down the hall to Milo's door. The steward takes out a passkey and slides it into the slot. The green light comes on, and I push the door open slightly with my elbow, careful not to touch it with my hands.

"Thank you so much. My wife would *kill* me if she knew how much I had to drink," I whisper as if there's a real woman in the room sleeping.

"I completely understand, sir. Have a great night," he says as he walks on down the hall.

I push the door open with my foot, just enough to get inside, and it clicks closed. The room is dark. The only light is from the moon shining through a crack in the curtains. I allow my eyes to adjust while I pull on my gloves. Cautiously, I approach the bed.

Milo is passed out face down. I waste no time taking care of business. I place a pillow over his head, point the gun, and shoot.

Bang!

He knows what he did. He doesn't have to be awake for me to explain it to him. I exit and grab the tiny camera off the wall, and head back down to my room.

The ship docks at six, a few hours later. The first passengers begin disembarking for the day's excursions at seven. I wear khaki shorts, an island shirt, hiking boots, and haul my backpack over my shoulder. I look like any other tourist getting off the ship for a hike. The only difference is that I keep on walking the fifteen miles to my resort on the other side of the island.

Five hours later, I check in at the main desk and retrieve my luggage. I sent it ahead by messenger from the airport. I finally fall into bed for a much-needed rest.

Chapter 7
Sasha

The first full day of my forced vacation is spent lying in bed until nine. I haven't done that in years. When you live on the streets, you can't sleep for very long at a time because someone could steal you blind or kill you. After Ethan took me in and I got off the drugs, I learned how important it was to take better care of myself—how to eat right and take care of my mind and body.

I also discovered how difficult it was to relax enough to fall into a deep sleep. Initially, I could only manage a few hours of sleep each night. When I did get to sleep, it was full of nightmares. Now that I've gotten my life together, sleep comes much easier. I only have an occasional nightmare, and it's usually because something or someone triggers it.

I guess the exhaustion of traveling and the tranquility of this room helped me relax. I run my hand over the untouched side of the white duvet and wonder if I'll ever find someone to share my bed with. I roll onto my back and inhale deeply. I point my toes and stretch my arms up over my head, and get ready to start the day.

The warm Caribbean air smells clean and fresh as I stand in

the doorway to the balcony. The crystal blue-green waters are breathtaking. The scene is almost magical.

I order room service and begin my yoga routine. Yoga has helped me to center my mind and body. I sit cross-legged on the patio, stretching as the sounds of the water calm my thoughts. I move into salute to the sun, child's pose, and cat-cow to warm up my muscles. Continuing with warrior one and two, I complete extended side angle and triangle pose, before there's a knock on my door, and it's time to eat.

When I'm done with breakfast, I put on my yellow bikini and head to my cabana on the beach. I spend most of the day watching people paddleboard, parasail, and ride Jet Skis, and I read more of my dirty book. I decide I couldn't come to the Caymans and not put my toe in the water, so I finally wander to the water's edge. The water is so warm I can't resist wading in farther. It's like bathwater—soothing and relaxing. I bop around for a while before heading back to my room for a shower. My first day on the island was relaxing and calm.

∽

Day two played out pretty much like day one did. Over-sleeping, yoga, breakfast, beach time, reading, and a nap. Yeah, it was relaxing, but I can't believe some people come to the beach to just lie around and do nothing. I might die of boredom before it's time to leave. Tonight, I decide to have dinner at the on-site restaurant.

∽

I look in the mirror and swish the skirt of my baby-blue dress. The scalloped neckline highlights my sun-kissed skin, and I finish the ensemble with white sandals. My hair is pulled back in a soft braid. I take one last look at the innocent traveler, and I'm off to the restaurant.

I'm informed there's an hour wait, so I take a seat at the bar.

"Fancy meeting you here," that familiar grumpy voice says.

You've got to be fucking kidding me.

"Are you stalking me?" I say snidely, not bothering to turn to look at him.

"I saw you come in. You can sit with me if you'd like."

"Thanks. But no thanks." Why won't this guy get the hint?

"Really? I'd love the company." His voice is sincere but I'm not falling for his games.

"Don't you have a computer to go tap on?"

"I already took care of my business. I'm just killing time until the plane can take me the hell out of here."

"Oh, so you want to *use* me to kill time?" I snap and turn around to look at him. "No thanks."

"C'mon. Give me a chance." He reaches his hand out to me. He looks like a lost puppy standing there with his windswept hair and those ocean blue eyes. *One dinner can't hurt anything, can it?*

"Only because I'm starving, and I don't want to wait an hour for a table." I take his hand, and he helps me down off the stool.

I let him guide me through the restaurant to a table in the middle of the room. He holds the chair out for me, and I sit.

"Thank you," I say sweetly. *All this goodie-goodie shit is getting on my nerves. I can pull out my own damn chair.*

"Here, you can use my menu. I know what I'm ordering."

"Thanks." I hold the menu up in front of my face and ask, "What are you going to order?"

"The cowgirl ribeye." I snicker behind the menu.

"What's so funny?"

"*Cowgirl* ribeye," I say, lowering the menu and laughing out loud.

"I like Cowgirl..." When the words slip past his lips, he realizes what he just said, and he laughs too. We're trying to stifle our laughter when the server comes to take our order.

I'm fanning myself as I go back to looking at the menu. I'll be damned if I'll eat a salad to look all cute. I'm starving, so I'm gonna eat. The server motions for me to give my order first.

"I think I'm going to have the beef sirloin with lobster and asparagus."

"Very nice choice, and to drink?" she asks.

"Cabernet Sauvignon and a Coke on the side, please." Joe lifts an eyebrow at me, considering what I just said. She turns to him for his order.

"I'll have the cowgirl ribeye with herb butter, carrots, and mashed potatoes."

"And to drink?"

"I'll have what the lady's having." *He's such a copycat.* I raise my brow at him.

"I'll be back shortly with your drink order."

"You looked at me like I was nuts, and then you turned around and ordered the same thing. I don't get you."

"I just thought, if you think it's good, maybe I should try it. I'm always up for trying new things."

"Oh." Not sure if that was a compliment.

"What do you do for a living?" he asks.

"I'm a personal assistant."

"Where?"

"Outside of Johnsonville." *That's all you're getting from me, buddy boy.* "What do you do?"

"I'm in finance. In New York," he says, his eyes shifting to the left. *He's lying.* I can read a lie from a mile away, and I think Joey boy is full of shit.

The server places our drinks in front of us along with a basket of warm bread wrapped in a cloth.

"Are you going snorkeling or parasailing while you're here?" I ask, reaching for a slice.

"Nah, I don't have a death wish. If you do it, I'll come watch you." He takes a sip of his wine.

"I wasn't planning on it. I spent the past two days lounging by the water in a cabana. I watched some crazy people doing those things though."

"Sounds relaxing."

"It was boring as hell," I whisper, leaning over the table.

"Since we're both bored, why don't we be bored tomorrow together?" he asks.

I shrug. *Do I really want to spend more time with Joe the liar?*

"I'll think about it," I say with another shrug.

The serving staff brings our food shortly thereafter. Up until then the conversation has been basic and almost nil.

I cut into my medium-rare steak and take my first bite. "Oh my God, this steak melts in your mouth. Mmm." I swear my eyes just rolled back in my head from pure ecstasy. "How's your cowgirl doing over there?" I smile mischievously.

"She... It... is divine." He holds up a piece on his fork to show me. I'm glad we've found something we can laugh about.

"I missed you on the flight from Miami," I say, cutting my steak.

"I came by way of cruise ship."

"Cruise ship?"

"Yeah, I had that meeting I told you about."

"Your meeting was on a cruise ship?"

"Uh-huh."

"Why didn't you stay on the ship instead of coming here?"

"I'm not a fan of ships." His eyes shift to the left. *This guy is just a big ole fat liar.* He's making me want to find out what he's hiding.

"Makes sense. What do you want to do tomorrow?" I ask as he instinctively reaches for his computer.

"No. Not the computer," I snap, shutting him down.

"Why not? Don't you like technology, Sandy?" he teases playfully.

"I like technology just fine, but not at the dinner table."

"Fair enough." He slides it back down into his bag, and the server brings the check.

"I got that," he says as we both reach for it. We sit there looking at each other, holding the check between us.

"I'm very capable of paying for my own dinner," I say.

"I'm sure you are, but I invited you. Please, it's my treat."
He pulls on the paper harder.

"I don't feel comfortable—"

"I don't think I started on the right foot. Let me do this to
make up for all the tap, tap, tapping on the plane." His face
lights up with an ornery smile. For one long second we just
stare at each other.

"Fine." I can feel the heat in my cheeks, and I let go of the
check.

We leave the restaurant and head to a table on the terrace.

"Are you sure you want to be bored with me tomorrow?" I
ask.

"Yeah, why not? Neither one of us wants to be here, so why
not *kill time* together?"

"I want to be clear, then. We're just *killing time*. Under no
circumstances will it be anything else."

"Anything else?" He looks confused. "You mean sex?" I
nod my head. "No, no, no, no, I don't have time for that."

"Good, because neither do I." I'm kind of offended he
wasn't at least interested.

"Can I tap now?" Joe asks, motioning to the computer.

"Yes, you may." I motion for him to continue and cross my
legs.

He taps away, and soon, he has some options for things we
can do tomorrow. "We could go horseback riding on the beach,
tour some caves, take a ride in a glass-bottomed boat, hiking…
Oh, here's one that could be fun."

"What?"

"A tour of the oldest rum distillery and the Tortuga rum
factory."

"I pick rum!" I raise my hand and wave it around like an
idiot, and we laugh.

"Me too. Let me see if I can book it."

He has booked us on the tour for tomorrow morning at ten.
He puts his laptop away, stands, and holds his hand out for me
to take. I get to my feet, and he walks me to my room.

"Thank you for letting me join you for dinner. It was nice to see the eyes behind the computer screen."

"You're very welcome. I'll see you at the boat dock at 9:45."

"Okay, sounds great. See you then," I say. He turns, and I watch as that delicious ass walks out of view. He's just someone to kill time with. *Keep telling yourself that.*

Chapter 8
Joe

'm walking back to my room on the south side of the complex, and I'm wondering if I should've leaned in for a good night kiss. No, we agreed to just hang out together on this beautiful, romantic island all alone. My phone rings.

"Yeah."

"How did it go?" the deep male voice asks.

"It went as planned. Thanks for leaving me the present. I found it right where you said it would be."

"Do you still have it?"

"Yeah. What do you want me to do with it?" I ask.

"I have another job for you."

"Another party...here?" I smile and nod as I pass an older couple on the path.

"Yeah."

"Okay, send me the details."

I'll need to do some research tonight if I want to spend the day with Sandy tomorrow. I stow my phone back in my pocket and let myself into my room. I unlock the little safe and make sure the Glock is where I left it. I climb up on the bed and lean against the headboard with my computer in my lap, and try to do a little research on my next mark.

⟿

The bright morning sun fills the sky while I watch for Sandy to meet me at the dock. I see her walking in the distance. She's wearing white shorts, a pink crop top, and little white tennis shoes. Her black hair is pulled tight in a high ponytail, and it's bouncing around in the breeze as she approaches. She has on oversized sunglasses, and a tiny purse hangs from her shoulder to her hip by a thin strap. Her pouty pink lips are glistening in the sunlight, and I wonder what it would be like to suck one into my mouth. *We're just killing time.*

She gives me a little wave and calls out, "Hey, you."

"Hey." Like an idiot, I wave back.

"I thought you said you didn't like boats."

"I don't like *ships*. There's a difference."

"Okay, if you say so." She giggles.

"Are you ready to board, milady?" I gesture to the ramp.

"Why yes, kind sir," she purrs. I take her by the hand, and we begin to ascend the steep ramp. When we're halfway up, a wave comes in and causes the boat to rock, knocking her off her feet and into me. I grab her by the waist and steady her back on her feet.

"Thank you," she says quietly. I feel like I was just struck by lightning.

"Sure, no problem."

We take our seats on the stern, and the boat gradually fills with the small group of passengers taking the tour.

⟿

We tour the rum distillery first. We learn all about the distillation process and get to try a few samples at the end of the tour.

"That was interesting. They gave us a lot of information," I say as we're walking back to the boat.

"I would've liked to try a few more samples, but yeah, it was good."

"Maybe we'll get more samples at the Tortuga Factory. Come on let's go before we miss the boat," I say, giving her arm a little tug.

Everyone loads back onto the boat, and we head for Tortuga. Just the name *Tortuga* makes me think of Captain Jack Sparrow, and how it would be really cool if he made an appearance.

This tour is a little longer, so we begin with a late lunch. We make small talk with the other couples, but we don't go out of our way to form lasting friendships.

This tour is just as enjoyable as the first. The guide makes learning fun, and lots of samples help.

After a few shots, the group is relaxed and feeling good. We shop in the liquor store. Since our purchases are duty-free, we decide to stock up. Sandy buys four bottles, and so do I.

"Ooh. Let's get a rum cake and eat it for dessert." She's almost vibrating with excitement.

"Where are we going to eat it?"

"We could eat it in my room. I have a dining area."

"Sounds like your room is bigger than mine."

"Maybe we'll have to visit both rooms and compare," she suggests with a wink.

Did she wink at me? I think she winked at me. I hope she winked at me. You're acting like a girl. Cut it out.

"Sounds like a plan," I say, trying to be cool.

The boat pulls into the dock, and all of our drunk asses stumble down the ramp. The bottles of liquor clang together in our bags. We wave goodbye to the other passengers, the captain, and the crew like idiots. I take Sandy's hand, and we head for her room.

"It's been fun *killing time* with you today." Her hand is soft and warm in mine.

"I think so, me too, you," she slurs out, and we laugh.

"I think you're drunk, Sandy."

"No. I think you're drunk, Joey." She swipes her key card and leads me inside.

"Holy shit! Your room is huge!"

"I told you my boss's wife set me up." She steps out of her shoes and puts her bags on the counter.

"Shit. You weren't kidding. She really set you up nice. Look at that view." I stand in the balcony door. The sun is setting over the sea, and the view is stunning.

"Let's eat the cake out there." She points to the balcony in an exaggerated gesture.

We each take a bottle of rum and place it on the patio table. The cake sits on a plate between us, and we sit across from each other.

"Dang it, I forgot the glasses," she says. As she starts to get back up, I grab her hand.

"We don't need no stinking glasses, matey, argh," I say in my best pirate voice. I take a swig from my bottle and slam it on the table. We both laugh, and she picks up her bottle, clanks it with mine, and takes a swig. "I haven't had this much to drink in a really long time."

"Me either," she agrees. "Remember what the guy at the gift shop said about the cake not having enough alcohol in it to make you drunk."

"Yeah. So?" I ask.

"We could soak it with rum and eat it with a spoon," she says excitedly.

"What the fuck?"

"Wanna try it?" She gives me a sly grin.

"I'm up for anything once." I wave my hand for her to proceed.

She pours the rum across the top of the cake, and we lean in close to watch it soak up the liquor. We hold our spoons out like children waiting to dig into a bowl of ice cream.

"One, two, three, go!" she yells. We each scoop up a big, soggy bite of the sloppy goodness and shovel it into our mouths. Her eyes grow wide, and she lets out a loud moan, "Mmm… that's delicious."

I nod my head in agreement and go in for a second bite.

"How come you didn't wear your glasses today?" she asks

nonchalantly out of nowhere. Well, shit. I can't tell her they were part of the disguise I was wearing when we met. My brain reels.

"I. Uh. I only need them when I read." I blurt out, hoping she'll buy it.

She nods her head once and seems to accept my answer, before she takes another bite. When we're full of cake and three sheets to the wind, we sit on the loungers and watch the dark waves roll onto the beach.

"Joe," she hums,

"Hmm."

"Don't you find me attractive?"

"What? Of course I do. Why would you say that?" *I can't believe this gorgeous, dark-haired woman just asked me such a silly question.*

She closes one eye and looks down into her bottle. "Well, I know we said we would just *kill time* together, but I'm attracted to you," she says softly.

I set my bottle on the ground beside my chair and sit up, dropping my legs between our chairs. I take her hand in mine.

"Sandy, you're a *beautiful* woman, and I haven't been able to take my eyes off you since I saw you walking down to the dock this morning."

"Oh," she says shyly.

"You're so out of my league. I wasn't sure you wanted anything to do with me like that."

"What do you mean by 'out of your league'?" Her brows scrunch up with confusion.

"You're so classy and dainty. You're unlike any woman I've ever been with. I'm not sure I'm good enough for you."

I stand and gesture to sit on her lounger. She pulls her legs out of the way, and I sit, pulling her legs onto my lap. I rub her bare feet and run my hands over her calves. She lets out a little moan at my touch. I lean over and place a gentle kiss on her lips, then back away to look into her caramel-colored eyes.

"What a great way to *kill time*," she purrs.

Chapter 9
Sasha

I'm *so* drunk. We've been taking drinks from our bottles of rum all evening. When he kissed my lips, I thought I was going to explode from the blood whooshing around in my head. We agreed no sex, but kissing is okay, right? I keep telling myself we're just *killing time*.

"Whoops, I'm empty," I mumble, tilting my bottle upside down and holding it up high to look inside. We wobble our way to the kitchen, laughing. Joe comes in behind me and wraps his arms around my waist. He puts his nose in my hair and takes in a deep breath. He brushes my hair off my shoulder, and I lean my head to the side to give him better access as he places hot kisses down my neck. I turn in his arms to face him, and our lips meet in a rush of heat, and the room begins to spin. That's the last thing I remember.

I groan as the morning light fills the room. There are no room-darkening curtains in this place, that's for sure. My head pounds as I squint and look around. I take in a deep breath when I realize there's a heavy arm lying across my stomach.

Oh shit. I turn my head to the right, rub my eyes, and stare at the lumpy covers. I don't remember anything after the kitchen. How did we get here like... this?

"Joe... Joe," I whisper, shaking his arm.

"Hmm?" He groans as he pulls me closer.

"Joe," I say, shaking him again. "Wake up."

"What's wrong?" He rolls over onto his back, throwing his arm over his eyes. "What the hell did we do last night, drink all the rum in Tortuga?"

"I think so," I agree. I lift the covers and look beneath to find our naked legs wrapped around each other. What *did* we do? I quickly steal a peek at his manhood and see how huge this man is. *Oh my God. I would know if that had been inside me, wouldn't I?*

He takes his arm down from his face and looks up at the ceiling. "I don't remember much after the kitchen, do you?"

"Not really. Did we...?" I ask cautiously.

"Did we what?" He turns to look at me. I lift the covers and gesture to our naked bodies. His eyes grow wide.

"Did we have... sex?" I whisper like it didn't happen if I don't say it loud enough.

"I don't remember." He squints.

"Me either," I admit, and we burst out laughing. "It was the rum. We'll blame it on the rum."

"Oh...the rum." He rubs his hand down his face and onto his jaw. "I haven't been that drunk in years."

"Me either. But seriously. Do you think we had sex?" I ask. We raise the covers together again and look at our naked bodies now lying side by side. I get a glimpse of his tattooed chest this time.

"I don't feel like I had sex. How do you feel between your legs? Sore? 'Cause you'd be sore if we had sex." I raise an eyebrow at him, but he keeps babbling. "You'd know it if we had sex 'cause I like it rough." His eyes grow wide, and his lips snap shut.

"Oh, really?" I question as I glide my hand between my legs.

Joe's eyes watch my fingers disappear between my thighs. "I don't feel sore or wet."

"Whew. That's good." He lets out his breath.

"Why is that good? Don't you want to have sex with me?" I ask, feeling appalled.

"Baby, I want you to remember when I fuck you."

My breath gets stuck in my throat. I'm not sure how to respond to his words because I definitely want to find out what it feels like to have that big dick between my legs. I throw the covers back and sit up.

"Oh my God, my head is splitting. How much did we drink?"

"At least a bottle each, not to mention the cake," he recounts.

"Oh... the cake." My stomach roils. "I gotta pee." I stand and turn to look at Joe, but he's already rolled back over and pulled the covers up over his head.

I leave the bathroom with pain reliever for both of us and grab some water bottles from the fridge. I hold his out to him.

"Here, take these. It should help your head." He groans from under the covers, but he concedes and sits up on his elbow. He pops them in his mouth, takes a hit off the water, and flops back down.

"Let's go back to sleep," he grumbles as he grabs me by the arm and pulls me onto the bed.

"I can't go back to sleep," I say. "Once I'm awake, I'm awake."

"We're on vacation, just try...for me." He sticks out his lips all pouty, and my heart sinks. *I do feel like shit.* What will it hurt?

"Fine, I'll try." I push him over, and he spoons me with his naked body. His warmth envelops me, and we both doze off to sleep.

Chapter 10
Joe

I stretch and feel her side of the bed, but she's not there anymore. I lift my head and look around the room to see Sandy out on the balcony in some weird yoga pose. It makes me smile to see her in those tight yoga pants with her ass in the air. She looks up, and our eyes connect. She drops her pose and stands with her hands on her hips and says, "About time you wake up, sleepyhead."

"Ugh. Morning," I groan.

"Come and stretch with me." *Where'd she get all the fucking energy from?*

"Nope."

"Why not?"

"Because I'm not all bendy like you are." I wave my hands in the air.

"You don't have to be all bendy. It's about clearing your mind and opening your body to the day."

"Nah, I'm gonna keep my mind closed and go take a shower."

"Okay, but I ordered breakfast, so hurry up." I throw back the covers and start to walk naked to the bathroom. I can feel her eyes on me, but I don't turn around.

"Like what you see, Princess?" I close the door behind me before she can answer.

I emerge fifteen minutes later with a white towel wrapped around my waist. "I need to find my clothes."

"I think they're behind the chair."

"Wonder how they got there?" I ask.

"Who knows? I found mine in the kitchen." She giggles.

"When I was showering, I had flashes of us dancing on the balcony. Do you remember doing that?"

She scrunches up her face. "No. But I remember eating cake out there and watching the water in the lounge chairs. I remember you rubbing my feet and kissing me."

"Maybe tonight we can do it all again, *without* the alcohol." I focus on those pouty pink lips of hers.

"I think that would be nice. Besides, I want to be wide awake when you fuck me with that big dick of yours." She grins.

"Wow. Where the hell did that come from?"

"Well, you said I would know it if you fucked me because I would be sore. Let's test your theory to see if it holds up. You know, *to kill time.*" She casually throws those words over her shoulder as she walks into the bathroom and closes the door.

After I pick my mouth up off the floor, I look for the rest of my clothes. Room service arrives and sets up breakfast on the small dining table. Sandy comes out of the bathroom wearing blue jeans, a lavender tank top, and those cute little white sneakers. Her hair is braided into two ponytails this time, and she has on that damn pink lipstick.

"Breakfast is served," I announce with my arms out. *Why do I act like such an idiot when I'm around her?*

"Great, I'm starving."

We chow down on pancakes, fresh fruit and steaming hot coffee.

When I'm done, I lean back from the table. "So what do you want to do today? Do I need to go get my laptop?"

"No!" She puts her hand up to stop me. "I know what we can do today."

"What?"

"Do you ride?"

"What do you mean... like... motorcycles?" My voice cracks a little. Never in a million years would I have thought those words would come out of her dainty little mouth. She nods her head.

"Yeah," I say warily. "Do you?"

"Sure do. I think we can rent some bikes for a few hours. Let's go explore the island."

"Sounds like a plan to me. I'll go back to my room and change clothes, then we can go."

I turn to leave.

"And Joe..."

"Yes."

"You can leave the laptop in your room today, okay?"

"Fine. See you in the lobby in thirty?"

"Perfect."

I pull on my black T-shirt, dark jeans, and hiking boots, and tuck my black leather gloves into my back pocket. There's a custom motorcycle touring company up the road, so we start walking. When we get there, we're told all the bikes are booked for the day, except for one custom Harley Davidson. We look at one another.

"We'll take it," we say in unison.

The attendant rents us two helmets to go along with the Harley, and we head for the parking lot. She beats me to the bike and throws her leg over. Reaching her hand out for the keys, she casually says, "Hop on."

"Uh... No..." I draw out the word. "Do I look like a fuckin' backpack to you?"

"Well, I'm not a backpack either," she snaps.

"You're better suited to be one than I am." I hold my arms out wide. Her eyes scan my body.

"Fine." She lets out a huff.

She climbs off the bike, and I hand her a helmet. I pull on mine, throw my leg over the bike, start her up, and give it a good rev. She taps me on the shoulder to ask me if she can get on, and I nod my head. As I put my hand out to help her climb on, she throws her leg over and sits down. She puts her sneakers on the pegs, taps my shoulder to tell me she's ready, and I begin to move forward.

When I start to pull away, I tap her leg to tell her to hold on to me. Her hands slide slowly around my middle and hold me tightly. My jeans suddenly become too tight, and I have to adjust myself.

We pull onto Esterly Tibbetts Highway and stay on the roads we think will have the best scenery: Crewe Road, Shamrock Road, and Bodden Town Road. It takes about an hour to go from one end of the island to the other. We make a brief stop at the blowholes and continue to Barefoot Beach. When we pull in and stop, we can see the crystal-clear water and the spectacular view. This beach is more secluded than the public beaches. We remove our helmets and hang them off the handlebars, kick off our shoes, and roll up our pant legs. Hand in hand, we walk to the water's edge.

"This entire island is incredible." Her eyes are wide as she scans the water, taking in every wave and grain of sand.

"It *is* beautiful." I can't take my eyes off of this woman, because *she* is so beautiful. No, she's fucking breathtaking.

She turns her head and catches me staring at her. A blush falls over her cheeks, and she lowers her head. I turn her body to face mine, and with one finger, I lift her chin so I'm looking into her dark chocolate eyes.

"Please don't look away from me."

I place a kiss on those soft, sweet lips, and her hands move to my hips, fingers sliding into my belt loops. She pulls me closer and kisses me back.

"I've been waiting all day to kiss you again." I nuzzle my nose into her neck and breathe in her cherry scent.

"Me too," she coos.

"C'mon, let's walk." I take her hand in mine, and we saunter down the beach. We kick water at each other and pick up shells and chuck them back into the sea.

"I think my forced vacation just got a lot better," she says.

"You do? Why?" I tease.

"Because I'm finally getting to see a different side of Grumpy Guy."

"Who's that?"

"You, silly. I called you that in my head when we were traveling."

"Why did you call me that?" I chuckle.

"Because you didn't even look at me on the entire first flight. You had your nose stuffed so deep in that computer of yours; I'm surprised you could breathe."

"I was trying to get my work done." She doesn't need to know I was researching a mark.

"Then you ate my french fry before you even knew my name."

"I was hungry." I wink at her.

"And let's not talk about all the tapping," she teases.

"I won't touch my computer again around you for the rest of the trip. But…"

"But what?" She stops walking.

"But I'll need something else to keep my fingers busy."

"I think that can be arranged," she says with a smirk, and I kiss her again. We stand on the beach, making out like teenagers. My hands roam down her jeans-clad thighs and up to her tight, round ass, and my cock twitches in my pants.

"We should probably go," I urge, pulling her down the beach toward the bike.

Chapter 11
Sasha

Climbing back on the bike, he pulls my legs closer to him this time, and I snuggle into his back the best I can with my helmet on. My hands are clasped together on his chest, and he rubs his gloved fingers across mine.

We're on a straight stretch of road, and I grind my center against him. I feel him take a deep intake of breath beneath my fingertips. Wetness grows between my thighs as his hand slides over my leg and squeezes my ass. Then he pats my thigh as if to say, *Be patient, we'll be there soon.*

Maybe grinding on him is too much while he's driving the bike. I run the fingers of my right hand down his neck and across his broad shoulder. He winces as if he thinks I'm going to tickle him, but I don't. My fingers travel along the seam of his tight black T-shirt until both of my hands are resting low around his waist. My pinky finger moves ever so slightly over the bulge in his pants, and I know he wants me as much as I want him. I saw his body under the covers, and this man is hung like a horse. The thought of having him inside me sends chills down my spine.

We return the motorcycle to the rental company and start

walking back to the resort. The anticipation of what I hope is coming soon is driving me crazy.

"Joe."

"Yes?"

"I...I..." I stammer like a moron. He stops walking.

"What's the matter, Princess?" Genuine concern is etched on his face as he takes my hand.

"When we started killing time, we agreed no sex."

"Can't we change our minds? I mean, we are the ones making the rules here." He waggles his eyebrows at me.

"I know. I'm just a little nervous." I'm not nervous about having sex. I could fuck his brains out right here, right now. I'm nervous because I'm about to have sex as *Sandy*. How does *Sandy* have sex? Is she as shy as she puts on? Is she vanilla? How am I supposed to *act*? It's been a long time since I've had sex with someone I cared about. *Care about?* What the fuck? I don't even know this guy, and I'm talking about having feelings for him. It's just sex.

"It's just been a while, ya know." That sounds like a vanilla answer Sandy would give.

"It's okay, Princess. We don't have to do anything you don't wanna do." He pulls me in for a hug, and I relax into his touch. He keeps his arm around my shoulders, and we continue to walk.

"Hey, do you care if we stop by my room so I can grab a few things?" he asks.

"Sure, as long as it's not the computer." I point my finger at him.

"No computer." He rolls his eyes. We walk through the lobby and out the other end of the building, then continue down a path lined with tropical plants and flowers. This resort is stunning, and I'm trying to soak in everything it has to offer.

He stops in front of the door. "This is my room. It's not as big as yours," he apologizes as he pushes it open for me. I walk inside and look around the room. It's just a smaller version of mine, and it's just as stunning.

"It's beautiful. I don't know what you're complaining about."

"I'm not *complaining*."

I watch him as he moves around the room. He leans down and pulls on the handle of the little safe nestled inside the cabinet under the television. *I wonder what he's hiding in there.* He grabs his backpack off the table, pulls his laptop out, and looks at me as he sets it carefully on the bed. He throws in a few toiletries and some clothes, and zips it back up.

"Lead the way." He gestures back at the door. We exit his room and walk in the direction of mine, holding hands.

"You still seem nervous," he says, squeezing my hand.

"Maybe a little."

"Are you a virgin?" *What kind of fucking question is that?*

"Me? No. Are you?"

"Oh, hell no." He laughs.

"Why would you think I'm a twenty-seven-year-old virgin?" I ask.

"Well, you said you were nervous..."

"I just don't know what you want." I huff out a breath.

"What I *want*. What are you talking about?"

"Yeah, you know, how should I *act*?" I don't have sex with people in character. Maybe this is a mistake.

"Act? I don't want you to *act*, Sandy. I want you to be yourself."

"What if I don't know who *I am*?"

"As long as you don't fake it while I fuck you, I'm good."

"What's that supposed to mean?"

He stops and takes me by the shoulders. Staring into my eyes, with a deep growl in his voice, he demands, "I want to hear all the sounds you make when you come, and every time you scream my name, it needs to be *real*."

"You think you can make me scream your name?" I raise my eyebrow to him and put a hand on my hip.

"Oh, I know I can, Princess."

"Prove it," I purr.

"I believe that's a challenge." He smirks.

"Maybe it is," I tease. He places a quick peck on my lips, and we stride off to my room.

I unlock the door, and as soon as it clicks closed, he drops his backpack to the floor, and his lips are on mine with a vengeance. Kissing, licking, sucking. We're both too worked up to worry about niceties. My hands grab the bottom of his shirt, and I pull it over his head, throwing it to the floor as he spins me and pins my back against the wall. Our breathing is heavy and ragged as our hands explore one another.

He wraps my braid around his fist and gives a little tug, and my neck opens up for him. Heat runs over my skin at the thought of how he could control me like that. My eyes graze over the tattoo on his muscular chest, and I want to lick it, so I lean forward, and I do. He groans as I lick and outline the phoenix with my tongue.

He unzips my jeans and pulls them down my legs, and I step out of them. Dropping to his knees in front of me, his fingers trace the band of my panties, and my breathing becomes shaky. He puts his nose on the tiny scrap of fabric between my legs and takes a deep breath.

"You smell so fucking sweet. Are you wet for me, Sandy?" he asks as he runs his finger over the fabric.

I nod my head as my fingers instinctively go to his wavy brown locks, and I pull, causing a moan to slip from his throat.

"Please, Joe," I pant.

"Gary," he says quietly.

"What?"

"My real name is Gary. When you scream my name, I want it to be Gary."

I'm confused as fuck at his confession. I knew he was lying about something. Could this be what it was? I suddenly feel the need to confess.

"Sasha."

"What?" He leans back to look at me.

"My real name is… Sasha."

We're both liars, but that doesn't matter right now because my panties are sliding down my legs.

Chapter 12
Gary

My brain is so fucked up right now. Sandy's *real* name is Sasha? But I don't give a shit because I told her I would make her scream my name, and that's precisely what I'm going to do.

"Widen your legs for me, Sasha." She does as I command. "That's my good girl." Her hands move back to my head, and she runs her fingers through my hair. It sends chills down my spine. "My girl has a praise kink, doesn't she?" A moan leaves her lips, and she pulls my hair harder. Her hips rock, begging me to touch her, to lick her.

The view of her neatly manicured pussy makes my cock ache against my zipper. I use my thumbs to spread her open for me, and lap my tongue through her center.

"You taste as sweet as you fucking smell."

Flattening my tongue, I lick her leisurely, like I have all the time in the world. But I can tell Sasha is looking for so much more. When I slide a finger into her center, she clenches around it, and her legs tremble.

I grip her tighter with my other hand to steady her.

"Oh God," she moans, and her fingers tighten on my hair.

"I need you to yell *my name*, remember?"

"Fuck. Gary," she moans as she writhes beneath my touch. It wasn't quite a yell, but we'll get there.

She squirms as I suck her needy clit into my mouth. She uses her grip on my hair to move me where she needs me, and I oblige. She grinds her pussy on my face, and I can't get enough of her sweet cream.

I add a second finger and curl them ever so slightly to work her G-spot.

"Oh fuck!" she yells as I flick my tongue on her clit, but I don't release the pressure with my mouth. She stiffens, and her pussy flutters around my fingers, but I don't stop. I can't help but smile as her body jumps at each lick as I tease her through her orgasm.

~

I stand and kiss her fiercely. Tasting herself on my tongue, she sucks it into her mouth with fevered desire. I grab her ass in my hands and lift her to my waist. She wraps her legs around me, as I carry her across the room and set her down on the bed. I remove her tank top and toss it aside. When I release the clasp on her bra and those glorious tits fall free, my cock demands the same.

As if she's reading my mind, her hand moves to my jeans and palms my hard length. Her hands on me make me feral. I want everything she will give me. She unbuttons my pants and lowers the zipper. My pants ease down my legs, and my cock springs to attention. A wicked smile lights up her face, and she licks her lips.

She lowers her mouth to my tip and licks away the precum. Her hooded eyes look up at me, and I release a shuddered breath as those pouty pink lips surround my tip. I've dreamed of her wrapping those pink lips around me since we were on the airplane.

She runs her tongue up and down my length as she cups my balls. Her grip is firm but not too much. She wraps her hot mouth around my dick and sucks me down her throat. I'm not a small man, but she takes everything I give her down that glorious throat of hers. I rock into her, lost in how her hot mouth feels. I realize I'm approaching the point of no return. She's going to make me come. That can't happen. Not yet. I pull her off my dick with a pop.

She wipes her mouth with the back of her hand, and her expression turns innocent. She bats those big eyes at me and says, "Is there a problem?"

"No, Princess. No problem. I wanted to make *you* scream tonight, remember?" I point at the bed. "Get in the middle of the bed and spread those gorgeous legs for me." She does as she's told and lays her head on the pillow. I love how she obeys my every order without hesitation.

"Good girl," I praise as I climb on the bed and kneel between her tanned, toned legs. I suck one nipple into my mouth, and a soft moan comes from her throat. I suck a little harder, and her nipple peaks in my mouth, and her hips rock up into me. Moving to the other breast, I give it the same attention as the first, and she's panting with need.

"Are you on birth control?" I pant.

"Yes. Are you clean?" she retorts.

"Yes. Condom?"

"No," she answers.

"But I always wear a condom."

"Good to know." She smiles. "But I need to feel all of that big dick of yours inside me." I think my brain just exploded.

"I wouldn't want to disappoint you." Pushing into her hot slick center is going to feel fucking amazing. I spread her legs wider with a hungry growl, and I notch my cock at her entrance and push in about an inch.

"Gary," her voice is scratchy.

"Yes, Baby."

"Please." She's writhing beneath me.

"Please, what, Sasha?"

"Make me scream your name." That's all I need to hear. I grab her hips and push into her further.

"Oh my God," she groans as she looks up at me with wide eyes.

"What's wrong?" I ask.

"You're so fuckin' big." *Not like I've never heard that one before*. But coming from her lips, it sounds so innocent.

"Your mouth can take me, so can this hot pussy," I push in deeper, and her legs lift around my waist. "That's it, you can take it," I say, as I push the rest of the way in and hold steady while her body adjusts to the feel of me.

"Oh shit!"

"You're taking all of me so well." I can't take it much longer. "I'm gonna move now, Baby." She nods, and I begin to rock into her, rolling my pelvis in circles as I go, and her hooded eyes open.

"That feels amazing," she purrs.

"Did you expect anything less than *amazing* tonight?" I grin, and she bites her lip.

"Relax, Sasha. Get out of your head. Just feel me inside you." She closes her eyes, and I pump in and out of her. "Tell me what you need."

"Deeper," she demands, and I swear my cock swells inside her even more. Her velvety channel feels amazing against my cock. I've been treating her like she's a porcelain doll or some shit, but I think she wants it rough like I do. I take her left leg and put it on my shoulder so I can fill her deeper.

"Yes, like that. Oh, Gary." I move into her faster.

"More," she moans, and my strokes become harder, and I can feel her body start to clench around my dick.

"Come for me," I rasp. And as if on cue, she tightens down on me like a vise.

"Gary, yes, Gary. Oh shi..." Her pussy clenches me so tight, I come fast and hard, filling her with my cum.

She's lying in my arms after we both come down from our high.

"So Sasha, huh?" I croon, rubbing circles on her arm with my finger as she lets out a hum.

"Yeah, sorry about that. A girl has to protect herself. The world is a dangerous place for a single woman these days."

"I can understand that."

"What about you, Joe? What's your excuse?"

"The same type of thing for me too, I guess. No one can hurt you if they don't know who you really are."

"I like Gary better, anyway."

"Sasha is much better than Sandy. It's sexy," I say, kissing the top of her head. "What do you want to do tomorrow to *kill time*?"

"Do we have to *do* anything? I mean, can't we just stay in bed all day and fuck?"

This woman surprises me the more I get to know her. "That was straight to the point."

"I enjoyed myself tonight. Didn't you?" she asks.

"Hell yeah, I enjoyed myself."

"I could do it again," she agrees with a smile.

"Fuck yeah. Over and over." She lets out a laugh.

Have I met a woman who can finally keep up with my sexual appetite?

"We have a plan, then. Stay in bed all day and *play*," she purrs as she mounts me.

"I think I like this *killing time* thing."

Chapter 13
Sasha

We sleep in the following morning and wake tangled in each other's limbs like we did the first morning. We order brunch and enjoy it on the balcony while soaking in the breathtaking view. I'm wearing his black T-shirt from our ride yesterday, and he's wearing a pair of gray shorts that hang low on his hips, allowing a good view of his deep V.

"Water?" he asks, as he carries the tray full of empty dishes inside and puts them out in the hallway for the staff to pick up.

"Sure." I walk in behind him and drop down on the bed.

Gary grabs two bottles of water. Handing me one, as we sit facing each other on the bed.

"Let's get to know each other better," he suggests.

"Okay, how do we do that?" I pull my knees up under me.

"We'll take turns asking each other questions."

"What kind of questions?"

"We can start with the usual boring ones. You know, like, what's your favorite color and stuff like that. We can get more personal as we go on."

"Okay, let's give it a try. You go first," I say.

"Favorite color?"

"Black. You?"

"Blue."

"Typical male answer," I say, waving him off like it doesn't count. "Do you have any siblings?"

"Yes. One sister. Her name is Ellen. You?"

"No. I'm an only child. Favorite song?"

"Easy one. The acoustic version of 'Judgement Day' by Five Finger Death Punch."

"Ooh, that's a good one."

"You?" he asks.

"Same band, different song. 'Welcome to the Circus.'"

"Oh yeah, that's a good one too. Interesting. We both like the same band. Not at all what I thought you would like." We sit in silence for a moment while he processes our answers. "Next question, favorite childhood memory?" he continues.

"Pass."

"What do you mean, pass? You can't pass," he argues.

"Why not? We should each get one pass."

"You can't make up new rules once we start the game," he declares.

"That's a rule." I stare at him in challenge.

"We're getting to know each other here. C'mon, you have to have *one* good memory?"

"Not really. You answer the question, then. What's *your* favorite childhood memory?" I ask, and he blows out his breath.

"Going to a giant amusement park which shall remain nameless."

"Really? How old were you?"

"I was twelve, and Ellen was ten."

"I bet you had the perfect parents with 2.5 children, a dog, a cat, and the proverbial white picket fence."

"Nope. I had a deadbeat dad who left my mom with two small children. I was three, and Ellen had just turned one. I don't even remember the piece of shit. My mom worked two jobs to keep food on the table. She won the trip in a raffle at the local corn festival. It was five days and four nights when she didn't have to worry about how to feed us or whether we were safe from the local drug dealers."

"Oh." I didn't see any of that coming. "Where did you grow up?"

"Missouri. Stop ducking the question. What's your good memory?" he asks firmly. I crinkle my nose and try to think of something from my childhood that didn't suck.

"Maybe the time I stayed all night at my friend Miranda's house when I was ten. She was allowed to have four friends sleep over on her birthday. We played with makeup, curled our hair, ate pizza, and stayed up half the night."

"See, you found one. Your turn to ask."

"What's your deepest, darkest fear?" I ask.

"Snakes. I fucking hate snakes. You?" he asks. I inhale and speak my truth in one long breath.

"I'm afraid I'll die, and they'll bury me, but I won't really be dead, and I'll wake up in the coffin buried alive."

"Wow! You don't play fuck around, do you? Why would you think something so terrible?"

I swallow down the saliva pooling in my mouth. "I used to have nightmares about it."

"Let's try a lighter question," he offers.

"Sounds good to me."

"If I could do anything to you in bed, what would it be?

"Control me."

"Damn. You didn't even hesitate. Why?"

"Because I'm always the one who has to be in control. My job is very demanding. I have to keep my emotions in check. Just once I would like for someone else to be in control."

"I could do that for you."

"Really? You think you could control me?" I smirk at him and take a drink of my water.

"I know I can." There is so much confidence in his voice. I almost believe he could do it.

"What about you? If I could do anything to you in bed, what would it be?" I ask.

"Sensation play," he replies without a moment's hesitation.

"What the hell is that?"

"Your partner engages your senses. It can be through taste, touch, smell, sound, or sight. It can be just one of your senses at a time, or you can engage more than one. There can be pain *or* pleasure involved," he says.

"I take it you've done this before?" I ask.

"Yes. Do you want to try it?"

"Do you have to tie me up to do it?"

"Not at all. It's not a bondage thing unless you want to add that element to it," he explains.

"Okay, I'll try it," I agree tentatively.

He rubs his hands together. "Alrighty then. I'll have to get some things together before we start. Let me see what you have around here first."

I'm not sure what I just agreed to, but he looks pretty excited.

Chapter 14
Gary

gather the items I can use from around the suite and place them on a tray I found in the cupboard. I cover it with a towel so Sasha can't see what I have.

"Are you about ready?" she asks.

"Someone's anxious." I chuckle.

"Maybe a little nervous. What do I do first?"

"First, you're going to take off all of your clothes and get comfortable on the bed." She doesn't even hesitate. She stands from the bed, removes my shirt, and lies down.

"Just one pillow, please," I instruct. She does as I say without hesitation, removing the extra pillow from beneath her head and tossing it to the floor. I bring the tray of items over to the bed and place them on the nightstand.

"What is all that stuff?" She leans up to try to peek, and I playfully slap her hand.

"Now, now, now. That's part of the fun. You don't know what's coming until it touches your skin. I had to improvise a little bit, so bear with me."

"Okay." She smiles reluctantly and lies back on the pillow.

"Close your eyes." I keep my voice calm and melodic. "I

won't do anything to hurt you *tonight*." Her eyes pop open, and she looks at me. A devious grin spreads across my lips. She smiles awkwardly and resumes her position.

"First, I'm going to put some music on in the background." 'Adorn' by Miguel plays quietly on my phone.

"Is it okay if I use the belt from your robe to cover your eyes?"

She opens one eye to peer at me. "Yes," she says quietly and shuts her eye again.

"I'm going to stimulate your senses tonight. Do you trust me?"

"Yes."

"I want you to pick a safe word."

Her eyes spring open just as I approach her with the cloth belt. "You said there would be no pain involved."

"There won't be," I say calmly. "But we don't know each other very well. I could still do something or say something you're uncomfortable with. A safe word will stop everything. It can be as simple as red or something out of the ordinary you wouldn't say in a sexual situation."

"I'll just use red, if that's okay?"

"Of course it is. *You* are in control, Sasha."

"I don't want to be in control," she snaps, way too fast.

"You won't be in control of what I do to you, but you'll always be in control of the scene. It's *your* body," I say in a soothing tone.

"I understand."

I tie the sash over her eyes. She's so fucking beautiful under my control. The sight of her sun-kissed body lying out before me makes my cock twitch in my shorts. *Down boy, you have to wait your turn.*

"Take a deep cleansing breath in for me." She does as I instruct. I lower the tone of my voice and speak in calm, even words.

"I'm going to use the first item on you now. Are you ready?" I ask.

"Yes," she whispers. Removing the towel from the tray, I reach for a feather I found in a floral display. I start by slowly running it over her legs, making circles and gliding it back and forth over her skin. Her skin is covered in goose bumps.

"How does that feel, Sasha?"

"It feels soft and gentle."

"What do you think it is?"

"A feather."

"Good girl." I continue to run the feather over her arms, shoulders, and neck. I take my time and try not to rush the experience. I place the feather above her right breast and roll it between my fingers. It spins on her nipple and it hardens in front of my eyes. She lets out a small whoosh of air.

"You're doing great. How do you feel?

"Relaxed."

"That's good... good." I move the feather up to her face and run it ever so gently across her furrowed brow until her muscles release and all the tension is gone. I tickle the tip of her nose with it, and she giggles softly. I place a peck on her lips and ask, "Are you ready to try another?"

A breathy, "Yes," comes from her lips.

I put the feather back on the tray and pick up the long, wide-toothed comb I found in her bathroom. I gently drag the comb over her arm, careful not to scratch. She winces a little, so I soften my touch. The wince turns into intrigue as I continue to pull it lightly over her other arm, up to her neck, down her chest to her stomach, and over each leg. I'm careful not to tickle her feet.

"How are you doing, Princess?

"I'm fine."

"How does it feel?"

"Interesting. It's a sensation I can say I've never had before. Oh...and I think it's a fork or a comb or something like that."

"Good guess. It *is* a comb. You're doing great, just breathe." A proud smile pierces her pretty pink lips. She takes in another cleansing breath in anticipation of the next object. I slide an ice cube from the bowl on the tray and place it at the base of her neck. Shivers run up her arms, and her nipples stand at attention.

"That's cold. Ice... Ice... It's Ice," she sputters as she flinches, and I try to stifle a laugh.

"You're correct, it *is* ice. Now I want you to concentrate on how it feels on your skin, not on how *cold* it is. Try to control your breathing and not let your mind take over."

I allow the ice cube to lead me across her skin. I watch as it melts, and the droplets slide down her body and fall to the sheet below.

I hear her occasionally take a cleansing breath to center herself, like she did on the balcony doing yoga. The first cube melts, and I dip my hand into the bowl for another. I slide it up her calf to the back of her knee. She tenses as it rolls across the tender skin at the top of her thigh. I watch as her mouth opens, as if she wants to say something, but then it closes. I bring the cube up to her hip bone and hold it there, watching the droplets slide down her skin and pool in her belly button.

One more cube to go, and it's all for those perky tits of hers. I start by moving it across her ribs and glide it up the space between her breasts to her collarbone. I make sure I don't leave it in one place too long before I circle back around to her breast. When it lands on her hard nipple, her breathing shudders.

I lower my lips to her ear and ask in a whisper, "How does this feel, Princess?"

Lost in her mind, she answers, "Amazing."

"I have one more thing for you. Are you game?"

"Yes."

"Spread your legs for me, Princess." She dutifully obliges. It feels like I've earned her complete trust with this exercise. Climbing onto the bed, I take her right leg in my hands and run my stubble over the bottom of her foot, and it jerks back.

"Hey! That tickles, and that's your *face.*"

"It won't all tickle. I promise. And you're correct. It *is* my whiskers."

I lower her foot down to the bed and raise the other, rubbing my chin back and forth along the bottom of it also. She giggles, and her leg tries to jump out of my hold. I place it back down on the bed. I move between her feet.

I use the sides of my face to caress the insides of her legs, moving back and forth between her legs. The right side of my face rubs the inside of her left leg. The left side of my face runs over her right. I work my way slowly, methodically, up to her thighs. Making my way up her body. When I reach the tender skin at the top of her leg closest to her pussy, she whines with need at my touch. I can smell her arousal, and my cock begs me to stop, but I continue.

"You're so needy for me, Sasha," I growl.

"Y…Yes… You're driving me crazy." Her voice trembles.

"That's the reaction I was going for, Princess." She pouts as I continue my climb up her soft body, never giving her pussy the attention it demands.

I continue to climb up her body and hover over. She lifts her hips upward, trying for more contact, but I won't give it to her.

"Not. Yet," I clip.

When my lips land softly on the crook of her neck, her hands slide around my body.

"Kiss me," she coos breathlessly. "I need you."

"Don't you want to play my game anymore?" I tease. She shakes her head. I run my tongue over her lips, and she calls mine inside. Desire rips through me, and I need to taste her pussy…now.

"You've been such a good girl for me tonight. I think it's time for your reward, don't you?" Her head nods. "I'll be back," I purr, and she grabs me tighter.

"Where are you going?"

"Down."

"Oh." Her breath hitches, and she releases her hold on me.

I rub my hands over her body, warming her flesh as I go, until I land between her legs once more.

"Damn, Sasha, your pussy is weeping for me," I groan.

I push her legs open farther and gently brush my whiskers over her clit, and her body trembles. Careful not to scratch too hard, I move back and forth gently. Her hands slide over the sheet.

I hold her pussy open wide, and I rub my whiskers back and forth through her folds. Her body quivers, and she moans.

"Do you like the way that feels, Princess?"

"Shit! Gary!" she cries out. The sensation almost too much for her body to handle after our relaxation session.

"Do you want me to stop?"

"No! Fuck no!" Her voice is desperate. Causing me to smile.

My tongue finds her clit. It's engorged and begging to be sucked. I slide my lips over it and suck while grinding my chin into her opening. She bucks her hips while her hands now fist the sheets, as her orgasm sweeps her away.

She needs a chance to process everything I did to her today. I remove the makeshift blindfold and kiss her softly. I lie down beside her, pulling her close, and she melts into my chest.

Her right arm snakes across my stomach. "That was so intense."

"I'm glad you enjoyed it, Princess."

"I felt so vulnerable with the blindfold on, but I knew I was safe with you. Thank you."

"Of course."

"Why do you call me Princess?" she asks, running her hand back and forth over the tattoo on my chest.

"I think I started calling you that because I thought you were stuck-up."

"Do you still think I'm stuck-up?" Concern etches her voice.

"Not since I've gotten to know you better. But you were very prim and proper on the plane. I definitely thought you were out of my league."

"Why do you keep saying that?"

"Let's just say, you're not like the other women I usually spend time with."

"What kind of women do you spend time with?"

"All kinds, but they usually don't stay around very long?"

"Why? Because your nose is always buried deep in your computer?" She chuckles.

"My work keeps me very busy, yes. And it's very confidential."

"Most people's financials are."

"What? Oh yeah, 'cause I'm in finance, right?"

"That won't affect me because we won't be seeing each other after this week anyway," she says.

"You're right," I agree. Not sure if that's a good thing or a bad thing.

"Just so you know, in the real world, I'm not a prim and proper bitch."

"I never said you were a bitch." *Where the hell did that come from?*

"Oh. Well, you know what I mean. I didn't want to go on this vacation at all."

"Why did you come, then?"

"Because my boss made me."

"Made you?"

"Yep. I didn't have a choice. My boss's wife is the one who told me it might be more fun if I made it a game," she confesses.

"What do you mean, a game?"

"She told me to wear different clothes and act like someone I always wanted to be, so I created 'Sasha the Vacationer,'" she says the words as if she's introducing Superman, and I can't help but laugh.

"Why did you want to become 'Sasha the Vacationer'?" My voice mimics hers.

"I guess because she's the total opposite of the real me. She's fancy and sophisticated. She gets to wear pretty clothes and is always polite."

"So you're not always prim and proper?"

"Nope."

"How do you normally dress?"

"All kinds of ways. For work, I dress professionally, but when I'm off duty, I dress more relaxed."

"I liked Sasha the Vacationer," I say.

"But the question is…now that you've met the *real* me, do you like her?"

"Are you being *the real* you right now, or are you in character?"

"I left the character behind after we came back from the ride. Sandy felt so…fake. It felt so easy being around you, that she just fell away. I didn't *make* it happen. It just… happened."

"I like *the real* Sasha." I move her hair out of her face and kiss her lips tenderly, and she cuddles back into my side.

"Was Joe a character for you too?" she asks.

"I guess. It was more for my job than for fun."

"For your job?"

How do I explain this to her, without telling her what I really do for a living?

"I change my persona to fit the job I need to do."

"I think I understand what you mean. Is this the *real* Gary?"

"Baby, this is the most real I've ever been with a woman in my entire life." I pull her tighter to my side. I can't get close enough to this woman.

"How old are you?" she asks.

"Thirty."

"Old man," she giggles.

"I'm not old. Just experienced."

"Vintage."

"Am not."

"Are too." Now we're both laughing.

"How old are you?" I ask.

"Don't you know, you never ask a lady her age." She pushes me away. "Wanna go to the beach for a bit. I have a cabana we could hang out in."

"Sure, let's go."

I wear my blue board shorts, and she has on a little red bikini that makes my mouth water. We lounge around, laughing at the people trying to paddleboard, people screaming their lungs out parasailing, and surfers taking nosedives. I think I even nodded off there for a few. I don't think I've ever been this relaxed.

After a few hours of beach time, she asks, "I think I'm about roasted, wanna go back inside?"

"Sure."

We gather up our belongings and head back to her room.

We eat dinner and spend the rest of the evening lying in each other's arms and enjoying each other's company.

"I didn't think I would have any fun on this vacation, but, Baby, you've made this trip unforgettable."

"I like it when you call me that."

"What... Baby?"

"Baby... Baby Girl... Sweetheart...I've never really had anyone call me sweet names before."

"Surely you're exaggerating?"

"I didn't have a very good life until a few years ago."

"Bad childhood. I know all about that shit," I say.

"You wouldn't understand."

"Enlighten me." She pulls away from me. "Please." I take her hand in mine. "You're safe with me, Sasha. Tell me."

"My life hasn't always been like this." She points at the surrounding room. "This is my first vacation ever."

"Ever?"

"Until the other day, I'd never even been out of the city."

"Oh."

"I can't tell you this stuff," she says as she tries to push me away again.

I cup her face with my hands and kiss her. "I wanna learn everything about you. Something tells me we're very much alike."

Chapter 15
Sasha

I lie back on the bed and look up at the ceiling. Crossing my arms over my body, shutting myself off to him.

"I had a hard life growing up. My parents weren't good people. My dad would lock me in the closet for hours at a time while he beat my mom. He would punch her and kick her until she was so bruised and broken, she couldn't walk."

"Sasha, I'm so sorry."

"Mom started doing drugs when I was around nine. Trying to escape the abuse, I'm sure. When he found out she was spending his hard-earned money to get high, he was furious. But it was okay for him to spend money to drink himself into a stupor. It was a circle of unending pain, and it kept escalating. I told you my favorite memory was when I was ten."

"Yeah."

"Well, that's because when I turned twelve, my whole life changed."

"How?"

"One night, they had a big fight. She was to the point she just checked out on life, ya know. He came home, and she was so high I don't think she felt it when he hit her. That's when he... he... he came into my room for the first time."

"Sasha. Shh, you don't have to...I understand." He scoots up against the headboard and pulls me into his arms.

"You don't want to hear this." I try to move out of his hold.

"Hey." He holds me tightly. "Hey, look at me." My eyes connect with his. "You can tell me anything. I would never judge you."

I take a deep breath and keep going. "The next morning, when I got up for school, she was still lying on the couch. I tried to wake her up, but she was cold... so cold." I close my eyes. "She left me alone with him." Tears stream down my face.

"Oh shit. You found her...dead?"

"Yeah. He never even checked on her. He just got up for work and left."

"I called 911, and they took her away. I never saw her again."

"Not even for a funeral?"

"Nope. He had her cremated, and that was it."

"I'm so sorry, Baby."

"For three years. Three long years, he treated me like shit. When I came home from school, I had to cook, clean, do laundry, and at night... he would come into my bed. I was just a kid."

"Did he beat you like he did her?"

"Yes."

"How did you get away from him?"

"I killed him." His body stills.

"Did you just say what I think you said?" he whispers as if someone else could hear him. I nod. *Why am I telling him all this shit?* It just keeps spewing out of my goddamn mouth, and I can't control it.

"You little whore. Let me in!" he screams through my bedroom door. The pounding keeps getting louder and louder.

"No! Leave me alone!" I yell.

The door bursts open so hard that the frame breaks. In the blink of an eye, he's standing in the middle of my bedroom. His face is beet red. His breathing is out of control, and his fists are clenched by his sides. I huddle under the covers, the butcher knife from the kitchen under my pillow.

"Did you think you could just lock the door and keep me out?" He laughs manically.

"Please, leave me alone. I don't want you to hurt me any-more."

"Shut the fuck up! You belong to me. I can do whatever I want to you."

"I'm your daughter!"

"You are whatever I say you are, you little bitch."

"I hate you!"

"Hate me all you want, but you're going to do what I want." He stalks toward the bed and climbs on top of me. I'm trapped with my arms beneath the covers. I try to struggle, but the only thing I can move is my head as he tries to stick his tongue in my mouth. The smell of cigarettes on his breath floods my nostrils. I buck my hips up. He's so drunk, he loses his balance and falls beside me on the mattress. This is my moment. I have to take it if I ever want to be free.

I grab the knife from under the pillow and jump up on my knees above him. With all the strength I have, I plunge the knife into his chest. I pull it back out and raise it above my head to stab him again. I take in the scene as he screams in agony. There's blood covering his shirt, the blanket, my hands, the wall...everything.

His breathing is ragged. He's seconds from death when he says, "You're not my real daughter."

"What the fuck, Sasha. What did you do?"

"I stabbed him again." My voice is cold and there is no remorse. He deserved everything he got that day and more.

"Fuck."

"He was the only father I ever knew. All those years, he treated me like I was his daughter, *until he didn't*. I don't know if he knew I wasn't his daughter all along, or if she just told him that night. Maybe that's why he chose to come into my room for the first time that night. To get back at her. I guess I'll never know."

"How did the cops not find out what you did?"

"I packed a bag, burned the house down, and ran like hell."

"No one ever came after you?"

"Nope. I guess they figured I died in the fire. Who cares about a kid from a family like mine?"

"Where did you go?"

"I lived on the streets."

"All alone. At fifteen?" he asks.

"You learn to survive. I made friends with some of the kitchen staff at restaurants around the city. If I stopped by at closing time, they would give me leftovers. I stayed in a few shelters and on a few couches, but I never stayed in one place very long."

"Who's your real father?"

"I have no idea." He comforts me by running his hand over my arm, playing with my hair, and placing soft kisses on the side of my head, never letting me go.

"I don't know why I felt the need to tell you my life story. We had such a great time today," I say, feeling embarrassed at my release of information. I never shared this in group sessions or with my counselor. Not even with Ethan.

"Maybe the scene we shared helped you release your pain."

"I don't trust a lot of people, Gary."

"Then I'm one of the lucky ones." He presses his lips to my forehead. "Wanna go walk along the beach and look at the stars?"

"I'd love to."

⌒

We walk along the dark beach. The sound of the waves crashing against the shore is calming, but all I can think about is how stupid I was for sharing so much information with Gary. *If that's his real name.* He didn't do the thing with his eyes, so I *think* he's telling the truth about his name. What in the hell possessed me to tell him I killed my father? He could be FBI, CIA, DEA, or any other three-letter word. I'm lost in my thoughts.

"Hey!" He taps me on the shoulder. "Are you okay?"

"Yeah, I'm fine. Just lost in the beautiful moon, I guess."

He puts his arm around me, and we walk back to the room.

Chapter 16
Gary

Last night couldn't have been more awkward between us. I think she feels like she gave away too much of herself to me. Today is our last day in paradise. I need to make it memorable, but I have some business to take care of first. She stirs beside me. Her hair hangs loosely over her face. I tuck a strand behind her ear and stroke my knuckle over her warm cheek.

"Good morning, sleepyhead," I croon, and she opens her eyes.

"What time is it?" she asks with a groan.

"Almost eight."

She stretches and cuddles back deeper into my side.

"How are we going to *kill time* today?" She yawns.

"I hate to say this, but I'm going to have to leave you for a few hours. I got a message from work, and I have some business I need to take care of on the island before we leave."

"That's okay... I'll find something to get into while you're gone."

"I'm really sorry."

"Work comes first. I know that as well as anybody," she

says as she pulls away to get up. I grab her hand and pull her back to me.

"Don't go. I have a surprise for you."

"A surprise? What kind of surprise?" she beams.

"I booked you a massage."

"You didn't have to do that."

"I know I didn't *have* to." I snuggle my nose into her neck and breathe in her sweet scent. "I wanted to spend our last day together, but then this work thing happened and messed up everything. I want you to have a good last day on the island. Go enjoy your massage, and I'll meet you for dinner this evening."

"Which restaurant do you want me to meet you at?"

"I'll text it to you later."

"Ooo. Mysterious," she says, waggling her eyebrows at me. "I'll pack while you're gone, so I don't have to waste time doing it later."

"See, we have a plan."

She gets out of bed and leans down, placing a chaste kiss on my lips before heading into the bathroom for a shower. I lie there, missing the warmth of her body already. I hear the shower turn on, and all I can think about is how much I don't want to leave her tomorrow. *Dammit! This trip isn't over yet. We still have time, and I want to spend every minute of it I can with her.*

I jump out of bed, cross the room to the bathroom, and turn the doorknob. The shower is on, and fog is forming on the mirror. I open the shower door, and Sasha is sitting on the floor. Her back is against the wall, and her knees are curled up tight to her chest. Her head is buried in her knees while the spray runs over her body.

"Baby, what's wrong?"

Her head pops up and her eyes grow wide.

"What are you doing?" she asks.

"I was going to surprise you with some shower sex, but I think you surprised me instead. Are you okay?" I close the shower door and sit on the tile floor beside her, the hot water pouring over our both of us now.

"I'm fine. I was just thinking."

"You do your best thinking naked on the shower floor, do you?" I ask.

"You could say that." Her voice is sad, and she won't look at me.

"What were you thinking about?"

"About you, and why I told you all that stuff."

"I told you. I won't tell anyone. After tomorrow, we'll both go our separate ways, and we'll never see each other again." I wrap my arm around her and pull her in closer.

"Gee, that makes me feel so much better."

"I just mean—"

"I know what you mean. We were just *killing time*. We both knew what this was. You have your life in New York, and I have mine in Johnsonville. But it's still going to be hard to say goodbye tomorrow."

"Sasha. I need you to know that I-I've never spent this much time with one woman before."

"What?"

"I know it's been fast, but I think I have feelings for you. I'm sorry."

"You're sorry?" *What the fuck is he saying? He's sorry he has feelings for me?*

"I'm not sorry because I've caught feelings for you. I'm sorry because I can't keep you in my life."

"Oh."

"My work takes top priority. I have a bigger relationship with my fist than I do with anyone else."

"My vibrator would agree with you." She chuckles lightly. "I know we can never be anything after tomorrow. I'm just not sure how I can say goodbye to you." She rests her forehead on her knees.

"Look, let's try not to think about it." I stand and pull her to her feet. "Let's just enjoy each other's company while we have it and try not to think about leaving until we have to."

"I'll try, if you will," she says, but she doesn't sound very convincing.

"Deal." We stand in the shower, shaking hands like idiots.

I gather both of her wrists in my hand and pin them above her head. "Now, what about that shower sex?"

"Yes, please." She sighs.

"Turn around, spread your legs, and let me see that sweet ass of yours."

"Yes, sir." My dick springs to life at the sound of that fuck- ing word.

"Say that again."

"Yes, sir."

~

"I really need to get moving. Someone hasn't let me have my computer in days."

"Who, me?" she teases.

"Yes, you." I need to finish the research on my mark and make our dinner reservations for later tonight.

"Enjoy your massage and dress fancy, Baby, because we're celebrating." I kiss her plump just-fucked lips. "There's that beautiful smile." One last peck and I'm gone.

~

I sit down on the bed in my room and start my research. As my fingers touch the keys, I can't help but laugh out loud when I hear the tap, tap, tapping sound. She's right, it *is* loud.

I spend the next hour going through the encrypted emails IT sent me about Raymond Russo. He owes a lot of money to some very powerful people, and I'm here to take care of business. Poison is their weapon of choice. An exchange was arranged for me to turn in the gun for the poison.

I spend just as long arranging dinner plans for this evening. There's a knock.

"Mr. Johnson?" a male voice comes through the door.

"Yes."

"I have the pelican you ordered."

"Is it room temperature?"

"Yes."

"Come in," I say, opening the door since he answered the code correctly. He rolls the dining cart inside and shuts the door behind him. He lifts the cloche and reveals a vial. I take it with my left hand and replace it with the Glock and the nine bullets in my right. He replaces the cloche and rolls the cart back out of the room.

"Have a nice day, sir," he says as he leaves.

All I need to do is pour the contents of the vial into whatever Russo is drinking, make sure he takes a drink, and then get the hell out of there. The poison takes about ten minutes to take effect. By then, I'll be long gone, and Russo will be dead. It will look like a heart attack.

I'm wearing the same suit I wore on the plane, along with my glasses. I've shaved off my stubble and styled my hair. I slide the vial into the pocket of my suit jacket and text IT.

> I'm ready.

THEM

> You'll only have forty-five minutes before the cameras come back online.

> Is he there yet?

> Yes. He's sitting at the bar on the right. He's wearing black pants, a blue Oxford shirt, and a polka-dot tie hanging loose around his neck.

> Copy.

> Get it in his drink and get the fuck out.

> I'll text when it's done.

I make my way to the bar, and he's sitting where they said he was.

"Hey, man," I say casually, sitting down on the barstool to his left.

"Hey," Raymond replies.

"What'll it be?" the bartender asks.

"Scotch on the rocks." He leaves and comes back with my drink. I hover over it, keeping my head low.

"Man, I wish there was a game in this godforsaken place," I complain. The dude is a gambler, he knows what I'm saying.

"Yeah, me too," Raymond speaks up. "This place is boring."

"How long have you been here?" I ask.

"Two days."

"Wait until you've been here four like me, you'll be going stir-crazy." I take a sip of my drink. "You here on business?"

"No, I needed a few days to lie low. I mean to get away from my ole lady, ya know?" He tosses the rest of his drink back.

"Yeah, they can be needy bitches, can't they?"

"You're telling me."

"Let me buy you another drink," I offer.

"Thanks. Gotta take a piss. Be right back." I signal to the bartender to bring Raymond another drink. When he sets it on the bar, I reach into my pocket and pop the lid off the vial. When the bartender turns his back, I dump the contents into the drink and go back to nursing my glass. Raymond stumbles back to his place at the bar, and I push his drink toward him without a word.

"Thanks, man."

"No problem." Raising my glass, I toast, "To freedom."

"To freedom," Raymond repeats, taking a big swallow of his whiskey. That's my cue to get the fuck out of dodge.

"Well, buddy, I'll see ya around," I say.

"Hey, thanks for the drink, man." I nod my head, and I'm out the door.

Chapter 17
Sasha

The hour massage Gary booked for me was heaven. I'm so relaxed. I feel like I'm floating back to my room. When I walk past the bar, I swear I see Gary. He's dressed in the suit he had on the day we met and those damn fuck-me glasses. This must be the business meeting he was talking about. I don't want to interrupt, so I make my way back to my room and take a quick shower before dinner.

My phone dings with a text.

GARY

Meet me on the beach at six.

Where?

You'll see me when you exit the bar where we had our first dinner together.

Okay. See you soon.

My bangs are pinned back in a clip, and the rest of my hair hangs down in thick, wavy curls. My makeup is soft, and I'm wearing the pink lipstick Gary likes. My dress is solid white with a gathered skirt, and it floats around my legs as I walk.

I exit the bar and see Gary straight ahead, just like he said. He reaches his hand out to me.

"Good evening. Sasha, you look stunning." He kisses me on the cheek, and he draws me into him for a hug. I can't take my eyes off the gorgeous scene behind him. The table is set with crystal stemware and white china plates. The breeze gently moves the tablecloth, and the candlelight flickers.

"What is all of this?" My voice is stunned and quiet. He's so handsome in his khaki pants and a loose-fitting white cotton shirt unbuttoned halfway. His tan skin is even darker by candlelight.

"I wanted to celebrate our last night together."

"This is amazing."

"Have a seat," he says as he pulls out my chair and gestures for me to sit.

"No one has ever done anything like this for me before."

"Well, I had to make our last night of *killing time* special." His smile falters. "I'm sorry. We said we weren't going to mention it."

"It's okay. We're both thinking it."

The six-course meal is magnificent. Once a week, the chef cooks an extravagant meal for a select number of guests. Somehow, Gary arranged for *our* food to be served on the beach. I'm starting to wonder who this man is and how he managed to persuade a top-level chef to give us special treatment.

The server pours our wine, and Gary stares at me. I look over my shoulder, wondering what the heck he's looking at.

"Are you okay?" I ask.

"I can't take my eyes off you." His words make my cheeks heat, and suddenly, I feel shy. "You're so beautiful."

"Gary. Stop." I'm not sure where all this bashfulness is coming from, but I'm uncomfortable as hell.

"I'm sorry I had to bail on you today."

"It's all right. Work comes first. Besides, I kept myself busy."

"What did you do all day?"

"I did a little yoga on the balcony. Went down to the cabana for an hour or so and soaked up a little more sunshine. Then I had lunch, packed up my room, and laid out my clothes for tomorrow's trip. How was your meeting?"

"It went exactly as planned."

"What else did you do?" I ask.

"Well, since a certain someone wouldn't let me have my computer, I had to prep for the meeting, and then I made to-night's arrangements."

We make casual chitchat throughout dinner. Neither of us has room for dessert, so while the server packages it up to take back to the room, we decide to take one last moonlight stroll on the beach.

Gary scoots back his chair, and before I can get up, he drops to one knee in front of me.

"What are you doing?" I gasp.

"Helping you take your shoes off." His smoldering eyes look up at me.

"You're crazy."

This man can make anything sexy. He releases the buckle on my shoe. Takes the back of my calf in one hand and removes my shoe with the other. He runs his hands over my calf and my foot, then lowers it back to the ground. It feels so erotic. He repeats the motion with the other shoe and then helps me to stand.

"That was nice," I coo. Gary grins and slips off his loafers, then rolls up his pant legs. He takes me by the hand, and we head for the beach. The moonlight shines over the water. The families have all left, and just a few couples are walking along the seashore.

"Are you going back to New York tomorrow?" I ask, loving the warm water rushing across my feet.

"New York?" He sounds confused.

"Yeah, you said you work in New York."

"Oh yeah, yeah," he backpedals. "I fly Miami to St. Louis and then on to The Big Apple." *He's lying again.*

"It's back to the grind on Monday for me too," I add awkwardly. All this forced talking is starting to make me queasy.

"I'm sure they'll be glad you're back," he says.

"I guess." This whole conversation is fake, and I can't stand it anymore. I let go of his hand and stop walking.

"What's wrong?"

"I don't wanna make small talk anymore. Can't we go back to my room and just *be* together like we were before? No questions, *no lies*, just us."

His brow furrows when I say no lies.

"We can do whatever you want, Princess." He reaches for my hand, and we head back to the table. We put on our shoes and grab the dessert box. He guides me down the gravel path with his hand on the small of my back.

The first thing we see when we enter the room is my bags packed by the door. We both stare at them for a long second. He closes and locks the door and moves into me. His hand wraps around my neck and he pulls me into him. His kiss is gentle and sweet.

"You know, no one has ever treated me the way you do," I say.

"Well, they should. You're an amazing person, Sasha." He swipes my tongue with his and sucks my lower lip into his mouth. "I've never felt this way before."

"What way?" I ask.

"*Needy* for someone. Like I can't get enough of you. I don't take my time with women, Sasha. I'm usually out to get a release and be on my way."

"Oh, so you're just a big ole ho bag off the island then?"

"I wouldn't say that. I just don't take the time to get to know many women, and when I do, something always gets in the way."

"We were *killing time*, so you spent more time with me."

"I think it started that way, but it turned into so much more when I started to get to know you." I want to tell him he doesn't really know who I am. He can never know the truth about what I do for a living or who I really work for. I can't bring him into my world and keep him safe. "I couldn't wait to get back to you today after my meeting."

"Gary," I whisper.

"Yes, Sweetheart."

I place my palms on his chest and push him back against the door. "I want you to scream *my* name tonight." His breath hitches, and a dirty grin spreads across his face.

"Well, if you insist."

I unbutton his shirt the rest of the way and push it off his shoulders. I run my hands up his muscular chest and take his face in my hands. Pulling him into me, I place a chaste kiss on his lips and waste no time dropping to my knees in front of him.

I run my hands over his strong legs as I push his pants to the floor, leaving him in just his boxer briefs. I want to memorize every inch of his body like he did with me last night. My hand lands on his erection. It's already as hard as steel in my hand. When I cup his balls and give a little squeeze, a deep moan vibrates from his chest.

"Oh, Baby Girl, you don't know what you do to me." *I know what I'm gonna do to him.*

"I'm going to drive you wild."

My mouth finds his dick still covered in his boxer briefs, and I breathe my hot breath through them. Finding my way up and down his thick dick with my hot breath, I can feel his ass cheeks clench in my hands.

My fingers curl around the waistband of his boxer briefs, and I tug them down. He steps out and stands before me in all his handsome nakedness. I look up at him, never breaking our gaze, as I wrap my mouth around his length and suck.

"Sasha," he hisses as his cock fills my mouth. I draw him in until he hits the back of my throat, and I gag. He pulls me off his dick.

"What's the matter?" I whine.

"I don't want to hurt you."

I chuckle. "You won't hurt me, Gary. I want you to make me your own personal cock sucking toy."

"Oh, shit," he groans when I pump his cock in my hand.

"Are you sure?"

"Mm Hmm," I agree.

"Tap me on my leg if it gets to be too much for you."

"I'll be fine," I assure him before sticking my tongue out again for his cock. When he feeds it into my mouth, I reach for his hands and bury them in my hair. He knows what I want. For him to control me. He wraps my hair around his fist and pulls it taut, causing a moan to leave my throat, and my pussy floods with my arousal. I push him deeper into my throat and suck him back out.

Starting to find a rhythm, I move my hands to his thighs and give them a squeeze. I want him to control the thrusts. I want him to use my mouth and find the pleasure he needs. My eyes begin to water, and a tear slides down my cheek. His thumb swipes it away as I get lost in the softness of his touch.

He hits the back of my throat, and it brings me back to reality when I choke on his thickness. I breathe in through my nose, and I swallow around him.

"Sasha. Oh, fuuuck, Sa…sha," he moans. "Baby, if you don't stop, I-I'm gonna cum down that sexy throat of yours." I look up at him and double-down my assault on his dick. I want to make him loose control like he does me.

Bringing my hand around, I grip his shaft and suck him deeper into my throat. I flatten my tongue and slide it up and down the underside of his cock, while I suck, and I feel his body tighten.

"Sasha. Oh shit, Sasha," he pants as he comes unglued for me. His eyes roll back into his head and thick ribbons of cum fill my throat. I swallow down every drop and run my tongue over his frenulum, making him squirm. His blown pupils connect with mine, and I know this is a memory he won't soon forget.

Chapter 18
Gary

I grip her shoulders and lift my queen off her knees.

"That was so fuckin' hot. Now it's my turn," I say, unbuttoning the top of her dress and sliding it down to her waist. "You looked like an angel coming to take me to heaven when you walked across the beach this evening." I slide her dress down over her hips and let it fall to the floor. I unbuckle her shoes, and she kicks them to the side with her dress.

"I love it when your hair is down." I remove the clip from her hair and let it fall around her face.

"The way your pink lips glisten in the moonlight." I swipe my tongue over her lips.

"Gary," she pants.

"Shh... Baby... Let me take care of you." I lift her naked body into my arms and lay her on the bed. Leaning over, I place soft kisses on her cheek and down her neck. She stiffens with surprise when I suck her nipple into my mouth and give it a little tug between my teeth.

"I haven't had my dessert yet,"

"We have dessert on the table."

I move my body between her legs and continue my descent

to her sweet, sweet center. "Not as tasty as this one."

My hands grip her thighs and spread them wide for me, and I inhale her delicious scent. My tongue places long, lingering swipes through her folds. Flattening my tongue, I lap up her juices.

"My dessert tastes so fuckin' good."

The sounds coming from her throat are making feral. I devour her like I can't get enough.

"I need your fingers, Gary." I like that she tells me exactly what she needs. I only want to bring her pleasure. My finger breeches her entrance, and she cries out for more. When another joins the party, her pussy grinds down on them. She pants and whines, moans and withers.

"You're so fucking wet, Sasha. Fuck."

My lips settle around her needy clit, and I suck as I crook my fingers and work her G-spot. Her orgasm explodes through her body and her legs clench around my head. For a moment, the sounds of her cries are muffled. When she looks down to see my head trapped between her legs, she giggles. "Oh God, I'm so sorry."

"It's okay. It was worth it to feel you come unglued on my tongue."

"Come up here," she coos.

I climb her body. "What can I do for you, Baby Girl?" I tease. My mouth hovers centimeters from hers.

Our breath is hot and all consuming before she says, "Fuck me. Fuck me hard, Gary. I want to feel you tomorrow, after you leave.

"Say please."

"Please. I need to feel your big cock inside me."

I plunge my tongue into her mouth and claim her. She's mine. Even if it can only be for tonight. I know she can feel it too when she raises her legs around my waist and pulls me into her.

"Now, Gary. Fuck me, now," she growls like a woman possessed. I feel like I'm burning from the inside out, and she's the only flame that doesn't consume me.

I take my dick in my hand and notch it at her entrance. She digs her heels into my ass cheeks. "Move… Now… Please…" she begs. I snap out of my pleasure-induced haze and thrust into her to the hilt in one hard push. Our moans fill the room.

"Yes. That's it. Gary. Oh."

Our movements are lust-filled and greedy. Her tight pussy clamps around my cock with such force that it's almost painful.

"Goddamm, your pussy takes me so well."

Her core pulses around me, and she writhes beneath my touch. I can't stop it this time as her pussy wrings another orgasm from me.

Her eyes flutter back into her head as little spasms surge through her core and into my dick. Nothing can satiate this need I have for her. I want to feel every shock as they flow through her. I want to watch her face as euphoria takes over. I want to hear all the sounds she makes. I love how she lets go and enjoys every sensation. I lift up to pull out of her, and she stops me.

"No. Don't leave me. Not yet." Her arms wrap around my middle, and she buries her head in my chest.

"I'll stay inside you all night, if that's what you need, Baby."

I envelop her body in mine and hold her. Just hold her. I've never wanted to stay connected with a woman in every way like I do Sasha.

〜

When she ready, she motions for me to pull out. I go to the bathroom and bring back a wet cloth to clean her up. Her eyes are closed, and she looks calm and relaxed. I lie down beside her, and she instinctively cuddles into my chest.

"I feel like I'm floating," she coos.

"Me too, Baby, me too."

Our limbs wind around one another, and I want to hold her in our little cocoon forever.

〜

We wake with groans as the sun shines through the billowing curtains, telling us what we both already know. Our time together is about to come to an end.

We both knew this couldn't be anything more than sex and fun when we started *killing time*. Sasha would never understand what I do for a living. She's so good and sweet. My world is too dangerous for someone like her, and I could never forgive myself if she got hurt because of me.

"Good morning." I place a kiss to the side of her head.

"Good morning," she sighs.

"Can you still feel me this morning, like you wanted?"

"Yes, and it feels delicious. Last night was perfect. Thank you." She runs her hand across my chest.

"I told you when we woke up together after the rum fiasco, you would remember it when I fucked you…"

"…with your big dick," she finishes with a giggle.

"I wasn't going to go there, but if we must." Now we're both laughing.

"We need to get moving," I say on an exhale.

"Yeah. I know."

We shower together until the water runs cold. We get dressed and we sit on the balcony. Watching the beautiful blue water and soaking every last moment we have together.

I don't want to leave her, but I've put it off as long as I can. "I need to go to my room and pack," I reluctantly say.

"I know," she says on a long sigh.

"Do you want to ride to the airport together?" I ask.

"Sure, that would be great."

"I'll meet you in the lobby at ten o'clock. Okay?"

"Yeah. I'll be there," she says, and I place a gentle kiss on her lips

I have less than an hour to pack my bags and clear my room. Sasha is already in the lobby waiting for me when I stroll into the lobby. Our bags are loaded into the waiting taxi, and we set out for the airport. She's nestled into my side. I can't believe I've found this remarkable woman, and I have to let her go. It's for her safety.

"Hey, we haven't checked our seat numbers. What are the odds we sit by each other on this flight too?" she perks up.

"Let's check." We both bring our tickets up on our phones and compare. "I'm in 12B. Where are you?"

"2A. Dammit," she says.

"That's okay. We can say another quick goodbye when we disembark."

We go through security and board the plane. Sasha takes her seat in first class, and I continue down the aisle to 12B with a sorry excuse for a smile on my face.

Chapter 19
Sasha

An older gentleman sits to my right, but I don't even acknowledge his presence. I'm being stupid. I know Gary is on the same plane, but it feels like he's already a thousand miles away. We have to say goodbye when we land anyway, so I might as well get used to it.

I lean my head against the window. I don't even notice the plane take off because my eyes are rimmed with tears. My mind is reeling with memories of the week with Gary. The tours, the dinners, the sex. It was all too perfect.

"Excuse me, Miss, is this seat taken?" a male voice says. I turn my head to see Gary standing in the aisle, pointing at the now empty seat.

I shake my head. He puts his backpack under the seat in front of him and sits down beside me.

"How... I mean... You got them to let you switch seats?"

"I paid the man beside you a thousand dollars to switch seats with me."

"You're crazy."

"About you," he says.

"No computer," I say, pointing my finger at him.

"No computer, *on this flight*." He laughs. He lifts the armrest and two seats become one. I scoot closer to him, and he wraps his arms around me. I could've climbed onto his lap and fucked his brains out in front of the whole plane, but I'm guessing that's not appropriate behavior on a commercial flight.

The curtains between first class and the rest of the plane are pulled closed. I notice there are only four other people in first class, so I have an idea.

"Meet me in the lavatory," I say in his ear. His eyes grow wide, but he doesn't tell me no. I move past him and down the short aisle to the empty room, where I make eye contact with the flight attendant in the galley. She smiles knowingly as I close myself into the tiny space.

It doesn't take long before the door opens and Gary squeezes inside.

"Oh my God, how are we going to do this? There's no room."

"Improvise." I reach down to unbutton his slacks and push them down only as far as I need to spring his cock from its jail.

"Aren't you a member of the Mile High Club?" I ask. "You fly all the time."

"Nope. This is my first time doing this."

"Mine too. Now, sit," I demand, and he obeys. I lift my skirt, push my panties to the side and mount his huge cock for the ride of my life.

⌒

What little time remains of our flight flies by, and before we know it, we're landing in Miami. My flight is scheduled to take off before his, so he walks me to my gate. When boarding begins, we squeeze each other's hands tightly.

"This is it," I say.

"Yeah, I guess so. Sasha…"

"I know. You don't have to say it."

"But… I want you to know how much this week has meant to me. I'll never forget you." He pulls me against his chest.

"I won't forget you either, Gary. Do great things in The Big Apple." I try to plaster a fake-ass smile on my face. Acting like it doesn't bother me to let go of the best thing that's ever happened to me.

"You do the same in Johnsonville." I wonder if he's going to call me "buddy" or "pal" next.

They call the final boarding call, and panic surges through my body. I crash into his arms for one more hug and turn to walk away.

He grabs my hand and pulls me back into him for one last glorious kiss. I float down the jetway, telling myself this is all for the best. I can't be with him. He wouldn't understand *taking care of business*, and I need to keep him safe.

Chapter 20
Sasha

Monday morning rolled around a little too soon, but I was up on time. Dressed back in my business attire. I'm ready to be Sasha "The Professional" again. My navy wrap dress and pumps fit the bill for today.

I walk into the office, drop my stuff on my desk, and see if the boss is in his office. I knock on his door, and he bellows, "Come in!"

"Hey, Boss. I just wanted to let you know I'm back."

"Thank fuck!"

"What's wrong?"

"No one can find shit around here. No one knows how to fix the damn copy machine. No one runs this place quite like you do. I'm so glad you're back." My heart fills with warmth at the thought that they needed me.

"Thanks, Boss." I turn to leave.

"Sasha."

"Yeah, Boss."

"Did you at least have a good time?"

"Yeah, I did. Thanks for forcing me to go on vacation."

"Same time next year?"

"I don't know if my heart can take it, but we'll see." Ethan looks confused, but I have work to do, and he wouldn't understand.

Lola rolls into the office around one o'clock to go to lunch with Ethan. As soon as she enters the office, she starts badgering me for information.

"Tell me all about your trip." She shoots me a cheeky grin.

"It was fine," I say, walking over to the filing cabinet.

"You look... different."

"Different?" I wave her off.

"You look like something changed in you while you were gone."

"I'm tan from lying on the beach."

"I don't mean your skin. There's something else different about you."

"Maybe something did happen."

"Tell me." She's giddy with excitement.

"Fine. His name was... um, Joe, and he's in finance out of New York City."

"New York City. Sounds like money to me."

"We didn't talk about money."

"Where did you meet?"

"He's the guy who sat beside me on the planes I texted you about."

"Oh. So you hooked up later?"

"Yes. At dinner the first night, by accident."

"What do you mean by accident?" she asks.

"We didn't make any plans to see each other when we got off the plane. As a matter of fact, he just left me sitting there. He was kind of a jerk."

"So how did you have dinner together?"

"I didn't make reservations at the hotel restaurant. When they said it was an hour wait, I went to sit at the bar. G... Joe saw me and asked me to join him."

"He sounds like he turned out to be nice after all."

"Yes, he did," I say with a smile.

She grabs me by the shoulders. "Oh my gosh! You're blushing! You like this guy... A lot."

"I enjoyed *killing time* with him."

"Killing time?"

"That's what we called spending time together at first, *killing time*. Because we both were forced to be there by our bosses." I give her a little side-eye.

"What did you do to *kill time*?"

I fill her in on the boat excursion we took to the rum distilleries, and I give her the bottle of rum I brought back for her and Ethan. I tell her about our drunken evening and waking up in bed naked together, and the motorcycle ride.

"He sounds perfect for you. When are you seeing him again?"

"I'm not."

"What the fuck! Why not?"

"Because we said from the beginning it was only for the week. We live in two different states."

"The distance is no big deal. He just needs to move here."

"He can't."

"Why the hell not?"

"You know what my side job is, Lola. He can never find out about that. I've never been seen or caught. The more people who know what I do, the riskier it'll be to help these women."

"I know that. But you deserve a chance at happiness too, Sasha."

"I don't think that's in the cards for me. He would never understand my line of work.

"But..."

"I do know I've never felt like this before. It would break my heart if he ended up disapproving of me or worse, getting hurt because of me. We both knew it was going to end, and now it's ...over." Her little pregnant body tries to hug the life out of me.

"We have to fix this. Call him. Text him. Something."

"I can't."

"Sure, you can."

"No, I *can't*. We didn't exchange phone numbers. We knew if we did, it wouldn't be a clean break."

"You're one tough broad."

"I have to keep him safe. I could never live with myself if he got hurt."

"I'm sure the IT guys can find him if you want them to."

"I don't want to, Lola. I can't."

"Let me know if you change your mind." She pulls me in for another hug. "Is Ethan busy?"

"No, you can go in." Lola goes into Ethan's office and shuts the door behind her. There's a lot of whispering, but I can't make out what they're saying.

Around four o'clock, my burner phone rings.

"Hey, Jerry, whatcha got for me?"

"Are you back in town yet, girly?" he asks.

"Yeah, and I need to get back to work. If you know what I mean."

"I have something for you, then. Her name is Katie Fulkow-ski. Her boyfriend is Tony Manillo. They call him Manny. I'll text you her phone number. She's asking for your help."

"What did he do?"

"A little bit of everything. Beat her, terrorized her, and almost ran her off the road, chasing her after an evening out with friends. She's scared to be in the same room with him. Afraid he'll put her in the hospital again. He's pretty evil, Sasha."

"How does she want me to do it?"

"She doesn't care. It's your choice. But, Sasha."

"Yeah, Jerry?"

"He's from one of Freddy's rival gangs, the Ravens."

"The Russians. Does Freddy know?"

"No, and I don't think we should involve him. The less he knows, the better."

"Okay. I'll call and talk to her."

"You need to be extra careful on this one, Sasha."
"Jerry, you're the one who taught me how to be careful."
"I mean it, girly. These guys are dangerous."
"I'll be okay. I'll text you when it's done."

I speak to Katie, and she's skittish as hell. This boyfriend of hers is a real piece of work. I had no problem accepting the job. She thinks she's being followed, so she won't meet me in person. She's holed up in a crappy motel on the edge of the city. I tried to get her to let me take her to the shelter, but she refused. Instead, she's agreed to go when the job is done.

Now, how to do it?

Chapter 21
Gary

've only been back in my condo for a few days when the phone rings.

"Yeah?"

"We have a problem," the boss snaps.

"No, how was your trip? Did you enjoy yourself? Did you hook up with any hot chicks?"

"Oh yeah, where are my manners? You can tell me all those things tonight at the club, but first, I have a job for you."

"Fine. What's up?"

"I need you to take care of some business downtown. There's a guy causing trouble on the corner of Rogers Street and Green. He's been shaking down our customers and working them over pretty good. I need him gone."

"What's he look like?"

"Blond-haired ponytail-wearing fuck boy. About six foot two, 180 pounds. He drives a red-and-black Triumph Rocket 3GT, and his helmet is red with a black devil painted on the back."

"Name?"

"Hewey Rivers."

"Do I need to get rid of the body?"

"Nope, shoot him on the street and let him lie there. It'll send a warning to the rest. They need to know I'm not fucking around."

"Drive by or sniper?"

"Do it how you wanna do it. I don't give a shit."

"Get Daniel to shut those cameras down in the area tonight."

"Will do."

"I'll take care of it and meet you at Scarlett's when it's done."

"Then you can tell me all about the hot chicks you hooked up with." He laughs.

I walk to the end of the hallway to where a bookcase fills the wall. I pull the second book to the right on the top shelf and hear a click. I pull on the shelf and it slides open, revealing my weapons room.

As I walk into the space, I breathe in the earthy scent of gun oil. The walls and carpet are black. The shelves are backlit with soft white light, as are the clean, shiny mirrors lining the counters. This is my favorite spot in the house. I built it to hold my ladies. They line the walls. Each with its own place of honor. To the right behind the door is my pride and joy. My grandpa's Chiappa Triple Threat—Eleanor.

"Hello, ladies. Daddy's home," I croon. My fingertips glide over the guns hanging on the wall. They stop on the MP7 fully automatic submachine gun. Her name is Josie, and tonight is her night. I take her down to clean and ready my weapon.

There's not much of a character involved in tonight's activities, but I still have a routine.

I pull on my black leather pants, black T-shirt, black leather jacket with a diagonal zipper, black biker boots, and black riding gloves. I pick up a fully loaded Josie, turn out the lights, and lock the room up tight. With Josie tucked safely inside my jacket, I proceed to the garage where my black Ducati Nera is parked. I pull on my plain black helmet and leave the garage.

Dressed in all black, I feel like Batman. But tonight, I won't be saving the world, just taking out the trash.

Coming to a stop on the block parallel to Rogers Street and Green, I can see the dickhead through my hands-free binoculars under my visor. It has to be him, blond fuckin' ponytail and all. He's roughed up one of our customers, and they are lying on the ground. He has mounted his bike and is getting ready to pull away from the curb.

It's late evening, and there aren't too many people on the street for a Thursday night. I pull Josie out of my coat, flip off the safety, and hold it out of sight in my lap. I rev up my bike and start down the street toward Hewey.

When I get within range, I raise Josie and fire, hitting him several times in quick succession. His body jerks with each hit. He loses control of his bike and falls to the ground, with it resting on top of him. I shoot a few more rounds as I pass by and leave him for dead on the side of the road. I don't want to backtrack and get caught by a camera, so I jump on the highway and head for home.

I park safely in the garage and return to my gun room. I clean my lady and place her back in her spot on the wall. "Another job well done, girl." I remove my black leather everything and take a quick shower.

Dressed in dark blue jeans, a gray Henley, and my blue jean jacket, I grab the keys to my pickup truck and head for Scarlett's. When I arrive, I head straight to the VIP area, where Max and Franco are sitting with the boss.

"There he is! It's about time you come back from your vacation," Max hollers as he throws back a shot of who knows what.

"Why? Did you miss me?" I ask batting my eyelashes at him.

"No, weirdo." He gives me a little shove. "We want to hear about all the pussy you got on the island."

"Nah." I wave him off.

"What do you mean, nah? Come on man, tell us," Franco pushes for more.

"I mean no. I'm not telling you shit." I raise my hand to Vinny, the bartender, for a drink.

"Come on, dude. We live vicariously through your hook ups."

"She must not have been any good," Max jokes. I rise from my chair so fast it crashes to the floor and grab him by the neck.

"Don't you ever say something like that to me again," I growl. His eyes are wide, and his pupils are blown as he tries to speak.

"M-M-Man, I was just pulling your chain. S-S-Sorry." I remove my hand from his throat and step back.

"Damn, you've got it bad," Franco says, shaking his head. My glare moves to him, and he stiffens.

"What the fuck are you talking about?" I hiss.

"She must've been amazing for you to act like that."

"She was. Now, can everybody just shut the fuck up, please?" I take my drink from Vinny, shoot it back, hand him back the empty glass, and bark, "Another." Vinny looks into the empty glass and heads back to the bar.

"Hey, you two, go get laid or something, and let me talk to lover boy over here." The boss waves them away.

"Whatever," they grumble as they leave us.

Vinny brings me my second drink.

"Keep 'em comin'." I fix my chair and sit back down at the table.

"What the hell happened down there?" he asks.

"I sat beside this prim and proper woman on the first two legs of the flight down. We spent a little time together while our planes were delayed, and I thought that was it."

"But…?" His voice draws out the word.

"But after I got the job done on the ship and settled into the resort, I saw her again at dinner. I invited her to eat with me. And…"

"Good God, man! What? What!" he demands.

"We ended up spending the entire trip together."

"Oh. Shit."

"She can hold her liquor, rides motorcycles, and fucks like a goddamn queen."

"I don't understand what the problem is. When are you gonna see her again?"

"I'm not."

"Why the fuck not?"

"Because when we started *killing time* together, we agreed it was just for the trip, nothing else. I can't share my life with someone as sweet as she is. She wouldn't understand what I do for a living."

"Maybe someone sweet like her is exactly what you need."

"Nah, man. I would be worried about her all the time."

"So you're just gonna be alone for the rest of your life?"

"Maybe."

"Man, you know that's not realistic, right?"

"Why not?"

"Because everyone needs somebody. Even this dumbass needs someone."

"It doesn't matter because I don't know how to find her," I say.

"You're telling me you didn't exchange phone numbers or anything?"

"Nope."

"Damn, man, you're an idiot."

"No, I'm not. I need to keep her safe. I liked her." I throw back my drink and raise my hand to Vinny.

"What's her name?"

"Sandy."

"Damn, even her name sounds innocent."

"See, told ya."

"Are you going to drink yourself under the table tonight?"

"Yep. Is that okay with you?"

"Do I have a choice?"

"Nope. And the job went like clockwork, by the way."

"Yeah, I know. Daniel told me."

Chapter 22
Sasha

Taking someone down takes planning. It's not just about how I change my appearance and what I drive, but it's also about where I do it. How will I do it? What weapon will I use? How do I get in? How do I get out without being seen? Jerry taught me it's all in the details.

I've spent the last few evenings following Manny around. He's always surrounded by an entourage of deadbeats. They seem to finish off their evenings at an old garage off Highway 81. I decide I'm going to do it there. I don't need to be in character for this one because they'll never see me coming. I want it to be painful and slow, so I'm going to use my paintball gun.

A paintball gun doesn't sound deadly. But it can be, depending on what types of balls you use in it. I'll be using three different types tonight.

The first paintballs will be filled with oleoresin capsicum liquid, commonly known as liquid pepper spray. It'll burn their eyes and keep them temporarily disabled while I get the dragon eggs ready. A dragon egg holds two chemicals, aluminum and lead oxide. When they combine upon impact, it will cause a fire.

The third and final ball is specifically for Manny. It contains a small amount of white phosphorus. When air comes into contact with the chemicals, they will self-combust, causing a fire that cannot be extinguished. It has to burn itself out. If there is enough of it, it will burn everything in its path: fabric, skin, bone, wood, metal, anything.

I lay out my weapon of choice and line the paintballs up in the order I want to use them. I decided to wear all black tonight. I pull my hair back into a braid, so my helmet will fit better. Black leather pants, boots, jacket, and gloves. There's nothing on me that's not black, including the black makeup that covers my eyes and nose when my visor is up. I load up my pockets and head for my bike.

Opening the garage door to my townhouse, I throw my leg over my Kawasaki Ninja 400 ABS. I had it repainted, so it's all black, and the slip-on exhaust helps reduce noise and makes it sound rumbly and deep. I follow Highway 81 and slowly pass by the garage. His bike and two others are out front. I ditch my ride behind some trees down the road and hike through the woods to the back of the garage.

I look through a window in the back, and sure enough, the usual three suspects are there. I take cover in the trees and get ready. I load the pepper balls first.

I shoot ten pepper balls through the window and watch for their reactions.

They hear the window shatter and look around to see why. Then it hits them. They rub their eyes and start to cough uncontrollably. Their faces turn red, snot runs from their noses, as they walk around aimlessly.

Dragon eggs at the ready.

I shoot one at the gas tank of a motorcycle off to the left of the garage and another into a desk full of papers on the right. Both ignite like clockwork, and the flames begin to grow. The three of them are blinded and coughing, trying to find a way to escape the fire.

White phosphorus ball loaded and at the ready.

I set my aim on Manny and shoot my shot. It hits him square in the back, and he screams in pain as the phosphorus ignites. My job here is done. Nothing is going to stop this fire now.

I hike back to my bike. When I drive past the garage, it's fully engulfed in flames. I call Jerry on my headset and head for the motel to pick up Katie.

"It's done," I report.

"How'd you do it?" he asks.

"Death by paintball."

"Girly, where does your mind come up with this shit?"

"I had an excellent teacher."

"I didn't teach you shit like that!"

"No. But you taught me to think outside the box."

"Where are you?" Jerry asks.

"I'm heading to the motel to pick up Katie and take her to the shelter."

"Let me know when you're both safe."

"Will do."

I hang up the call as a fire truck screams past me. I dial Lola.

"It's done. I'm on my way to get Katie."

"I'll meet you at the shelter," she says.

"Copy that."

I pull into the seedy motel. I tap the door to her room four times, and she opens it a crack.

"Get your shit and let's get the fuck out of here," I bark. She should've already been safe at the shelter. It pissed me off that she refused, but it's time to get her the fuck out of here.

"Are you sure he's dead?" she asks tentatively.

"There's no way he could've survived the phosphorus. Come on, let's get you somewhere safe."

She picks up her meager backpack full of belongings, and we head to my bike. I didn't bring her a helmet, so I take mine off and put it on her.

"What about you?" she sounds worried.

"It's just a short ride. I'll be fine." I get on the bike and start it up. She climbs on the back and holds on tight while we continue down Route 26 to the shelter.

Ten minutes later, I'm typing in the code to the underground garage. The door opens, and we pull inside. I turn to watch the door close, park and turn off the bike. Lola is waiting for us in the doorway.

"Katie, this is Lola. She owns the shelter, and she's here to help you."

"Thank you," Katie says, as she breaks down and begins to cry.

"Come on. Let me show you around, and then you can get some rest," Lola says, leading her inside.

I head to the security office and check the cameras to make sure no one followed us. When it seems all clear, I go to the bathroom and take off my black makeup.

I keep extra clothes at the shelter for nights like this. When I bring in someone new, I like to spend the night, so they know they're not alone. Lola shows Katie to her room.

"It's going to be okay now. He's gone," Lola tries to reassure her.

"Thank you."

She hugs us both, and we leave her to get settled in. It's going to be a long night. The first night always is.

Katie closes and bolts the door.

Lola debates whether to stay the night.

"I have it covered. I'll stay until Marissa and the staff get here in the morning.".

I spent most of the night sitting in the hall outside Katie's door, listening to her cry. Around three in the morning, she seems to have fallen asleep. So I move down to the family room and try to get some sleep myself.

Marissa comes to work at eight and wakes me up with a little shake.

"Sasha, I'm here. You can go now," she whispers. I stretch, and my nose follows the smell of coffee to the kitchen.

"How did she do last night?" she asks.

"She cried until around three." She hands me a cup of the black gold.

"She'll be okay. It's hard for some of them to *feel* safe for quite a while, even after their abuser is gone. I'll keep an eye on her. You get to work."

"Thanks. Let me know if you need me." I finish my coffee and head out on my bike. I make it back to the townhouse, change into my Sasha "The Professional" clothes, hop in my white Camry, and head to work. Walking into my office, I see Freddy standing by my desk.

"Hey, what's up?" I ask, putting my bag down on my chair.

"Where have you been? You're late." His deep booming voice fills the small space. *He's not my boss. Ethan is.*

"Ethan knows where I was." My eyebrows tense from his tone. "What's wrong?"

"Did you take care of some business last night?" he questions.

"Yeah, why?"

"Well, the Ravens paid me a little visit at the ass crack of dawn. Accused me of taking out Tony Manillo and two of his flunkies last night."

Confirmation noted. I took out all three dirtbags.

"Yeah, it was me. Why?" My voice filled with satisfaction.

"Because they said they have video footage of someone on a black bike leaving the area."

"Video footage? Daniel was supposed to cut all the cameras in the area last night."

He looks down at the ground. "That was probably my fault."

"What the fuck! Why is it your fault?" I seethe.

"Because I had him working on a little project for me, and I think yours fell through the cracks."

"My LIFE fell through the cracks!" My words boom through the room. Ethan comes flying out of his office when he hears me raise my voice. He knows I don't yell in the office.

"What the fuck is going on out here?" he barks.

"Daniel didn't turn off the cameras while I took care of that scumbag piece of shit last night, and they saw me leave."

"Fuck, Freddy. What the hell?"

"Yeah, well, it gets worse," Freddy continues.

"How the fuck can it get any worse?" I replay the night in my mind. *How could it be any worse?*

"I had Daniel go back through all the footage he could find from last night with Sasha in it and scrub it, but he found something which might be a problem,"

"No. No. No. No. No." My hands cover my face as I pace around the office.

"What the hell's wrong?" Ethan asks.

"I took my helmet off at the motel. Fuck!"

"Why did you take off your helmet?" Ethan asks. "You never break your cover."

"I wanted to get Katie to the shelter as soon as possible. She wouldn't go until Manillo was dead. I only had one helmet with me, and she needed it more than I did. So I put it on her. They could've *kinda* seen my face."

"What do you mean, *kinda* seen your face?" Freddy asks.

"I didn't think I needed a full disguise for the job, so I only put black makeup on my eyes and face where the visor was. So part of my face would've been black, but the rest wasn't covered. And I didn't wear a wig."

"Dammit!" Ethan points at me and yells, "So you deviated from the plan not once, but twice! Sasha, you don't make these kinds of mistakes." Turning to Freddy, he continues, "And you! I thought we hired extra IT people so this kind of shit wouldn't happen. I wanted to ensure all bases were covered whenever we needed them. Why didn't he delegate the cameras to someone else?"

"I don't know, but I'll fucking find out." IT falls under Freddy's jurisdiction in The Organization.

"What do I do now?" I ask. "I have another job tomorrow night."

"Do you think they followed you?"

"We didn't see anything out of the ordinary on the security cameras at the shelter, and I didn't notice a tail this morning."

"Maybe they don't know who you are. All they said was that a black bike left the scene. They didn't say if it was a woman or a man. Keep the bike hidden for a while. And maybe stay away from the shelter unless it's necessary," Freddy suggests.

"I've never been seen before," I murmur, panic seeping in.

"We're not positive you've been seen yet," Ethan tries to reassure me. "Just change up your routine and keep your head on a swivel. Let Freddy or me know if anything out of the ordinary comes up."

"I will."

Chapter 23
Gary

It's been a few weeks since I've been back from vacation, and I can't seem to get Sasha out of my head. I know we said we would never see each other again, but I miss those damn lips so much. Maybe I could do a little search for her. My fingers slide over the keys on my laptop. Just once. No. Fuck, no. I can't do that to her. We promised.

I have to keep myself busy. My phone rings, and it's the boss. Before I even answer, he speaks.

"I have a job for you." *Thank fuck. Something to keep my mind off Sasha.*

"Okay. Details."

"Come to the office and I'll fill you in."

"Why can't you tell me on the phone?"

"It's kind of a different situation."

"I'll be there in twenty."

I walk into the boss's office, and the room is empty. I plop down in one of the leather chairs in front of his desk and wait. After a few minutes, I hear a commotion out in the hall and the door flies open. In walks the boss, and he's tailed by Max and Franco, who are dragging a guy I've never seen before.

"What the hell?" I say as I stand.

"Gary, this is Janson Banks." I stare at the guy. They're basically holding him up by his armpits. His face is bloody, and his nose is huge and black and blue. "*He's* your next assignment." My eyes connect with the boss.

"What do you need me for? It looks like they have the situation under control."

"Well, you see, Janson here has been stalking one of my waitresses at Scarlett's."

"Which one?"

"Maggie."

"She's the new girl, right? Twenty-one, dark hair."

"Yeah. That's her. You could say he tried to *hunt* her."

"Hunt her? I don't understand."

"Janson snatched Maggie after work one night and drove her out to the woods. He gave her a two-minute head start and told her to run."

"I was just trying to play with her."

"You have to be two consenting adults to primal play, you idiot. She wasn't a consenting player in the game. She basically ran for her life in those woods that night."

"Did you hurt her?" I ask. Janson squeezes his eyes closed and shakes his head. I turn to the boss. "Is she all right?"

"She had some cuts and scratches from running around the woods in the dark, and a twisted ankle, but she's fine. She's one smart kid."

"What do you mean?"

"She used what she learned and got away from him." The boss puts all of the female staff through training at the gym with Jerry. He teaches them tips and tricks to disarm customers and keep themselves safe. We have bouncers. Big bouncers. But they can't be everywhere all the time. If the girls can keep the troublemaker busy until help arrives, they'll have a better chance of not getting hurt.

"Would you like to tell the story, Janson, or would you like me to do it?" Janson hangs his head and begins the story.

"I thought we were playing a game. Really, I did!"

"The story, Janson!" the boss demands.

"I grabbed her in the employee parking lot at Scarlett's. I put her in the trunk of my car and drove her out to the woods by Dole Park. I took the ropes off her wrists and told her she had a two-minute head start. I watched her run off into the darkness. I brought my night vision goggles, so no matter where she tried to hide, I would find her. I watched her zigzag through the trees. Her chest was heaving with each ragged breath, and the sweat on her skin glistened in the moonlight." His voice starts to trail off as he remembers her body.

"Okay, you perv. How did she get away?" I bark.

"Oh yeah, right. She tripped over a tree root and twisted her ankle. She was trying to crawl behind a bush when I caught up with her. I won."

"You won?"

"Yeah, the game."

"Fuck. Keep going," the boss grumbles.

"I was crawling up her body to take my prize when she headbutted me. She broke my nose, man!"

"Aw, poor baby," I hiss.

"She used those heavy combat boots she wears to kick me in the balls. Then she stole my goggles and left me lying there on the forest floor in the dark."

"Good for her," the boss says.

"So what do you have in mind for this piece of shit?" I ask.

"Please. Just let me go. I'll never do it again!"

"Shut the fuck up!" I yell.

"I want you to take him out to the woods tonight and hunt *him* down, like he hunted down Maggie." A smile spreads across my face. This will definitely take my mind off Sasha for a few hours.

"I have the perfect gun for this little game."

⌒

Max and Franco deliver Janson to the edge of the woods

at Dole Park. Maggie is standing off to the side watching as I walk up. She points to the place where he set her free, and explains how she got away.

"Do you want me to hold him while you kill him.? I ask. She shakes her head. Her eyes are as big as saucers.

"Do you want to watch me do it?"

"No." She looks down at her hand as she plays with a piece of ripped skin on her finger.

"Do you want me to take care of him in the woods and tell you when I'm done?"

Her green eyes look up at me and she nods. "Is that okay?"

I take her hands in mine and stop the nervous picking. "I can do whatever you want, Maggie." He nods her head and the game is on.

Tonight, I'll be using my grandpa's 1916 Chiappa Triple Threat shotgun with 12-gauge buckshot shells. Janson's eyes are wide as he watches me prepare it. I load all three shells into their chambers at one time. It's a little trick Gramps showed me to intimidate your opponent.

"You don't have to do this, man, come on," he panics.

"It'll be fun. It's just a game, right?" I tease.

"I wasn't going to shoot her."

"No, you were just going to *fuck* her. Maybe I should fuck that fat ass of yours, Janson. Is that what you want?"

"No! Fuck. No!"

"I'm going to give you the same two-minute head start you gave Maggie, but I'll be able to find your sorry ass without any fancy night vision goggles." The moon is full and bright tonight, and it'll light my way through the forest. This idiot doesn't even have a chance. "Are you ready, Janson?"

"No. No. Please. Can't we talk about this?"

"Time for talking is over. Get ready…Set…Go!" Janson takes off running through the forest, knocking branches out of his way with his forearms. He makes so much noise, I know exactly where he is. Two minutes go by, and I enter the woods. Slowly, I move forward into the darkness and begin to stalk my prey.

After a few minutes, his footsteps stop, and I can hear his heavy breathing floating through the air.

"Why did you stop running, Janson?" I taunt.

"You know I'm going to catch you," I singsong.

"And when I do, I'm going to blow your fucking head off," I growl.

The footfalls begin again, and a loud thud follows when he hits the ground.

"Aw, you can do better than that."

He scrambles to his feet, but he's not running. He's... hobbling. He must've hurt a leg or foot or something.

"Did little Janson get a boo-boo?" I laugh like a lunatic. I can hear grunts and feet shuffling through the leaves.

"Do you need a break, Janson? Oh wait, you didn't give Maggie any breaks to catch her breath, did you? Never mind."

The movement begins again, but I can't help tormenting him. "You need to do better. I can smell your fear." My voice is deep and menacing now.

I can see him clearly in the distance. He's maybe fifteen yards in front of me.

"There you are," I croon. He turns around to find me, and he trips. Falling to the ground once again.

"Get up!"

He's whimpering. Tears flood his face. "Please," he begs. "Don't do this."

"I said, get up! I want to look in your eyes when I shoot you." He pushes himself up to stand, and when he turns to run, there is a giant tree in his way. He spins to look at me, back up against the tree. "Please," he cries.

"You're such a pussy. You have to kidnap a woman because you couldn't get her the right way," I taunt, giving his cheek a smack.

"It was a game," he pleads as I back away from him.

"It was *your* sick and twisted game that she didn't want to play." I raise my weapon and size up my shot.

"I know that now. Please, I'll never do it again. I swear."

"You won't get a chance to play again." I squeeze off the three rounds in rapid succession, and buckshot sprays across his body. His clothes immediately soak with blood from so many spots you can't count. He falls to the ground one last time with a thud, dead.

I turn and make my way out of the forest to where Max and Franco are waiting.

"You know what to do," I say as I walk past them.

"Yes, Boss," they agree in unison.

Chapter 24
Sasha

'm meeting a new client, Victoria, at the shelter to discuss the situation with her husband. She's waiting in Amelia's office when I enter.

"Oh good, you made it," Amelia says. "Victoria, I'd like you to meet Sasha. She's going to help you with your problem."

"Hi," she says timidly.

I sit down in the chair next to her and try not to spook her. "It's nice to meet you, Victoria. I know this is difficult for you, but can you tell me a little bit about what's been going on with your husband?" She squirms in her chair. She looks so uncomfortable. I hope she doesn't bolt on us.

Deciding to kill your significant other is difficult for most women. As a matter of fact, I haven't met one woman that hasn't been upset. Sometimes at the last minute they become remorseful and get a little skittish. Maybe he'll change and all that shit. But the fact is, once they make it to me, their life has already been a shit show, and they're screaming for someone. Anyone. To listen to them and help. I've only had two women start the consultation and then bolt. But they both came back after another round of beatings, and begged me to took care of business.

"It's okay, Victoria. We're here to help you. He can't touch you in here. You're safe," Amelia tries to reassure her. She nods and begins to speak.

"Please call me Tori. *He* called me Victoria," she clarifies.

"Of course, Tori."

"We've been married ten years. He wasn't always like this. We used to have a lot of fun and…loved each other." Tears fill her eyes. "But the last few years have been really hard, ya know? He works long hours and is under a great deal of pressure at work. When he comes home late, he takes it out on me. He's put me in the hospital three times. I've had various broken bones." She holds up her arm, and shows us her crooked fingers. "I've had two concussions, and the doctors said if I get another one, it could be catastrophic for me. I could go on, but do I really have to?"

"No. It's fine. You don't have to go on. What's his name?" I ask.

"Walter. Our last name is Fleming."

"Do you have any preferences on how I take care of the situation?"

"No, but it has to look like an accident."

"Why?" Amelia asks.

"Because of the way his life insurance policy is written. If there's any foul play, I won't get a cent. I need the money to live on, so it has to be convincing." She lays the folded insurance policy on the desk.

"Oh, it'll be convincing. Don't you worry. What does he do for a living?" I ask.

"He's an electrician."

"Hmm. I think I can arrange a little electrical accident."

"If it happens on the job, I get double the money."

"Nice."

"I'll pay you. Whatever you want after I get the insurance money."

"That's not a problem. I'll have Jerry research the policy and work out all of the details for us."

"Thank you so much." She bursts into tears. Relief spreads across her features. She crumples in on herself as Amelia comes around the desk and sits in the chair on the other side of her. "I can't take it anymore. Everything hurts. I can't sleep. I can't eat. I'm scared all the time. I pray to God every day that I don't get pregnant. I don't want anything to remind me of him."

"Shh, it's going to be all right. You stay here with us and we'll keep you safe."

"Thank you."

"I can see if our doctor can give you something to help you sleep if you'd like." Tori nods.

"May I see your phone?" She holds it out to me without hesitation. I check it for tracking devices, and when I don't find any, I ask, "Tori, is there any chance he put a chip in your body?"

"A what?"

"A tracking device. It's usually injected under the skin."

She scrunches up her brows. "Not that I know of. But... can you check anyway? I've been unconscious several times. I guess he could have. I never would've known it. I have so many bruises and pain."

"Yes, of course." Amelia gets on the phone with Ruck, and he instructs her to bring Tori to the clinic anytime she's ready.

I leave Amelia to get Tori settled in and start researching how to take care of her little problem.

Two days later, Jerry has verified the life insurance policy, confirming Tori's claim. It has to be an accident. He can't commit suicide or be murdered. She's still the beneficiary, and the policy is for $350,000. If it happens on the job, she does get double. With all the paperwork in order, I move forward with my plan.

I've rented an Airbnb across town under an assumed name and pretended to be the owner, and requested a repairman for a short circuit. Holden hacked into the company's dispatch system and assigned my job to Walter Fleming. Dillon is our electrical guru, so I had him set the scene.

I'm dressed in old, drab sweatpants, a baggy sweatshirt, and fluffy slippers. My hair is up in a curly blond wig piled on top of my head, and I have on wire-rimmed glasses. I finish off my character with a Chicago accent like Sue in the airport bar. There's a knock on the door.

"Yeah, yeah. I'm comin'," I holler before opening the door to find Wally.

"Are you the property owner?" he asks. His eyes squint as he looks me over.

"Yeah. What's it to ya?"

"Oh. I'm the electrician with Jackson and Merrill Electric. I believe you put in a request for a short circuit."

"Yeah. That was me. Come on in." I usher him inside and close and lock the door behind him. Leading him into the area where the breaker box is, I point and tell my story.

"Whenever I try to use the fan in the bathroom, all the lights go out."

"I see," he says. "Let me take a look." He opens the breaker box and studies the board. Pulling on this and that. "Can you show me the fan you're talking about, please?" he asks.

"Sure. It's in this bathroom over here." I lead him to the bathroom and push open the door, but I don't turn on the switch. I'll let Wally do that. I step far enough away that he can't accidentally take me down with him.

His feet land in the standing water on the bathroom floor. When his fingers connect with the switch, there's a bright flash as the arc fills the space. The smell of burning flesh fills my nostrils, and I step back even farther.

Dillon rigged the switch with more voltage than normally used in a bathroom. The electricity surging through his body causes his muscles to contract, his chest to clench, and his breathing to stop. His eyes are wide and look as if they could pop out of their sockets. As fast as it started, the electricity releases him and shoots him across the room. His head connects with the porcelain toilet bowl with a thud, and he falls to the floor in a heap.

Instead of calling for the usual cleaning team when I'm sure he's dead, I call 911 from a burner phone. The situation has to be documented for the insurance company. I frantically speak to the dispatcher, providing them with the address and circumstances. I leave the door open and vacate the premises, heading for the shelter.

I change my clothes when I get there and leave with Tori in tow. She must be at home when the police arrive to deliver the devastating news about her beloved Walter. She has already been instructed on how to act and what to say when they arrive.

Chapter 25
Sasha

I've been trying to keep busy, but I still find myself lost in daydreams about Gary. Was I an idiot to let him go? How can someone get under my skin after just a few days? I've had plenty of sex before, but no one has ever made me feel like he did. What was it he called it? *Needy.* Yeah, I'm fuckin' needy for him. I could always have Holden try to find him. No. I can't bring him into my world. I left him to keep him safe, and that's what I'm going to do, even if it makes me miserable doing it.

Chapter 26
Gary

I t's Saturday night, and I've been preparing the last few days to take out another mark, Salvadore Placato. Sal is a real piece of work. Hookers, drugs, gambling, you name it, he's got a hand in it. He lives on the west side of town with his wife and no kids. I've only seen the wife once, but she looked pretty beat up. Hopefully, getting rid of him will help her start a new life. He frequents Happy's Bar over by the college. I've been staking the place out, and tonight is the night to take care of a little business.

I'm dressed in a tweed blazer, white shirt, print bow tie, sandy brown wig, and black Harry Potter-shaped glasses. I'm going for that *Professor* vibe. I have my face shoved in a textbook, and I'm sitting in a booth in the back.

⌒

Sasha

I roll up to Happy's Bar and call Daniel.
"You've got my back tonight, right, Daniel?" I hiss.

"Yes, Sasha, I have the cameras at the bar and for a mile radius turned off already," he says confidently.

"You took them out at the motel down the street too, right?"

"Yes."

"Good. Is he here yet?"

"No, I haven't seen him enter the bar yet. I'll have eyes on you when you get a little closer."

"That makes me feel so secure," I say with a snark. He'd better do his fuckin' job tonight, or I'm going to break his little nerd neck.

"How are you dressed tonight?" he asks.

"Long red curly hair, black leather mini skirt, six-inch heels, and a burgundy shirt."

"Got it."

I exit the vehicle and walk around the corner to the bar.

"I see you," Daniel says.

"Copy that," I hang up and put my cell into my jacket pocket, the one opposite to my gun.

I walk into Happy's and do a quick scan of the room. There are only a handful of people in here tonight. It's a dive bar with not a lot of traffic. A couple makes out at a table in the corner, a geek reads a book in a booth in the back, and two bikers are sitting on the opposite end of the bar, paying no attention to me. I position myself at the bar where I can see the door, and I order a drink.

Salvatore Placato's wife, Pam, wants him dead. Sal has beaten the shit out of her for the last time. She showed up at the shelter a few days ago, beaten and broken. Ruck tried to calm her down, but eventually, he had to sedate her so he could tend to her injuries. Sal likes to pick up women and take them to the cheap motel down the street. So here I sit, ready and waiting.

It's nine o'clock. I've been here for more than an hour when Sal finally enters the bar. I circle the rim of my glass with my index finger, place it in my mouth, and suck it clean. I give my long red hair a flip, and it's like a beacon calling him home, as he moves in my direction.

"Hey, gorgeous," he croons.

"Hey, yourself, handsome," I purr.
"Can I buy you a drink?
"You sure can, sugar. Have a seat."

Gary

Looks like Salvatore found himself a little plaything for the night. She has so much curly red hair, I can't see her face. She turns her back to me as he slides onto the stool beside her and motions to the bartender for a drink.

The drinks are flowing, and he keeps moving closer and closer to her. She laughs and pushes him away with a tap of her hand to his chest. She has no idea what she's in for with this one.

They've been making small talk for a while when he stands, takes her by the hand, and helps her off the barstool. She picks up her leather jacket and pulls it on. He drapes his arm over her shoulders, and they walk out of the bar.

Sasha

So far, so good. Sal is picking up everything I'm putting down. He's so gullible. We walk down the street to the little motel. He leads me up the stairs to a room on the second floor. We enter, and I close and lock the door behind us. I don't give him any time to get the upper hand on me before I pull my gun from my coat pocket and point it at his forehead.

"What the fuck is going on?" Sal shrieks.

"Well, you see, Sal, Pam is tired of being your punching bag, and I'm here to teach you a little lesson."

"You're going to teach me a lesson?" He laughs.

"Mm-hmm," I hum in agreement.

"Is this a joke or something?"

"No joke, Sal." He turns to walk away from me. *He really thinks he's going to fuckin' walk away from me!* I cock the gun, and he stops in his tracks.

"You don't seem to think I'm serious, Sal." He shrugs. "Why don't you go over to the table and have a seat. We need to have a little chat."

"Why don't you just put the gun down, Tonya, while we talk?" All this red hair screams for a name like Merida, but I went with Tonya instead.

"Oh, I can talk just fine with this gun in my hand." I wave the gun at the chair for him to have a seat. He pulls the chair out and sits with a harrumph.

"I need to let you know how Pam feels about you before I kill you."

"I don't fucking care how that cunt feels about me."

"Why are you with her if you don't care about her?" I ask. "Why not just let her go, instead of beating her up all the time?"

"What I do is none of your business, bitch."

"I know guys like you. You need a punching bag to make you feel like a man."

"Shut the fuck up."

I press the gun to the side of his head.

"You piece of shit. I'm here to inform you that Pam isn't going to take your shit anymore."

I shove his head away with the gun, pull the silencer from my pocket, and screw it onto the end.

"When I get out of here, I'm gonna fix her once and for all."

"The only way you'll be leaving this room tonight is with an escort from the coroner." He scoffs in my face, and I'm ready to kill him now. "You're a very brave man, Sal. Do you know that?"

"Yeah. Why?" he says as he turns his head away from me, attitude pouring out of him.

"Because I don't let people talk to me the way you have, ever." Without another word, I shoot him in the leg.

"You fucking bitch! You shot me!"

"Oh, did lil ole me shoot big ole you?" I scoff in a sweet Southern drawl. I harshen my tone in a blink. "Are you taking me seriously now, Sal? Or do I need to shoot you again?"

Gary

I stay in the shadows and follow Sal and the red-haired woman to the cheap motel at the end of the street. I watch as her sweet ass swings from left to right as she climbs the stairs. Damn, what an ass. *Stop it! You're on a mission.* She follows him to his room on the second floor. She closes the door, and I hear the deadbolt click.

In a few minutes, a scream bursts from the room. Did he just hurt that woman? Is he a serial killer or something? I run to the door and kick it in.

Both of their heads snap to me standing in the doorway. The scene is a little different from what I imagined in my head.

Sal sits in a chair at the table, and the red-haired woman towers above him with a gun pointed at his temple. There's blood running down his shin, from what I can only imagine is a gunshot wound.

"Who the fuck are you?" they both yell in unison.

I enter the room, gun drawn on them both, and shut the door behind me. "What the fuck is going on here?"

"Gary?" the woman says tentatively.

"What did you just say?"

"Gary, is that you?" she repeats.

I remove my fake glasses and stare at the woman. Sal's head flips back and forth between the two of us. The woman pulls the wig from her head, and her long black braid falls down her back. I can't believe my eyes.

"Sasha? What the hell are you doing here?"

"What the hell are *you* doing here?" This can't be Sasha. The sweet, demure, delicate woman I met on the island. *There's no fuckin' way.*

"I have some business to take care of. Would you mind leaving us alone, please?" she asks as she points her gun at the door.

"Hell no! I'm not leaving you here with this piece of shit."

"I assure you." She chuckles. "I can take care of myself."

"I'm *not* leaving."

"Okay then, can you at least let me finish what I came here to do?" I hold my hand out for her to proceed, and she turns back to Sal. She points the gun at the side of his head and says, "Sal, do you have anything you would like to say?"

One...

Two...

Three...

Bang.

My mind just exploded, along with Sal's brains, out the side of his head.

Chapter 27
Sasha

I pocket my gun and walk over to Gary. His mouth is hanging open, and I wonder if he's in shock.

"What the hell are you doing here? You're supposed to be in New York City."

"Yeah, about that. I don't live in New York City."

"You don't?" *I knew he was a liar.* "Have you been following me?"

"No, nothing like that."

"Then how did you know I was here?"

"I didn't."

"You just happened to be at the same shady motel, on the same night, to talk to the same piece of shit?" I stand here with my hands on my hips, waiting for an explanation.

"No... I mean, yes... I mean."

"What *do* you mean, Gary? If that's really your name."

He takes a deep breath and starts to speak. "Yes, my real name is Gary. No, I didn't know you'd be here. No, I haven't been following you. Yes, I was following Sal. I was coming to take him out myself."

"*You* were going to take him out?"

"Yes."

"Why?"

"Because... It's my job," he grits. "I work for The Organization."

No... this can't be happening.

"I work for The Organization. How have I never seen you before?"

"I don't broadcast to the world that I'm an assassin for The Organization. Do you?"

"No."

"I work for Freddy," he says.

"I work for Ethan," I counter.

There's a long silence between us while all this new information soaks in. He's looking me over in my disguise, and I'm looking at him in his.

"Nice bow tie," I say with a smirk.

"Nice skirt, what there is of it," he goads. We walk toward each other, and our bodies collide. His lips are on mine. They are desperate and urgent.

"I missed you." He peppers kisses down my neck.

"I missed you too."

"I haven't been able to stop thinking about you," he croons.

"I never should've let you go in that airport," I declare.

Snapping back to reality, he says, "Mmm. I think we need to get out of this place before we get caught."

"Oh shit, you're right." I reach over and grab my wig. I pull my ponytail up into it and adjust it on my head. He puts on his glasses and adjusts his bow tie. We turn out the lights, leave the room, and start walking back toward the bar.

"We need to talk," I say.

"I agree."

"Where?"

"My place," he says.

"I have my car. I'll follow you," I suggest as we reach Happy's parking lot. "My car's the Escape over there."

"I'm on the Ducati." He gestures with his head in its direction.

"Nice bike. You owe me a ride."

"Anytime, Princess." We go to our separate vehicles.

When I get into my car, I call Pam.

"It's done. He'll never bother you again," I assure.

"Thank you, Sasha," she chokes out over the car speaker.

"Get some sleep." I hang up.

I call Daniel next.

"It's done."

"Who's with you?" he asks.

"How do you know someone's with me?"

"I saw them on our cameras."

"I thought the fuckin' cameras were off, Daniel?"

"I put one of *our* cameras up this afternoon so I could keep an eye on you."

"Ah. Gee, thanks," I say sarcastically. "Gary's with me."

"Shit," Daniel swears under his breath.

"Yeah, you and I need to have a little conversation, Daniel. You forgot my cameras the other night because you were doing a job for Gary, didn't you?"

"I'm so sorry, Sasha. Freddy ripped me a new asshole. It'll never happen again."

"You better hope they didn't figure out who I was." I hang up on him.

The last call I make is to Lola. I don't give her a chance to speak.

"I need to see you tomorrow morning, first thing," I order.

"Tomorrow's Sunday," she says with a yawn. "Do you know what time it is?"

"I need to see you tomorrow," I stress. Jaw tensed and teeth gritted.

"What the hell's going on?"

"Guess who interrupted my job for Pam tonight?"

"Oh God. What happened?" Her voice is more urgent now.

"Gary."

There's a pause. "Sasha, I can explain."

"Oh, you're gonna explain, all right. Does Ethan know what you did?"

"Not exactly."

"You set me up, didn't you?"

"Don't make it sound so bad."

"We *all* need to meet at the office in the morning, at eight," I demand.

"I'll make sure everyone's there." I don't let her get in another word before I hang up. I continue following Gary home. I yank the big wig off and toss it onto the seat.

Gary ushers me to park in his garage and puts down the door behind me. He lives in a condo on the East side of the city.

"Nice place," I say.

"Thanks."

"How long have you lived here?"

"I've been here a few years."

"A few years! How is this even happening?" I'm so confused. I run the damn place. How did I not know this man existed?

"I don't know how our paths have never crossed before," he says.

"Did you work for The Organization while Antonio Martinelli was in charge?"

"No, I came on after they split up everything. I went to work for Freddy as his enforcer first."

"Enforcer. Shit." I know what an enforcer really does. "That explains it, Freddy brought you into The Organization *himself*." Enforcers are like ghosts. Their identity is kept strictly confidential. An enforcer will torture and kill whoever, however, no questions asked.

I've heard stories about how Ethan tortured people when he was Antonio's enforcer. It was gruesome. Pulling out fingernails, cutting off toes and fingers, burning, slicing, stabbing, and shocking. A cold chill travels up my spine. I kill, but it's simple and quick.

"I've only recently become strictly his assassin. I mean,

I'll do whatever he wants, but that's my primary job now," he explains. "How did you get started?"

"It's a long story, but the short version is Ethan took me in, and Jerry trained me. I was stationed in Antonio's office as his assistant to watch him and gather intel. Since Antonio's death, I run things for Ethan and 'take care of business' on the side for women in the city and at the shelter."

"So personal assistant by day, assassin by night?" He chuckles.

"You could say that." My face turns expressionless. He takes that as a warning and wipes the smile off of his face. Coming in behind me, he wraps me in his arms. "I wish you would've told me."

"I thought I was keeping you safe by letting you go." I sigh. My head leans back onto his hard chest. "How would that conversation have gone, Gary? Hi. My name is Sasha. I can take you out in a hundred different ways. What was your name?" We both laugh.

"I get it. I was trying to protect you too," he says.

"I didn't want to drag you into this life. But... I guess since you're already a part of it... Maybe...."

"Maybe we could go back to seeing each other?" he asks.

"If you want to."

"Fuck, yeah, I want to." His hands roam up and down my body, and I grind my ass into his hard cock that's begging to say hello.

"Gary."

"Yeah, Baby."

"That *is* your name, right?" I ask.

"Yes. Is Sasha yours?"

"Yes, but I like it when you call me Baby."

"Baby, I want to fuck you into tomorrow."

"Yes, please."

Gary scoops me into his arms and carries me to his bedroom. Somewhere along the way, I kick off my heels before he tosses me onto the black comforter with a bounce, and he's on top of me. His tongue swipes over my bottom lip, and I open for him. He kisses me like he hasn't seen me in years. It's frenzied and fast.

"I've missed you so fucking much," he mumbles into my neck.

"I need you," I purr, pushing him back to look at him. "You look like a professor in this get-up." I remove his tie and toss it aside.

"And you look like a hot piece of ass in this outfit." A devilish grin shines on his face as he rips my shirt open.

"Oh, is that how it's going to be?" I rip open his shirt, and buttons fly all around us. He shakes out of his shirt and runs his hands all over my body, landing on my breasts. He tweaks my nipples through my bra, and I squeal.

I undo the button of his pants and lower his zipper.

"Take 'em off," I demand.

"Yes, ma'am." He stands and removes his pants and boxer briefs.

"Now you take off that tiny little skirt of yours."

"Yes, sir." I stand on the other side of the bed and remove what's left of my shirt, my bra, my skirt, and my thong.

"Why are you so far away?" he growls.

"Come and get me." I wink.

He wastes no time, climbing across the bed. It makes me giggle when he grabs me and pulls us down on the bed. His strong arms lift me above him, and I straddle him.

"Ride me, Baby."

"Why do I gotta do all the work?" I smile.

"You know you like to be in control."

"You know me so well."

"Fuck me, Sasha. Show me how you like it."

"You know how I like it. Hard and deep," I whisper.

I slide my pussy down over his hard length, taking exactly what I want. We both let out a moan as his hardness fills me.

"You look so fuckin' good riding my cock," Gary praises.

His strong hands knead my breasts while he rolls my nipples

between his fingers. The feeling sends tingles straight to my clit. I lean back and steady my hands on his thighs, slowly grinding my hips on his cock.

"That feels amazing, but I need you now!" He grabs me and flips me onto my back. His long, thick cock never leaving me.

"Oh my God, Gary!"

With his hands on either side of my face he growls, "Eyes on me while I fuck you, Baby." My eyes spring open to see his dark eyes looking back at me while the corner of his mouth curls. He nips at my lips.

"Haven't you figured out by now I'm not as sweet and innocent as you thought I was?"

"You'll always be Sweet Sasha to me."

I wrap my legs around his waist as he pounds into me hard and deep like he promised. My climax builds as a sheen of sweat begins to cover our bodies. "I'm getting close." I just need his dirty mouth to push me over the edge.

"I need to feel your tight pussy come around my cock." Gary doesn't disappoint. His words cause me to climax on a whole other level.

"Oh God, Gary. I-I-I'm…"

"That's my good fuckin' girl. I'm coming right along with you," Gary croons as he fills me with his cum.

With his semi-hard cock still inside me, he rolls us over. My body is splayed on top of his.

"I could stay like this forever," I murmur. My body feels boneless as I melt into him.

"Maybe now we can."

Chapter 28
Sasha

Gary and I enter Ethan's office first thing in the morning. Inside the room are Ethan, Lola, Freddy, and Amelia sit waiting for us.

"Good morning," I say, in complete control with no expression on my face. Gary stands to my right—arms crossed; legs spread like the enforcer he is.

"Good morning. I see you two have met," Lola says slyly.

"You know we've met, Lola. You set it all up," I accuse, pointing my finger between Gary and me.

"Now that's not exactly true," she argues.

"Please tell me then, what was your plan when you sent us on the same planes, seated beside each other, with rooms at the same resort, for the same week?"

"First, it wasn't just me. Amelia was in on it too," Lola says, pointing over her shoulder in Amelia's direction.

"Damn, girl, nothing like throwing me under the bus," Amelia counters with her hands on her hips. Freddy gives her the side-eye. Ethan and Freddy stand there, taking in the scene unfolding in front of them. Just letting the women go at it.

"If I'm going down, you're going down with me."

"Fine." Amelia addresses the group, "*We* thought you two would be perfect together, but you work for different sides of The Organization. *We* thought that if you could get to know one another, you might hit it off. When I found out Freddy was sending Gary to do a job in the Grand Caymans…"

Lola continues, "I told Ethan, if he could get you to take your vacation, I could do the rest."

"Thanks, Lo, throw me under the bus with Amelia," Ethan chimes in.

"So that's why you told me I *had* to take a vacation." I glare at Ethan.

"Guilty as charged," Ethan concedes as he looks at Lola.

"You arranged the tickets so we would be sitting next to each other and staying at the same resort," I say to Lola.

"Yes, I did. But you two did the rest," she blurts. I look at Gary, and we share a smile. "You said you had a good time." Lola gives me a little wink.

"You told her?" Gary finally speaks up.

I shush him. "Not everything."

Turning my attention back to Lola, "Why didn't you tell me you knew it was him when we were talking about the trip? I told you I met someone I really liked, but we couldn't be together."

"You said you met a guy named *Joe*. I thought maybe I was wrong, and you were talking about someone else. By then, we were in too deep, and I thought it best to keep my mouth shut," Lola admits.

My eyes connect with Gary's, and he nods for me to go on.

"So last night we were both sent to take out the same guy and almost shot each other."

"Oh no!" Amelia gasps as her hand flies to her mouth.

"That's enough of this bullshit!" Ethan barks. "Are you both all right?"

"Yes. She took care of business, and then we got the hell out of there," Gary says.

"So this is Sandy? I'm confused," Freddy chimes in. Gary and I look back and forth and burst out laughing.

"So you talked about me too?" I ask.

"Guilty as charged." Gary smirks and continues to tell our story. "When we first met, we both lied about our names. I was Joe, and she was Sandy. But when we decided we wanted more, we told each other our real names so it wouldn't feel like a lie anymore."

"Aw." Amelia and Lola swoon. My eyes snap back to them and scowl.

"Neither one of us wanted to put the other in a situation where they could be hurt, so we let each other go."

Freddy raises an eyebrow. "So how's this gonna work?" he asks. "They've worked for different sides of The Organization for a while now and never crossed paths. Will they both be able to continue in their current positions?"

"I don't see why not," Ethan says. "We just need to assign one person to keep their *business* in order. To make sure this kind of mistake never happens again."

"Not Daniel!" I yell. "That son of a bitch may have leaked my identity."

"What the hell?" Gary yells back.

"I'll fill you in later."

Freddy chimes in. "I agree. Daniel has too much on his plate. He was trying to take care of both of you by himself and all the details got to be too much for him. Ethan and I will assign one person we trust to handle both of your assignments. Does that sound fair?"

Gary and I look at each other and nod. "Yes," we say in unison.

"Fine. We'll meet again when we've made some decisions," Ethan says.

I turn to Lola and point at her. "I'm still mad at you."

"You can't be mad at a pregnant lady," she says as she rubs her tummy and makes a sad face.

"Watch me." I stride from the room with Gary in tow. We head down the hallway toward the elevator.

"So I guess we're kinda working together now," he says with a smirk.

"Guess so."

"Maybe we need to go back to my place and talk about it some more, hmm?" He pulls me in close and plants a kiss on my lips.

"I think maybe we should." This man knows how to make me smile.

Chapter 29
Gary

We arrive back at my house and park the Ducati in the garage.

"That was fantastic! I love this bike. Next time, you have to let me drive," Sasha says.

"I don't do the backpack thing, remember? Big guy here." I hold my arms out wide.

"Then you'll have to let me drive this, and you can drive mine."

"What do you drive?"

"A Kawasaki Ninja 400 ABS with slip-on exhaust."

"Damn, girl, that's a nice bike."

"Not as nice as your Ducati, but I like it."

"You know what I'd like to see?" I say as I pull her in tight to me and grip her ass.

"What?"

"Your naked body stretched across my bike." I smile and push the button to lower the garage door.

"I think that could be arranged." The words come out of her mouth smooth as silk. She unbuttons her jeans and pushes them down her legs. I can feel my dick hardening in my pants as she removes her shirt and bra. She's standing in my garage, naked. She walks over and mounts my bike backward, leaning back over the tank. She holds her arms above her head and arches her back. Seeing her creamy fleshing laying across my bike makes my dick fuckin' hard.

"Fuck, baby. You look sexy as hell." Still wearing my leather riding gloves, I walk over and take a handful of her hair and pull her head back, ravishing her throat. My other hand takes hold of her breast and kneads it in my gloved palm. I pinch her nipple, and she moans and grinds her ass into the seat.

"My needy girl likes a little pain with her pleasure doesn't' she? Her head nods. A groan escapes her lips when I smack the side of her breast. "Use your words, Baby."

Her glazed irises stare back at me. "I like a little pain with my pleasure… Daddy." My cock turns to steel.

"You can call me Daddy out here, but in the bedroom tonight, I want you to call me Master."

"Yes, Daddy." Her pupils are blown and that devious smile of hers has my cock weeping.

"Stand up and lean back against my bike." I hold out my hand to help her off the bike, and she does as she's told. I drop to my knees in front of her.

"Spread your legs as wide as you can. I need to taste you." She again does as she's told without hesitation. I hold open her silky folds with my gloved hands and sink my tongue inside her wet pussy.

"You taste so fucking good," I say in between licks and sucks. She throws her head back as I slide a gloved finger inside her pussy, and she rocks onto my hand. I add a second finger and lick her clit. "I want you to come for me, and then I'm going to fuck you on my bike."

"Yes, Daddy." She sighs heavily.

I suck her needy clit into my mouth, and she cries out, "Yes. Right there." I concentrate my tongue on the right side of her clit, where I know she likes it. Her body bucks, and it doesn't take long before she's coming all over my gloved hand. Her arousal glistens on the leather.

"That's my good girl," I praise as I stand and remove my jeans. My naked ass mounts my bike and comes to rest on the warm leather seat.

"Straddle my lap and take my dick in your hot pussy."

She puts one foot on the peg and swings her other leg over the bike. Facing me, she wraps her warm body around mine and slides her hot pussy down over my stiff cock. With her hands in my hair, she pulls me tight to her body. I bite her flesh over her collarbone and swipe over it with my tongue. She groans and squeezes my cock tight in her center.

"Lie back, Baby," I urge, lowering her down carefully. Her back is against the tank, and her hands grab the handlebars. I lean up and thrust into her. Her legs try to find purchase, but the angle is off, so I grip them in my hands, wrap them around my waist, and thrust into her like a man possessed. Seeing her splayed across my bike is like a dream come true. "Are you going to come for me again, Baby?"

"Yes, Daddy."

"This is just the beginning. Tonight, I'm going to make you mine. Your pussy is going to feel me for days." I moan, and she grinds her pussy onto me. My thumb moves to her clit, and her muscles tighten.

"Gary. I-I'm going to c… Oh!" She arches her back and convulses into her orgasm.

"Such a good… fucking… girl." My voice cracks as I remove my cock and pump it in my fist above her. Coating her breast and stomach in my release. "Oh my fucking God, Sasha. You look so fucking beautiful covered in my cum."

"Did you just claim me, Gary."

"You know I fuckin' did. You're mine now," I growl.

I know she can't be comfortable lying on the gas tank so I offer her my hand and help her from the bike. I remove the leather gloves, and place them on the seat. Using a clean shop cloth, I wipe the sticky cum from her body.

"Thank you," she says as she wraps her arms around my neck and kisses me possessively. I lift her to me, and she wraps her legs around me. Carrying her into the house and down the hall, I stand her on her feet beside my bed.

"Remember when we were on the island and played our game of questions?" I ask.

"Yes."

"You said you wanted to be controlled so you didn't have to think about anything. You didn't want to make decisions and didn't want to be in charge."

"I remember."

"Did you mean it?"

"Yes."

"I'd like to give that to you tonight, if you'll let me." Her eyes lift to mine, and she sinks to her knees and takes the nadu position, and my heart stops.

"Yes, Master."

"You've done this before?"

"Yes, Master."

"What's your safe word?"

"Red."

"I expect you to use it if you need to, Sasha. Don't try to take it if it's too much for you."

"Yes, Master."

Lifting her chin with two fingers, I command, "Eyes open."

Some Doms don't like eye contact. But I need it. I want to be able to connect with her on another level. We are new to this type of play, so eye contact is the best way to learn what she likes and, most importantly, what she doesn't like.

I brush her hair back out of her face, and I reach my hand out to her. "Put your hand in mine." She does as I instruct. I slide the hair tie from her wrist she usually keeps there and move around behind her. I braid her hair and attach the tie.

"You're all mine tonight." I growl. A shy smile forms across her lips as I use her shoulders to guide her to stand once more.

"Lie down on the bed." She does as she's told. I go to the closet and bring back a few items.

"Hold both hands out to me." She does, and I fasten one

black cuff to each wrist. I hook them together with the cuff clip and raise them above her head, then connect them to the ring on the headboard. I reach into the bedside table and retrieve one more cuff. This one is for her right ankle. I attach it and secure it to the chain at the foot of the bed. I want one leg free to move her where I want her.

"Will you be okay if I blindfold you?"

"Yes, I would like to try, Master."

"If you start to feel scared or anxious, I want you to say yellow, and we'll stop and take it off."

"Yes, Master. Thank you."

"You look so beautiful under my control."

I retrieve my flogger from the nightstand. The tails are about eighteen inches long, and they're made of soft leather. I trace it over her body so she can get used to the sensation before I use it on her.

"Remember our sensation play?"

"Yes, Master."

"What do you think this is?"

"A flogger."

"That's correct. I'm going to use it on you now." I don't wait for her to answer. I swat her with it on one thigh, and then the other. She moans. I do it a little harder, and her hips buck. I swat her chest and drag it gently across her face, watching as her breathing hitches.

"What color are you, Sasha?"

"Green, Master."

"What's your pain level?" I ask. She points one finger.

I apply a few more swats, a little harder to her thighs, and ask the pain level again. This time she shows me three fingers. That's exactly where I want her to be. Not to hard, but enough to bring a little pain.

"Good girl." I take a bullet vibrator out of its package, and her head jerks toward the sound when I turn it on.

"I don't want you to come until I tell you to. Do you understand?"

"Yes, Master."

I adjust the bullet to a low rumbling setting and run it through her folds, inserting it into her wet pussy. She lets out a hiss as her body responds to the pulses. She's trying to move her free leg to create friction, but I slap it away. A soft whimper escapes her lips. Her hips rock as I adjust the setting on my app, and the pulse quickens to a faster speed.

"Master. Oh, Master. I need to come, please," she begs.

"Not. Yet." I change the setting again. This time, it makes a wavelike vibration. The pulse grows higher and then back down low, over and over. I can see her body riding the waves of the vibrator, as if it were waves in the ocean. This one is too easy for her to control herself, so I change it once again. The next one has a strong, deep vibration, and she jumps with the sensation. It takes her immediately to the edge.

"Master. Please, I need to come."

"You can hold on a little longer." She lets out a frustrated moan, and I take the flogger back out, running it over her pussy. Her body jerks with surprise.

"Please, Master. Please," she begs and pulls on her arms. Her body is trying to move from side to side, looking for relief, but it's not coming.

"I can't... I can't wait anymore." Her body writhes with need as she continues to beg, "Please, Master."

I take the bullet out and run my finger through her now soaked pussy, and her body collapses on the bed. "The smell of your arousal is intoxicating." I bring my soaked finger to her lips. "You don't know what you do to me. How you lying here under my control makes my cock so fucking hard." I paint her lips with her arousal and that soft pink tongue darts out for a taste. Her body shudders as I run two fingers through her pussy once more for taste of my own. "I think you're ready to take my cock now, Baby Girl."

"Thank you, sir." I give the flogger a sharp, quick flick to her pussy, causing her to cry out in surprise.

"What did you call me?" I demand.

"I'm sorry. I'm sorry. Thank you, *Master*."

"That's better." I unhook her leg from the chain and flip her over. Her arms are now twisted above her head.

"Up on your knees, head down, ass up." She does as she's told, like the good little slut she is for me, and I climb on the bed behind her. Resting my cock at her entrance, I push into her with one stroke, and she cries out. I like how she's just as needy for me to be inside of her as I am to feel the warmth of her pussy around me. I hold her on my cock while she adjusts to the fullness, and I slap her ass.

"Thank you, Master!" she cries. I pull out and thrust into her deep for one stroke and halfway inside for two. *Smack*. Her pussy tries to pull me in deeper on the half strokes, but I don't allow it. She needs to release her control and let me run the show.

Her frustration rises as I continue to alternate strokes. One full. Two half. *Smack*. My fingers dig into her hips as I control the motion. With each smack of her ass, her body seems to relax farther into the mattress. Once she finally stops fighting for control, she seems to lose herself in the sensations and her mind shuts off. She's all mine now. Body and mind.

I turn on the bullet and place it on her clit, and she moans. She pushes back harder on my swollen cock.

"My little slut is so needy for me."

"Yes, Master."

"Say it!" my voice rumbles.

"I'm your needy little slut."

"What do you need, slut?"

"To come."

"Beg me."

"Please, Master. I need to come."

"That's my good little slut."

My strokes change to deep and slow, pulling her pleasure from her with each movement. "Come on my cock, Sasha. I want you so wet, it's running down your legs."

Her orgasm erupts through her. Body jerking. Pussy contracting. I can't contain myself any longer. I shoot my load deep inside her.

I run my hand down the length of her spine, soothing her. My eyes focus on where we're connected. At how good she looks taking my cock while our cum runs down her thighs. I hear what sounds like crying. Panic takes over my body. What have I done? Did I go too far? Did I hurt her?

"Sasha, what's your color, Baby? Tell me." I lean over her. I don't remove myself from her before I lean forward. My chest pressed against her back. I remove the blindfold. Her eyes are clenched shut, and tears stream down her face.

"Green," she says calmly. Her brows pinched like she doesn't know why I'm concerned. I use the back of my fingers to wipe the tears from her cheeks.

"Did I hurt you?" My voice no longer demanding but soothing and calm.

"No."

"Then why are you crying, Baby?"

"What?"

"Why are you crying?"

"I'm not…" Her eyes flutter open. "Oh. I didn't realize I was. I'm sorry."

"Don't you ever be sorry for how you feel." I move the wet strands of hair behind her ear. "Here, let me take these off." I remove the handcuffs and rub each of her wrists. When I pull out of her warm center to get up, she sinks into the large mattress.

I head to the bathroom for a warm washcloth and begin aftercare. I want to take care of her body, but I need to pay special attention to her mind and heart right now. Quickly, I clean her up and apply arnica cream to her backside and crawl in bed beside her. Pulling her onto my chest, I kiss the side of her head. Tears continue to pour down her flushed face.

"It's okay, Baby. I've got you. Let it out. I'm so proud of you." She lies in my arms and cries herself to sleep. Exhausted from our scene, I relax into her body. I have Sasha back in my bed, and this time I'm never letting her go.

Chapter 30
Sasha

'm awakened by the sun's glow peeking through the curtains. I'm wrapped in Gary's arms. I don't think either one of us moved all night.

"Good morning, Sweetheart," he says as he rolls out of my grasp and stretches.

"Good morning." I stretch alongside him. "Last night was amazing."

"Can you tell me why you were crying?"

"I guess I needed a release, and you gave it to me. Thank you."

He rolls onto his side and props himself up on his elbow. "I want you to know you're safe with me, Sasha."

I turn on my side, mimicking his stance. "I know I am. I can feel it when we're in a scene. I know you're there to protect me, and you would never hurt me."

"Have you ever been to a Dom before?" he asks.

"Yes."

"How was your experience?"

"Not as good as last night."

"What does that mean?"

"He wasn't as patient as you were. He was into inflicting pain more than I was receiving it."

"You mean he hurt you?"

"Not the first visit, but the second time, yes, he did. I had bruises and cuts on my skin, and he choked me until I passed out."

"Where did this happen?"

"Scarlett's." I can hear his teeth grinding.

"When?"

"About two years ago."

"Scarlett's is Freddy's club. Does he know this happened in his club?"

"Yes. He's the only person who knew until…now."

"What happened?" he asks.

I come rushing out of the back hallway and straight into Freddy's enormous chest. He grabs me by the shoulders and holds me at arm's length and looks me up and down.

"What the hell happened to you back there?"

"Nothing. I gotta go." I try to push him away.

"Come with me." He takes me by the hand and pulls me down the hallway, ushering me into his office and closing the door.

"Tell me what the fuck happened, dammit! Did you ask for this kind of treatment?"

"Do I look like I did?" I yell, holding out my wrists and showing him the marks the asshole left on me. He comes closer and uses one finger to turn my face from left to right, checking the marks he left on my skin.

"Who did this to you? I'll fucking kill them," he snarls with rage.

"Just forget it," I say, trying to push past him once more, but I don't get very far. I should know better than to try to get this brick wall to let me go.

"I'll ask you one more time, Sasha. Who the fuck did this to you?" He stares at me with his death glare.

"Quinn."

"I remember him. That dude was an asshole. What did Freddy do to him?"

I burst into his office two days later. "I want to see Quinn, dammit!" I yell at Freddy.

"Sasha, you don't want to see him."

"Yes, I do... I want to finish him off myself."

"I knew you wouldn't let this go. Come on."

Freddy drives us to the warehouse on the outskirts of town. It's a large empty structure where The Organization brings people they need to take care of. After walking around the side of the building to a metal door, we push our way inside. We walk to the center of the room, and there hangs Quinn. His hands are in metal shackles above his head. They're attached to a chain, and he's stretched out on his tiptoes. His head hangs off to one side.

Freddy walks up to his body and slaps his face.

"Hey, dumbass. Wake up. You have company." Slowly, Quinn moves his head, trying to focus his swollen eyes on me.

"You." His voice is gravelly and hoarse. "He's torturing me because of you!"

"Shut up, you piece of shit!" Freddy barks.

I stand back and look at the naked body hanging before me. The shackles are digging into the flesh on his wrists. There's a long trail of blood dripping down his arms. He's missing two toes on his right foot and three fingernails on his left hand. There are round marks on his torso, and all the hair around them is burned off. Maybe from electric shocks? Freddy has enjoyed playing with Quinn. Now it's my turn.

"You remember Sasha," Freddy says playfully.

"Yeah, I remember her." He almost sounds disappointed.

"So when she told you to stop the other night, what did your brain hear?"

"What?"

"When she was crying out the word Red as you slapped her across the face. What did you hear?"

"I...I...I don't know, Red?" he asks, confused by the question.

"So if you heard her yelling the word Red, why didn't you stop?"

"Because she wanted more. I knew she did."

Freddy grabs him by the throat. "Red means stop, you bag of shit. It means no more. It means I'm done. It means I've reached my limit. It means enough!" Freddy squeezes tighter as Quinn tries to speak, but no words come out.

"See, just like you're trying to tell me to stop, Sasha begged you to stop that night." Quinn moves his head up and down a smidge in understanding. Freddy releases his throat, and he gasps for air.

"I...I... I guess I got carried away."

"How many other times in my club have you gotten carried away and hurt a woman?"

"Maybe two or three? I'm the Dominant. These bitches want me to control them. To make them bend to my will. It's what they pay for." Rage is welling up inside me the more this asshole speaks.

I won't stay silent any longer. "NO! That's not what all women go to a Dom for. Some go to experience being controlled. But the Dom is also supposed to make you feel safe and cared for. A Dom is supposed to help you release your inhibitions and release control to someone you can trust for an hour of your life. Not to be beaten and bloodied. You don't know what you're doing, and you need to be stopped. You're done hurting women."

"Fine. I quit. Now let me down." He actually looks at Freddy as if he'll let him go now that he gave him the answer he wanted.

"Freddy, are you going to let him go?" I ask.

"Fuck no! He won't be walking out of here alive."

I walk over to the table and take the Ruger Max 9 pistol in my hand. Freddy releases the chain enough so I can reach Quinn.

"Do you have anything you want to say, Quinn?" I ask. A confused look fills his face.

One...

Two…
Three…
Bang.

"I'm so fucking proud of you. I'll have to thank Freddy for taking care of you. We should discuss our limits in the bedroom before we get too deep into our playtimes. I like being your dominant, but I don't ever want to do anything you don't feel comfortable with. Tell me what kind of things you like."

I cuddle in tighter to him. "I liked the flogger. It had a sting to it, but it was still sensual. I like to be spanked and restrained. The edging was hard, but the orgasm was phenomenal. I don't think I've ever come so hard in my whole life."

"You were so beautiful last night when you came for me. Your skin flushed with desire." He kisses the top of my head and holds me tight. "What don't you like?"

"Sometimes being blindfolded sends me back to the closet…into the darkness."

"Did it do that last night?"

"No. Last night, it was almost peaceful until you brought out the bullet." I laugh.

"I only want to give you pleasure," he croons.

"I loved everything you gave me last night." I place my hand on his hard dick.

"I was trying to control that," he says with a chuckle, looking at my hand.

"But I love to please you." *I gently kiss his lips.*

"I love the way your cock tastes on my tongue." *I lick the precum from his hard tip.*

"I love the way it pulses in my hand." *I squeeze his thick cock in my fist.*

"I love the way you moan my name when you come." *I lower my mouth to his shaft.*

"Sasha. Your mouth is so fucking perfect," he groans.

"Your cock makes me so wet," I whisper before I take his cock to the back of my throat, and Gary loses all control.

Chapter 31
Sasha

"Can you come in here, please?" Ethan calls on the intercom.

"Yes, Boss."

I enter his office, and he's sitting back in his leather chair. He points for me to sit across from him.

"I want to fill you in on the security changes."

"Of course."

"Freddy and I have chosen Holden to be your go-to person for all the business you and Gary need to take care of. He'll be responsible for anything you need to carry out your missions and to provide cover. Since you handle jobs outside of The Organization, you'll need to tell him when you have an upcoming job, so nothing overlaps. This means you can't go off half-cocked and do a job without telling someone."

"I'm perfectly capable of pulling off my own jobs. I've been doing it by myself for quite some time now."

"I'm well aware of how *capable* you are, Sasha. That's not what this is about. This is about making sure no one falls between the cracks again and gets hurt. You and Gary should never have pursued the same target. This arrangement will be safer for both of you."

"Does Gary know?"

"Freddy's telling him now."

"Okay, Boss, I'll give it a try."

"Thank you."

I stand to leave, but hesitate. "Did you know Lola was trying to set us up?" He fidgets in his seat.

"I knew she was putting you both on the same plane. You two did the rest."

"Thanks," I say, turning to leave.

"Sasha. She wasn't trying to hurt you. You help everyone else. She wanted you to find someone and be happy."

"I know. I'm just scared."

"Why are you scared?"

"What if something happens to him?"

"This new system will help keep you both safe."

"That's not what I'm talking about."

"What is it then?"

"What if I fall in love with him and something bad happens to him? I don't think I could handle it."

Ethan comes around to my side of the desk and holds me firmly by my shoulders.

"You can't go through life not letting love in because you're afraid. You have to live, Sasha. Fall in love and be happy. Take the extra precautions and don't do stupid shit."

"I'll try."

"Now get back to work. I'm not used to all this sappy shit coming from you."

"Blame it on your wife. She started it."

I take out my cell and text Gary.

> Did you meet with Freddy?

GARY
> Yes, are you okay with all of it?

> Holden will do a good job.

That's not what I mean. Giving up your freedom.

I'm not giving up my freedom

Sure, you are. Having someone looking over your shoulder all the time.

You sound more upset than I am.

I don't need somebody looking over my shoulder while I handle my jobs.

He won't be. He's there for support.

We'll see.

Do you want to come over for dinner?

I can't tonight. I have to work.

You have business to take care of?

No, I work at Scarlett's tonight.

You work at Scarlett's? Doing what?

I'm a Dom there. Two nights a week.

What the fuck?

You never told me that.

No wonder he's so good at all the things he does to my body

.

> There's a lot you don't know about me, Sasha. I'm sure you have things you haven't told me.

> I guess so.

He knows a hell of a lot more about me than I know about him. *Don't be clingy, Sasha. Let it go.*

> Talk to you soon.

> Later.

It sits in my gut all day. *He's a fucking Dom at Scarlett's.* Freddy's usually at Scarlett's on Friday and Saturday nights. He prefers to be present when the crowds are larger, ensuring nothing goes sideways.

I haven't been to Scarlett's since that night with Quinn two years ago. Could I go back there after what he did to me? Do I want to go back there? I'm stronger now. It'll be fine. I text Freddy.

> Hey

FREDDY
> What's up?

> Are you going to be at Scarlett's tonight?

> Yes, why?

> Could I tag along?

> Sure. But why?

> I haven't been there for a while and wanted to check it out. Unless I would be cramping your style.

The guys would love to see you.
Come after eight.

Who can I drink under the table
tonight?

We'll soon find out.

⌒

I get done at the office around six, go home, eat, shower,
and dress for the club. I wear my knee-length black leather
skirt, white silk shirt, and four-inch black heels. I pull my hair
up in the front and let the back hang free. I'm taking an Uber
tonight because I know I'll be drinking.

I have the driver let me out at the curb, and I stand on the
sidewalk looking up at the marquee. Taking in a deep breath,
I slide my proverbial mask into place and approach the door.
Frisco is bouncing tonight.

"Sasha, how are you!" he gushes, as he pulls me in for a big
hug.

"I'm good, Frisco. How have you been?"

"I'm good. It's been too long. You look gorgeous as ever."

"Thank you," I say, doing a little curtsy thing,

"Freddy and the guys are in VIP."

I say thanks again as he opens the red velvet rope guarding
the door and lets me in. I wave to Vinny behind the bar and
find Freddy, Max, Billy, Franco, and the new soldier, Tommy,
sitting in VIP.

"Hi ya, fellas."

"Sasha!" they all holler as they lift their drinks to me.

"Vinny, our girl needs a drink," Max yells across the room.
Vinny lifts his chin in acknowledgment, and they make room
for me to sit.

"Tommy, this is Sasha. Have you met yet?" Freddy intro-
duces us.

Tommy scrunches up his face. "I don't think so." Everyone laughs.

"What's so funny?" Tommy asks.

"I met you in the office a month ago when you came on board." I chuckle.

"No, I don't think so. I would've remembered you." He gives me a wink.

"I'm Sasha. I work for Ethan Martinelli." Just saying his name makes Tommy's face turn ghostly white.

"You're the lady from outside his office? No…" He shakes his head. Everybody laughs again.

"Yes," Max teases. He slaps him on the back and leans in close. "No one messes with Sasha. Do you understand what I'm saying to you, newbie?" He squeezes his shoulder so tight Tommy winces.

"I understand."

"I can take care of myself, Max, but thanks." I smile at Tommy.

Vinny brings my whiskey and sets it on the table in front of me.

"You're looking good, Sasha," Vinny says in his deep voice. Vinny doesn't have much to say to anyone usually, but he always takes a second to compliment me.

"Thanks, Vinny. Can you bring all of us a shot on me, please?" He nods his head and walks back to the bar.

"What's the occasion?" Billy asks.

"No occasion. Can't a girl just come out and have some fun with her coworkers?" We all laugh. It's obvious to me Tommy is the soldier I'll be drinking under the table tonight. Why else would a newbie be sitting in VIP with a leader of The Organization and his captains? Vinny sets the tray full of shots on the table. Everyone leans in and grabs one.

"What are we toasting?" I ask.

"To Sasha!" they all yell. We clink glasses and toss the caramel-colored liquid back.

Five shots in and a lot of laughter later, Tommy looks like he's feeling very relaxed. The terror has left his eyes, and now his cockiness emerges.

"You sure can hold your liquor," he slurs at me.

"I can?" I say, acting like a dumb girl. I turn my gaze to Freddy and wink. He knows exactly what I'm thinking.

"I bet I can drink more than you can," he boasts. *And there it is.*

"Oh, really? We'll have to see about that," I say. *Challenge accepted.* Freddy's hand goes up in the air, motioning for Vinny to bring a bottle.

Everyone steps away from the table, leaving just me and Tommy sitting face-to-face while everyone watches from a few feet away.

"How old are you, Tommy?" I ask, pouring us each a shot.

"Twenty-one." He smiles proudly as we hold our shots out to show each other and knock them back.

"Ah, you're just a baby," I tease, slamming my glass on the table.

"How old are you?" he asks.

"Oooh," the crowd jeers.

Freddy laughs and leans over Tommy's shoulder. "Don't you know you never ask a lady her age?" Tommy's face goes pale.

"Sorry. Sorry." He's rethinking his words as I pour us each another shot.

"You need to learn how to treat a lady, Tommy," I say. His eyes are wide as we throw back the next shot. Tommy makes another terrible mistake as we slam our glasses on the table.

"Yes, ma'am."

"Oooh," the crowd says once again.

"Now, what did I say wrong?" poor little Tommy asks.

"Don't you ever call me ma'am. I'm not some eighty-year-old grandma," I say gruffly. *There's only one person who can call me ma'am, and that's Gary when he's on his knees begging me for more.*

"Yes, Sasha."

"Better." I can tell he's about had enough. His eyes are droopy, and his face looks like it's sliding off his skull. Staring at each other, we lift our glasses once again. Shooting them back and slamming them down.

"You're doing pretty good, baby boy," I praise, patting his cheek softly.

"Don't... call... me...tha..." he says in slow motion as he passes out on the table in front of me.

"You did it again, Sasha!" Freddy says with a rolling laugh and throws my arm into the air like I just won a boxing match.

"Come on, big boy, let's get you home so you can sleep it off," Max says as he and Billy each grab an arm and lift him to his feet.

"He put up a good fight." Freddy laughs.

"Eight shots are pretty good for a newbie like him," I say. Just then, I see Gary come out of the brown door at the back of the club. He heads straight to the VIP section. When he sees me, he looks like a deer caught in the headlights.

Chapter 32
Sasha

"What are you doing here?" Gary asks as he leans over and kisses my cheek.

"Kicking Tommy's ass at shots, that's what she's doing here." Freddy belly laughs.

Gary looks tired. Like he's ready to crawl into bed. Standing, I put my hand on his forearm.

"Are you okay?"

"Yeah, sometimes it takes a lot out of me to give someone the experience they're looking for." I never thought about the Dom's side of the experience. I just assumed they enjoy bossing people around, but it seems to be more mentally taxing for him than I thought.

"Are you going home?" I ask.

"Yeah. I'm done for the night," he says. "Do you want to come home and keep me warm?"

"I'd like that." I turn to Freddy and say, "We're heading out."

"Hey, don't let her drive. She's had too much to drink," Freddy warns. Gary nods, and we head out.

"How much did you drink tonight?" he asks as we walk through the parking lot.

"I think Freddy said eight shots, but I had a drink before we got started, so…nine…ish."

"You *really* can hold your liquor, woman." He pulls me in and kisses the side of my head.

"I'm the champ around here, so of course I can. Freddy loves to watch me drink his newbies under the table," I say with a laugh. He leads me to a blue Camaro with a large white stripe down the center.

"This is nice. How many vehicles do you have?" I ask.

"A few." He smirks as he closes my door. He puts his duffel bag in the trunk, walks around to the driver's side, and climbs in. The car starts with a loud rumble, and we take off down the road.

⌒

We enter the condo from the garage, his arm around my shoulders. He looks wiped out.

"Are you sure you're okay?" I ask as he sits down on the couch.

"Yeah. She was a tough client."

"Tough client? What does that mean?"

"She likes a lot of complex rope play, rough spanking, and lots of degradation. It takes a lot out of me emotionally when I have to do that to someone."

"Let me take care of you tonight," I offer as I lay his head on my lap and run my fingers through his hair, lightly scratching my nails over his scalp.

"God, I love it when you do that," he moans.

"You take care of me when we have our scenes. Let me do that for you." Applying pressure with two fingers on each temple, I gently rub in circles, and he releases a long sigh. I use my fingers to pay attention to the space between his scrunched-up eyebrows. I massage the skin there until his face relaxes, and he looks near sleep. I place a gentle kiss on his lips.

"Let's get you to bed so you can relax properly." He lets out a moan and rolls onto his side, wrapping his arms around my waist and pulling me in tight. Like a child not wanting to go to bed.

"I don't want to let you go yet," he whines.

"I can hold you in bed. You'll be more comfortable." He inhales deeply, places a kiss on my stomach, and rises from the couch.

"Okay, come on." He takes me by the hand and leads me to the bedroom. I take my place standing on the right side of the bed, and Gary is on the left. We stare into each other's eyes across the bed while we slowly begin to remove our clothes for each other's viewing pleasure.

I unbutton my white shirt. The silky fabric slides down my arms and drops at my feet. He reaches behind him and pulls his black T-shirt over his head, and drops it to the floor. As if challenging me to take the next step, he raises a brow.

I unzip my skirt, and it falls down my legs. His hands go to the button on his slacks first, then he slides the zipper down. He pushes them down over his hips and steps out of them. Once again, it's my turn.

Reaching my hands behind my back, I release my bra. The straps slide down to my elbows, and they join my shirt on the floor. His eyes grow wide, and he licks his lips. I can feel my nipples hardening from his gaze.

"I guess it's my turn again since you don't wear as many clothes as I do," I say innocently.

"It's only fair." He reaches his hand out for me to continue.

Lowering my black panties down my legs, I stand naked before him. He slides his thumbs into the waistband of his boxer briefs and pushes them down his legs, and his hard cock springs free. As if on cue, we both pull back the covers and climb into bed.

"You know you drive me fuckin' crazy, woman."

"I'm sure I don't know what you're talking about." I give him my best sheepish expression and rest my hand on his chest.

"I'm helping you relax." I giggle. He flips me over so he's on top of me

"No, you're trying to get me all worked up." I flip him back over onto his back. His eyes are wide, and he seems amazed I could catch him off guard enough to do it back to him. Thank you, Jerry, for my training.

"I can help you relax and forget if you give me a chance," I purr. His arms drop to his sides, and he acts like he's asleep.

"That's not what I mean, you goofball. I can make you feel good, like you do me."

"Okay. Give it a try."

"Oh, is this a challenge?"

"I think it was."

"Give me a minute and I'll be right back." I turn on the small light on the nightstand, then cross the room and turn off the overhead light. I go to the living room to retrieve my purse. I take out my perfume and makeup bag, then I head to his bedroom closet. I grab one of his ties from the rack and a few other items, then put everything on the bathroom counter to get organized.

"Close your eyes, please, and remove one of those pillows from under your head," I order, walking out of the bathroom.

"Yes, ma'am." He tosses the pillow to the floor. In one quick pull, I snatch the sheet from his body to unveil his beautiful form. His cock is ready to play, but it needs to wait until I'm done pleasuring my man in other ways.

I speak in a soft, melodic tone.

"I'm going to use this tie to cover your eyes." I hold his tie up to show him.

"Yes, please," he answers quietly.

"I'll need your safe word." I wrap the tie around his head and secure it in place.

"Red," he says on an exhale.

I bring my items out of the bathroom and lay them on a towel on the nightstand. The first item I take from my carefully collected cache is my perfume bottle.

"Are you ready, Baby?" I ask.

"Yes."

I press the pump twice on the bottle, Daisy by Marc Jacobs. I don't want to overpower the room with the smell, but I want to engage his senses. He thinks he's so smart. I've done my research.

His nose begins to sniff the air. "I smell strawberries and gardenias. Oh, Baby, that's a good one. I love the smell of you." It makes me smile, knowing I'm giving him what he needs.

"Now for the next one. Are you ready?"

"Yes, please."

I pick up a fluffy makeup brush from my stash and gently glide it over his skin. It's as soft as silk. I run it down his arms, across his chest, and slide it down his stomach. When I reach his legs, I make small circles and lightly land on the tips of his toes, causing him to shiver a little.

"Hey, no tickling."

"Did you forget the whiskers you ran across the bottoms of my feet, hmm?"

"Touché."

I bring the brush back up his body, stopping for a moment on the head of his cock, making it twitch with need. I continue up his torso, landing on his neck, where I stroke it up and down. Then over his face, where I lightly brush the softness over his cheeks and eyebrows. Slowly, the tension leaves his face, and I think I'm on the right track.

"How are you feeling?" I ask quietly.

"Relaxed."

"What do you think it is?"

"I'm not sure. A paintbrush, maybe?"

"Close enough. It's my makeup brush." I boop him on the nose with it and giggle softly.

"Let's try another one," I say, taking out the flogger I found in the closet. I run it along his body in the same manner he did mine. Hanging it just above his skin, I let it touch him softly. At first, his eyebrows pull together, trying to figure out what it is, then they relax, and a small smile spreads across his lips.

"That's my flogger," he croons with a grin.

"Correct."

"What are you going to do with it?"

"Tell me what you want me to do with it." My voice is dark and sultry. His breath hitches as if he doesn't want to tell me what to do, so I give him a choice. "Do you want me to rub it gently all over your body, or do you want me to swat you with it?"

His answer is so soft it is barely audible. "Swat me with it."

"Have you been a bad boy?" I croon.

"Yes."

I'm going to give my man what he wants. I glide the leather pieces over him so they barely touch his skin. When I run it over his nipples, goose bumps skate over his flesh, and he shudders. Holding it above his cock, I brush it back and forth over his tip, and his cock twitches.

I step back and begin rolling my wrist, making the flogger spin. It hits his chest over and over lightly. Gary lets out a moan.

"Sasha."

"What's your color, Gary?"

"Green."

I continue this technique on his thighs to warm up his skin until it turns a light pink, preparing him for more.

"What's your pain level, Baby?"

"One," he says, and the thought of swatting him makes my pussy weep. I hold the flogger back farther and flick my wrist, and it makes a little crack as it comes in contact with his thigh. The sound sends electricity through my body. I'm just as aroused by using the flogger as he is by being touched by it. Little pink marks appear on his skin, and I run my finger over one.

"What's your pain level now, baby?"

"Two," he hisses. I need to go a little harder to get him where I want him.

I step back and aim for his chest this time. Pulling back, I swat him a little harder, and he flinches.

"What's your pain level now, Baby?"

"Three."

"Perfect." Now I know how hard to use it on him.

"Roll over for me. Head down, ass up." He doesn't hesitate. He rolls over for me and sticks his ass in the air and gives it a wiggle, causing a laugh to spurt from my lips. I swat him a little harder for it, and he groans. I warm his ass with the wrist rolls and then move a little farther away and flick the flogger over and over on his tan skin. The sounds coming from his mouth are delicious. His ass and upper thighs are glowing for me now.

"Okay, Baby, roll back over." He does as he's told and takes a moment while he repositions himself to rub his hard cock.

"You're giving me blue balls, Princess."

"I just have one more. Can you make it?"

"Yes."

"What's your color?"

"Green."

I don't have whiskers on my face like he does, but I do have a tongue. I start at his feet, planting a kiss on the top of each foot.

"Sasha."

"Shh…" I continue up his legs, licking, kissing, nibbling and sucking his skin. Working my way up his legs from left to right and back, I mimic what he did to me. Easing my way toward his cock.

As I approach his manhood, it's hard as steel, and he holds his breath in anticipation of my touch, but I don't touch him there. Instead, I continue past. A defeated groan comes from his chest. I run my tongue over his deep V and each of his hard, well-defined abs, continuing up his torso.

My tongue swirls over his left nipple. It's still pebbled from the flogger and then onto his right. His breathing is ragged, and when I make my way to his neck, his whole body shakes. I stop on his lips and kiss him hard and deep.

"Sasha…"

"I'll be right back."

"Where are you going?

"Down…"

"Oh."

His breathing stops as I lick the tip of his glistening cock. Precum has been leaking from the tip and lies on his belly. I lick over the crown and down his shaft, holding it in my hand firmly as I guide my tongue up and down his length.

"Sasha, I can't take it anymore."

"I got you, Baby." I straddle his lap.

"You've been such a good boy for me this evening. Are you ready for your reward?"

"Yes, Mistress." *Oh fuck. I like that word.*

"Say it again," I demand.

"Yes, Mistress." His voice is deep and needy.

"Fuck." Now I can't wait any longer. My pussy is dripping from the arousal this scene has caused me too. I notch him at my entrance and at a punishingly slow pace, I push myself down over his cock.

"Oh fuck!" he moans as his hands move to my ass, and he thrusts up into me harder.

"Say my name, dammit!" I bark. He's so deep inside me, I think I can feel him in my belly.

"Sasha. Sasha, fuuuuck. Sasha," he babbles.

A thumb comes to meet my clit, and he works me until I explode around him.

"Fuck, Baby. You feel so good coming around my cock." He's so deep in my center, I swear I can feel each pump of his cum as he fills me.

"Take the blindfold off," I pant. He yanks it off and slings it across the room.

"You're so mesmerizing when you're in control, Sasha." He pulls me down onto his chest, our breathing still coming fast and ragged. He gently caresses my shoulders and back while placing kisses to the top of my head.

"You're fucking amazing. Do you know that? How did you know exactly what I needed tonight?"

"I just gave you what you gave me. A chance to not be in control."

Chapter 33
Sasha

Lola is in the office waiting for Ethan to take her to another doctor's appointment. She's still trying to make up with me, so she's talking nonstop.

"How are you and Gary getting along?"

"Fine."

"Do you go out on dates?" I stare at her like she's insane.

"Yes."

"Are you going to try to find out who your real father is?"

"I don't know where to start," I admit, trying my best not to look at her.

"I can help you. I would like to make up for the whole Gary thing. If you'll let me."

I stop typing and look at her. She gives me those puppy dog eyes, and I let out a huff.

"What do I have to do?"

"Spit."

"Excuse me?"

"Yeah, all you have to do is spit into a little vial. It gets sent off to a lab, and they compare your results with millions they already have on file. Maybe you could find a match."

"I don't know?" I sneer.

"At the very least, it would tell you which country your family originates from."

"I guess it couldn't hurt. I don't have any idea where my parents came from."

"It's a start," she says.

"Okay, I'll try it."

"I'll get everything together, and we can do it tomorrow."

Ethan comes out of his office ready for the appointment.

"Hey, Baby," he says as he takes Lola into his arms and kisses her with purpose. "Are you two ready to go?" He rubs her belly.

"Yeah, Bennie's waiting downstairs. Sasha, I'll see you tomorrow," she says with a little wave.

The next day, around lunchtime, Lola appears in my doorway, waving a box in her hand.

"Can you meet me in the conference room, please?"

Following her inside, I close the door. "What is all this stuff?"

"This is a test from My Family and Me." She opens the box and lays everything out, and hands me a white tube with what looks like a funnel on top.

"Here, spit into this. Enough to fill it up to this line." I do as I'm told and spit.

"Okay, now what?" I ask, holding it out to her. She takes the tube from me, removes the funnel part, puts a tiny lid on top, and screws it on tight. She places it into a baggie and seals it.

"That's all there is to it?" I ask.

"Yup." She hands me a little blue card with a long number on it. "Don't lose this. You will need it to get the results."

"Okay."

"I'll drop it off at the post office, and we'll have some results in four to six weeks."

"Thank you for doing this for me," I say, as I start walking out of the conference room.

"Sasha, I really didn't mean to hurt you."

"I know, Lola. I'll get over it. Please, just don't ever lie to me again."

"I won't. I'm sorry." She follows me to the elevator, and I push the button for her.

"How did your doctor's appointment go yesterday?" I ask.

"This baby is cooking just fine. We're in the final stretch now."

"That's wonderful news. You could make it all up to me by telling me what the gender is," I tease, waggling my brows at her.

"Now, you know I can't do that. Ethan and I want it to be a surprise."

"I had to give it a shot."

The doors close Lola inside the elevator, and I walk back to my desk.

Chapter 34
Sasha

Four weeks go by, and Lola comes to the office. She's panting and her face is red as a beet. She has one hand on her hip, and the other is braced on the doorframe. She looks like she ran all the way here.

"Lola, are you okay?" I come from behind my desk and take her hand, ushering her to sit on the couch. "I'll get Ethan."

I run to Ethan's door and throw it open. His head pops up, and his eyes stare at me with anger, but before he can speak, I shout, "Lola's here, and she doesn't look good." Anger turns to concern as he rounds the desk and runs out the door.

"Lo, are you okay? What's wrong?" He kneels in front of her. It's so out of character to see Rocco Ethan Martinelli, Don Supreme of The Martinelli Organization, on his knees in front of anyone, let alone a woman. But their love is so strong, it defies all boundaries. He would do anything for her.

"The baby's coming. My contractions are five minutes apart," she pants.

"Why did you come here? Bennie should've taken you straight to the hospital, and I would've met you there."

"I want you to go with me," she whines. "And I have something for Sasha." He moves next to her on the couch and rubs circles on her back.

"Me?"

"Yes, it's a response to the test we sent to My Family and Me. I didn't open it. You do it when you're ready." She hands me a white envelope.

"Thank you, but you two need to go." Just then, Lola erupts into a guttural moan as a contraction takes over.

Ethan's eyes grow wide as she squeezes his hand tightly. When the contraction passes, he stands and pulls her up.

"We need to get the hell out of here. I don't want you having our daughter in the car on the way to the hospital." My hands fly to my mouth.

"Oh my God, you're having a girl!" They've been secretive during the whole pregnancy. They wouldn't even tell his sisters the sex of the baby, and he just let it slip.

"I guess everyone will know soon enough. Sorry, Lo," Ethan says.

"I won't tell, I promise." I cross my heart.

"It's okay. Let's go," she says.

"I'll take care of everything here. You two go. Get out of here." I shoo them out the door.

They leave the office, ready to welcome their baby girl into the world. I plop down in my chair, letting out a huge sigh. I look at the damn white envelope. *What the hell.* Gathering up my nerve, I decide to open it.

I pull the folded sheet of paper from the envelope, and I think I might throw up. I can breathe again when I see it's only the instructions to view the results on their website. It'll have to wait until I get home because I need to finish up here first.

⌐

I stopped off and got Chinese food on the way home. I set the bag of food on the coffee table, go to my bedroom, take my hair out of the tight bun, and shake it out. I change into some sweatpants and one of Gary's sweatshirts I confiscated the last time he stayed over. I grab a water bottle and sit on the couch. With the laptop in front of me, I close my eyes. *You can do this.*

Using the code on the blue card Lola told me not to lose when we first took the sample, I log in to the website and bring up my file. I scroll through the choices: ancestry report, DNA relatives, health, and lab results. What news do I want first? Let's see where I come from. I click on the ancestry report first.

A map of the world pops up with my results underneath. Seventy-five percent... Russian. *What the fuck?* Russian? I look closer and the results show I'm 75% Russian, 16.4% French and German, and 8.6% British and Irish.

"Fuck."

My mom couldn't have been Russian. She didn't have an accent or anything to suggest any Russian in her background. That means my biological father was a full-blown Russian?

"Russian." The word gets stuck in my throat as I try to wrap my brain around the information. There's a knock on my door. I walk over to it and say in my deepest, manly voice, "Who is it?"

I hear Gary chuckle on the other side of the door.

"The Big Bad Wolf, Baby, open up." I pull the door open and stare at him.

"Why did you answer like that?" he asks.

"I was trying to disguise my voice in case you were someone I didn't know."

"Oh, and you think *that* voice would discourage someone from breaking in here?"

"Well, I don't know, but it made me feel better." He takes me in his arms and kisses me, and I giggle.

"Hi," I coo.

"Hi." He closes and locks the door behind him. "Whatcha doin'?" he asks.

"I got the results from My Family and Me on my spit test."

"Spit test?" He laughs.

"Lola helped me do it. You spit in this little tube and send it away. Then they tell you where your ancestors came from."

"Sounds interesting." Turning the laptop toward him, he says, "So tell me what I'm looking at here."

I point at the results.

"See here, it says I'm 75 percent..." We both say in unison, "Russian." He turns and stares at me with a dumbfounded look on his face.

"Now you know how I feel."

"Your parents are both Russian?" he asks.

"There was nothing about my mom that screamed Russian, ever. No accent. Nothing."

"For you to be 75% Russian, your mom had to be Russian. Your dad makes up half of your DNA and so does your mom."

"Fuck. I'm Russian."

"Looks like it, Baby."

"Did you connect with your father?"

"I didn't get that far. Here, let me see." I turn the laptop toward me again and click on DNA Relatives. Five people come up.

"Five. That's all?" I say disappointedly. My head falls into my hands, and Gary turns the laptop back his way.

"Let me see." There's a long pause while he looks at the screen. "There are five accounts listed. Four people share 0.32% of their DNA with you. They didn't list their names, just letters and numbers. Like they don't want to be identified. The last one says... Aunt."

"What?" I lift my head. Scooting in closer to him. "Show me."

"Yeah, it even shows her name, Lilith Frazier, 25% shared DNA." He points at the screen.

"I have an aunt? I have an aunt. I have an aunt! Oh my God, I can't believe this. I have an aunt!"

"Baby, you have an aunt," he says as we both laugh and hug.

"My head is spinning. She has to be related to my mom. Lilith doesn't sound Russian to me, does it to you?"

"No, not really, but..."

"I wonder if I can talk to her somehow?"

"I think you..."

"I wonder if she would want to meet me?"

"I think..."

"Maybe she knows who my real father is? Or how they met? Or who my mom's parents are? Or where I'm from..."

"I ..." My thoughts are swirling around me like a tornado. Gary grabs me by the shoulders and forces me to look at him.

"Sasha, you need to slow down and think about this," he snaps. I take in a deep breath.

"You don't think she'll like me?"

"Baby, don't you dare go there. She will *love* you. That's not it. I'm thinking about the whole assassin thing and working for the Mafia."

"Oh... Yeah...Right. I wasn't thinking about that. I wouldn't want her to get hurt because she's associated with me."

"Let's take this in logical steps, okay?"

"Okay."

"Look." He points back at the screen. "You can click on this icon and ask her if she wants to connect first. Then if she connects back, you can send her a message to try to share some information."

"Okay. Okay. That sounds like it makes sense." I hold my breath and click the icon. It changes to read *Invitation sent* and I release my breath. "Now we wait. Want some Chinese food?"

We share my dinner, and we're lying on the couch together watching Netflix. After about an hour, my computer dings.

"What was that?" We both look at each other. "It can't be. Not this soon." I lean over and grab the laptop and place it on Gary's chest with an oof.

"Oh. My. God. She accepted my invitation." I sit up and move the computer onto my lap. "What do I do now?"

"Ask her a question."

"Which question? I have so many."

"Start with something small, like is your sister Samantha Matthews?"

"Yeah. Yeah, that sounds good. Short and sweet. Straight to the point." I type it into the message section and hit send, hoping she's still connected and will see it before she exits the website.

"Come on, lie back down and try to relax." I do as he says and cuddle back down into his arms, trying to concentrate on the movie again.

Five minutes later, there's another ding. I leap up from the couch, and Gary laughs at me.

"I'm excited, so sue me." Sure enough, there's a message.

LILITH

> I'm Samantha's older sister. Are you her daughter?

I stare at the screen.

"What should I write back?" I whisper, as if she can hear me.

"What else do you want to know?" he answers. I think for a moment and reply to her.

> Yes. Do you have any other brothers or sisters?

> No. Would you rather text?

I don't hesitate. I dash to the closet, grab one of my burner phones, and quickly look up its number.

"Are you sure this is a good idea? You don't know anything about this woman."

"I know, but it's just a burner phone. She can't trace it. If I don't want to communicate anymore, I'll destroy it." I type the phone number for the burner into the message section and hit send.

"If, you're sure."

"It's kind of exciting. Don't you think?" My heart is pounding with excitement.

"Yes, it's exciting, but you need to be careful. Don't go off meeting her or doing something without me."

"I won't. I promise." The phone chimes with a text.

> Do you know where my sister is? I would love to see her.

> > I'm sorry. My mother died fifteen years ago.

> How did she die?

> > Drug overdose.

> Can I contact Troy?

> > No, he died in a fire twelve years ago.

> Who raised you?

> > I raised myself. I had no other family.

> I'm so sorry.

> > When was the last time you saw my mom?

> 1996.

> > Was she married to Troy then?

> No

> > Was she married at all then?

No

Do you know who my real father is?

Troy

No, he's not. Do you know who my real father is?

She stops replying. I'm a little disappointed, but I did just tell her her sister is dead. About an hour goes by, and the phone finally chimes.

Yes

Who?

The phone goes off again, and I check the message.
"What the fuck?"
The room begins to spin. I drop the phone. I can't breathe. I can't hear. I can't think. Gary picks up the phone and reads the text.
"Holy fucking shit!"

Chapter 35
Gary

Sasha's face is as white as a sheet. She's just sitting on the couch staring into nothingness. I think she's in shock. I text Freddy.

We have a big problem.

FREDDY

What's up?

Sasha got her DNA results back.

What does that have to do with me?

You'll never believe who her real father is supposed to be?

Who?

Boris Petrov

I'll be there in twenty.

Fifteen minutes later, Freddy walks through Sasha's front door.

"Tell me everything."

I tell him all about the test she sent off, the results being 75 percent Russian, the lady she connected with, and the messages they sent back and forth.

"She hasn't sent any more messages since she got the one with his name on it."

"Good. We need to talk about how she's going to handle this." He looks at Sasha, who's still in a daze on the couch. "What's wrong with her?"

"I think she's in shock. I was afraid to touch her."

Freddy and I walk over and sit on either side of her. I take one hand, and Freddy takes the other. He turns her head to look at him, but there are only vacant eyes staring back.

"Sasha..." She just stares at him. "Sasha." He taps the side of her face, and her brows furrow. "SASHA!" he barks, and she blinks. "Are you okay?"

"Boris Petrov is my father," she murmurs.

"I heard," he says like he's talking to a child.

"What am I going to do?"

"We'll figure it out."

"He's the head of the Russian Mafia, Freddy."

"I know who he is, Sasha. What does he know about you?"

"I don't know."

"We need to find out."

"How do I do that?"

"You're going to need to text your aunt back."

"What am I supposed to say? Um, yeah. Do you know if the head of the Russian Mafia knows I'm his daughter?" Sasha snarks.

"Well, maybe don't say it *quite* like that. We'll help you. Where's the phone?" Sasha gives him the phone. I look over his shoulder as he types out a message.

FREDDY

> I'm sorry it took me so long to respond. I'm a little taken aback by your message.

"Taken aback? Who the fuck says *aback*, Freddy? Give me the phone." I snatch the phone away. Before I can begin typing, the phone chimes with a text.

LILITH

> I'm sure it's upsetting to know your real father is such a dangerous man.

Sasha seems to come back to life and takes the phone back from me.

SASHA

> Does he know about me?

> When Sam found out she was pregnant with you, Boris was no longer in her life. She was already dating Troy, and she told him you were his child.

"Explains why Troy treated me like I was his daughter all those years. He never acted like I wasn't, until the night my mom died."

> Are you certain she never told him about me?

> I left before you were born.

> Why did you leave?

I got married. Tell me what happened to Samantha.

Troy started beating her when I was nine.

Why?

I don't know why he started beating her. We were a pretty normal family until then.

Did they argue?

Sure.

About what?

I don't remember. I was a child. I would hide in the closet when he hurt her.

When did the drugs start?

It started with pain medicine after he broke her arm.

He broke her arm?

He broke a lot of her bones. He would get mad because she did drugs, and then he would get drunk, and they would fight.

Why didn't she take you and leave?

I don't know.

Are you okay? I know this is a lot.

I'm fine. How are you? I'm sorry your sister is dead.

I'm going to let you go for tonight. I need to process all this. Can we text tomorrow? Let's say, seven?

That would be fine. Thank you.

"It sounds like she wants to know all she can about her sister. Tomorrow, when you talk to her, try to get her to talk about your father," Freddy advises.

"I will," she says.

"Keep me posted. I need to get back to the hospital. It's killing Amelia waiting for this baby to come."

"Oh, I forgot to ask. How's Lola doing?"

"She seems good, but Ethan is a wreck. He doesn't think it should be taking so long." He chuckles. "Call me tomorrow and give me an update."

I walk him to the door and out into the hall.

"Keep an eye on her, Gary. Sasha thinks she's invincible. Don't let her meet this woman alone. I don't trust any of it."

"I won't. Thanks, Boss."

When I get back inside, Sasha is cleaning up the kitchen.

"I'm beat," I say.

She comes around me from behind and squeezes me tight.

"I'm sorry I freaked out on you there for a minute."

"A minute? Try twenty."

"Twenty? Really? It was just a little overwhelming."

I turn her around to face me.

"I know, Baby. I'm here for whatever you decide to do about Lilith."

"What do you think I should do?"

"I think it'll depend on what she says tomorrow. Let's go to bed."

"To sleep?" She snuggles her nose into my neck.

"We don't have to sleep if you don't want to." I kiss the top of her head.

"I don't wanna sleep. I wanna do you." I lift her into my arms and carry her to the bedroom.

Chapter 36
Sasha

Gary and I arrive at the hospital to welcome Baby Girl Martinelli to the world the next afternoon. I open the door slowly and pop my head inside to make sure it's okay if we come in. Ethan is standing beside the bed, looking down at Lola holding their new little bundle of joy. He waves for us to come on in.

"Congratulations. How's everyone doing?" I whisper, slipping into the room.

"Momma and baby are doing just fine," Ethan says as I hand him the flowers we brought. I move over to take his spot and squeeze Lola's hand.

"Hi, Momma."

"Hi." She sounds exhausted. She pulls back the blanket to give me a glimpse of the baby.

"Oh, my goodness, she's beautiful. What did you name her?"

"Alessia Anne Martinelli. Anne was my mother's middle name," she says proudly.

"It's a beautiful name." I stare into the face of this tiny little human and wonder if I'll ever get to experience this kind of unconditional love in my lifetime. How can an assassin have a child? How could I ever keep them safe? There's no way any of this is ever happening for me.

Gary and Ethan shake hands and stand at the foot of the bed. I lean in close to Lola.

"We're not going to stay, but I wanted to come and say thank you."

"For what?"

"For helping me do the spit test."

"Did you find out something?" She squeezes my hand.

"Yes. Good or bad, I found my mom's sister."

"That's amazing!" she whisper-shouts.

"Yeah, I thought so too…" I hesitate.

"But…"

I move in to speak into her ear.

"She says my father is Boris Petrov." Her face turns stark white. She knows what kind of ruthless killer the man is. We've both heard the horrific stories. His torture methods can't be erased from my brain.

"I don't know positively from DNA, but this lady sounds pretty convinced it's him." I back away from her slowly.

"Sasha."

"It's okay, Lola. I'll be fine. But you know I can't come around you and the baby again until I figure this shit out."

"I understand."

I take hold of Gary's hand and catch a glimpse of Ethan. His brows are furrowed, and his eyes are tight slits now. The happiness on his face from before has been replaced with darkness. Gary obviously told him about our new friend, and I'm sure he's furious I came here around his family. He steps in front of me.

"If you need anything, you tell Holden, and it's yours. Do you understand?" I feel like I was just punched in the chest. He's concerned for…me.

"Why?"

"Because you're *family*, Sasha. Don't you know that by now?"

"I mean… I never—"

"You might be a badass killer, but you have the best heart of anyone I know. Now, get the hell out of here and keep us posted on what she says in your next text exchange." He hugs me, and I'm not sure what to do with myself.

Gary tugs on my hand, and we head down the hall. After we get into the elevator, Gary pins me to the wall. Lifting my chin with his index finger, he looks me in the eyes, and his playful demeanor slips away.

"Hey, what's the matter?"

"I didn't know they considered me…family." He pulls me in for a long hug instead.

"You told me on the island you don't let people in. Maybe if you open yourself up a little, you would see how many people really care about you." Tears tickle the corners of my eyes. *Don't cry, don't cry, don't cry.* Enough of this weak shit. I take a deep breath, lower my mask back into place and kiss him back.

"I'll try." The burner phone chimes.

Gary and I stare at each other. I pull the little phone out of my pocket and check the message.

LILITH

Can you text now?

We make it to the parking lot before I text back.

I'll text you when I get home in about twenty minutes.

Okay.

"I thought you agreed on seven?" Gary asks.
"We did."

"I wonder what changed?"

"Maybe she's just as anxious as I am."

"Or she has some other plans."

"What's that supposed to mean?" I say defensively as we climb into the car.

"I'm just saying you need to be careful. What if this is a catfishing scam or something?"

"How could she be catfishing me? Her DNA matched mine. You can't fake that, Gary." I'm getting aggravated by his skepticism.

"You and I both know how powerful Petrov is." I know he's trying to be the voice of reason here, but it really pisses me off when I know he's right. I sit back against the seat with my arms folded over my chest. She has to exist. She just has to.

As soon as I lay my purse on the table at home, I start texting Lilith.

> Is now a good time?

LILITH
> Yes.

> This is a lot sooner than seven. What happened?

> I couldn't wait any longer.

I turn and give Gary the stink eye, as if to say, *See, I told you so*.

> Are you ok? I know yesterday was a shock.

> It was. But I have questions.

Please ask me.

How do you know he is my father?

My sister told me. He was her first love.

How long were they together?

A few months.

Why did they break up?

She was fifteen, and he was twenty. His father arranged for him to marry another. They could never be together.

Sitting on the couch with Gary, I lean back onto his chest, sharing the texts with him.

"She was as old as I was when I killed Troy. I knew she was young when she had me, but I thought she was in her late thirties when she died. She would have been…" I try to calculate her actual age. "She was only twenty-eight. But she looked so much older."

"Drugs make you look older, Baby, especially meth and heroin," he confirms. I sit staring at the burner phone. Do I even want to know more?

"I don't know if I can do this."

"You don't *have* to do anything."

"I know, but… maybe I need to." Taking in a deep breath, I text again.

What do you want from me?

Nothing.

Really?

> I was trying to connect with family.
> I'm all alone.

"She's trying to make you feel bad for her," Gary says. "Don't let her."

> I'm sorry. I can't be your family.

> Please. Can we meet? I need to see your face.

> I don't think that's a good idea.

> Do you look like my sister?

> I think so.

> Please, just once.

"I don't know what to do, Gary." I toss the phone on the couch.

"Say no, Sasha. I have a bad feeling about this."

"I'm so curious."

"I know, Baby, but I don't think you should do this."

My brain is telling me yes, but my gut is telling me no. I want to meet her. Look into her eyes. See if they're my mother's eyes. But it could put Gary and me in a lot of danger. What if she's working with Petrov? What if he wants me dead? What if this is a trap? What if he already knows who I work for? Fuck! I don't know what to do.

"Will you go with me?" I ask Gary.

"Of course I'll go with you. If you want this to happen, arrange the meeting outside of the city. Away from where we work and live."

> How do I know you're not working with Petrov to get to me?

I could never hurt you.

You don't even know me.

You're the only family I have left.

Let me think about it.

Thank you.

"What are you going to do?" Gary rubs my arm.

"I want to meet her, but—"

He cuts me off with his hand. "That's all I need to know. Because if you want to meet her and you don't, you'll regret it. All the what-ifs will eat you alive. So we might as well make it happen."

"Thank you." I snuggle into his chest.

"Anything for you, Sasha, you know that."

"Where should we meet?" I ask.

"How about the warehouse?" he suggests.

"Do you want to scare the shit out of her?"

"Yeah. You're right. How about...the motorcycle bar out past Highway 81?"

"Can't be there."

"Why not?"

"Because I did a job out there a while back. Remember the one when Daniel dropped the ball?"

"That's where it was?"

"Yep."

"Damn. Okay. I know, let's go in the other direction. The Golden Giraffe."

"That's a strip club."

"It's in neutral territory. The Russians don't hang out on the other side of the city, and who would ever think we would meet an older lady there?"

"How old do you think she is?"

"I don't know, like seventy."

"Gary, she has to be fifty at most."

"Not what I was picturing, then."

"I guess not." I shake my head and send her a text.

> Can you meet me tomorrow at eight?

Where?

> The Golden Giraffe.

I'll be there. I have short brown hair, and I'll wear a red scarf.

> I have black hair. I'll be wearing a black leather jacket.

I can't wait.

"I can't believe you told her your actual hair color," Gary chimes.

"Fuck."

Chapter 37
Gary

Holden has surveillance set up all around the Golden Giraffe, with soldiers stationed inside for backup. We're all wearing earpieces, so we can communicate in case something goes south.

"No sign of a red scarf," Holden reports.

Sasha and I walk into the club and have a seat at a table in the center of the room that the crew prepared for us. It's outfitted with microphones, and the cameras are focused in close. The table is round, with three chairs strategically placed for the best views.

The music is blaring, and the strobe lights are flashing when Lilith walks into the club at 8:04. You can't miss her. She looks like an older version of Sasha in a short wig. I hear Sasha let out a breath beside me when she sees her. Their eyes connect, and she stands and walks a few steps to meet her.

"Lilith?" She holds out her hand.

"Sasha?"

"Yes. It's nice to meet you." Sasha ushers her to the table. Holding her hand out toward me, she says, "This is my, uh, my Gary." *Yeah, we'll have to talk about that one tonight.*

We haven't taken the time to define our relationship yet. I feel strongly for her. Shit, I may even love her, but I don't know if she's there yet. Sometimes I think she regrets sharing so much of her past with me, when I haven't told her much about myself. Not to mention what we both do for The Organization. But I do know I'll protect this woman with every ounce of my being. I would kill Petrov for her if she would let me.

"Nice to meet you. Won't you sit down?" I gesture to the chair. Lilith sits and looks up at Sasha. My eyes quickly scan the room to see if anyone followed her into the club.

"You look just like your mother," she says in awe.

"Thank you, so do you." Sasha removes her jacket and hangs it on the back of her chair like she always does and sits. Her aunt keeps her scarf pulled up tight around her neck.

"Thank you for meeting me." She continues to stare like she's memorizing every freckle and line. Her hand propped up under her chin in amazement.

"Would you like a drink?" I ask.

"No, thank you. I can't stay long."

"Well, let's get to it, then," Sasha says. "Please, tell me about my parents."

"Your mother was very young when they dated."

"How did they meet?"

"It was a small town. Everybody knew everybody else. They'd known each other their whole lives."

"May I ask how old you are?" Sasha asks.

"Forty-eight." Sasha eyeballs me with an "I told you so" look.

"Did she love him?" Sasha continues.

"I think she thought she did. She was only fifteen. He was older and very smitten with her."

"Was he always a dangerous man, like he is today?" I ask.

"Yes. He was always very possessive. If you messed with what he considered his, you would pay the ultimate price."

"He's only gotten more deadly with age," I state. She nods her head in agreement. Her eyes shift briefly toward me and back to Sasha.

"You said his father made him marry someone else. Who was it?" Sasha asks. Lilith begins to squirm in her chair, tugging the scarf up tighter around her neck. Her eyes scan the tables in front of us.

"A girl from our town."

"Didn't he like her?"

"No, he didn't want to marry her. He wanted your mother."

"Did my mother have an arranged marriage also?"

"No. I was the oldest, so our father made me marry a terrible man. I married for the family, so Samantha wasn't forced to."

"So she married Troy for love?"

"I'm not sure if it was for love, exactly. When she found out she was pregnant, they hadn't been dating very long. She told him the baby was his. When our father demanded they marry immediately, Troy didn't protest."

There's something about this woman that's not right. She's unsettled, and her eyes aren't focused on the conversation anymore. They're shifting around the room as if she's searching for someone.

"Are you afraid?" I lean in close and ask.

"No. Why would you ask me that?" She chuckles, an awkward sound.

"You look… uncomfortable."

"No. I'm fine."

Why don't I believe her?

I hear the conversation between Holden and the guys in my ear. They continue to search the bar but haven't found anything to be concerned about.

"Did Petrov ever find out my mother was pregnant with his baby?" Sasha asks, bringing Lilith's focus back to her.

"Not at first." Her eyes spring back to Sasha.

"What do you mean, not at first?" Sasha asks.

"She was eight weeks along by the time she told our father. She and Troy were basically thrown in front of the town priest and married. That didn't hide the fact that you were a full-term, eight-pound baby. Boris isn't a stupid man. He went to see

Samantha when you were two months old. He knew instantly she lied, and you were his daughter."

"How?"

"Because you had his jet-black hair and big brown eyes."

"So I do look like him."

"Yes, but I can see Samantha in you too. You have her nose and olive skin. And how can anyone miss those cheekbones and your beautiful smile?" Sasha seems to soften, but quickly snaps back harder.

"So he knows I exist. Has he looked for me?"

"How would I know that?" Lilith asks, shifting in her seat again.

"Because he sent you here, didn't he?" Both of us stare at Sasha. Lilith's mouth hangs open, and when she speaks, her voice is shaky and broken.

"He didn't... send me. I did the test. On my own. Over a year ago." Her voice is becoming more and more panicked.

"But he told you to do it, didn't he?"

"I... don't know what you're trying to say?" Sasha reaches out and pulls the scarf from Lilith's neck. Bruises in the shape of fingers cover her skin.

"Was he the one who hurt you, Lilith?" Lilith grabs the scarf back and hastily winds it around her neck.

"You don't know what you're talking about." Sasha and I look at each other and back at Lilith. "I had to do it."

"Had to do what?" Sasha asks.

"He's been trying to find you for fifteen years. This was the last thing he could think of to try to find you. He had almost given up, too, until you connected with me yesterday."

"But everyone thought I was dead. Why would he think I was still alive?"

"He couldn't convince himself you were gone. He said he could *feel* you were still alive." Her face sneers slightly, like she's jealous.

"Why didn't he *feel* Troy beating and raping me, then?" Lilith's mouth snaps shut.

"I didn't know he was doing that to you."

"He started coming into my room when I was twelve years old." Her aunt's hand flies to her mouth.

"That pig!" she spits.

"Petrov knew my mother died. Why didn't he come and get me?"

"I guess because you still had Troy. We didn't know he was hurting you, Sasha. I swear."

"Yeah. Well. He was. It doesn't matter now. I have a new life. I'm happy. I know everything I need to know about Boris Petrov, and I want nothing to do with him. So you can go back to wherever you came from and tell your boss that for me."

"He's not my boss." She lowers her eyes.

"Who is he to you, then? Why are you doing all of this for him?"

"I don't have a choice, Sasha. He's my... husband."

Chapter 38
Sasha

"Your husband! What the fuck, Lilith? You didn't think you should've led with that little piece of information instead of talking in circles?"

"I told you I was forced to marry a terrible man. I just didn't tell you it was Boris."

"He strangled you. He put those marks on your neck."

"Please, I don't want anything from you. I just wanted to meet my niece. You're the only family I have left. I don't know what Boris wants with you, but I know it won't be good. There's nothing good in that man whatsoever."

"I've heard about the things he does to people," I say.

"I've seen it with my own eyes. I'm not sure why he's kept me around all these years. Sometimes I just wish he would kill me and put me out of my misery."

"I *can* help you," I lean in closer. "I have experience making bad men go away." Gary shoots me a glare, but I can't look at him right now.

"No. You have to stay away."

"Does he know you're here, Lilith?"

"He knows everything, Sasha. He'll hurt me for meeting

you and not telling him where to find you. But I don't care. I needed to look into your eyes just once."

"He's coming for me, then."

"He has always been coming for you. I'll never tell him anything about you. I'll die first." Before I can say anything else, she stands. "I have to go."

"But—"

She cuts me off. "I'll never contact you again, Sasha. I just wanted to meet you." She pulls me in for a tight hug, then turns and strides from the club.

"Follow her and see where she goes," I say through the microphone. I see two of the guys leave, hot on her heels. I motion to the server to bring us two whiskeys, and we sit back in our chairs.

"What the fuck was all that?" Gary finally asks.

"She's scared to death."

"I could see that, but why would she risk meeting you? She had to know he would punish her, and she just put your life at risk." The concern in his voice makes my mask falter slightly.

"I can't see how she's survived all this time with him. I can't fathom the pain she's endured. We have to get her away from him."

"Are you fucking crazy? He'll kill you. How do you know she wasn't being controlled by him tonight?" he asks.

"I don't, but Jerry taught me how to read body signals, and she was putting a lot of them out there. Searching the room, shifting in her seat, the scarf she wouldn't let go of. The weirdest thing was the way she was staring at me, like she'd seen a ghost."

"What do you want to do now?"

"I think we need to meet with Freddy and Ethan to find out what they'll *allow* me to do. I would like to take him out, but I'm not sure how that will affect The Organization."

"Let me do it." Gary takes my hand. "Let me kill him for you."

I pull my hand away from his. My voice is sharp. "I'm

perfectly capable of taking care of my own business." I harden my stare at him. *Who the fuck does he think he is to tell me I can't do this?*

"I know how qualified you are, Baby, but this is your *father.*"

"He's not my fuckin' father. He's a monster, and I deal with monsters every day."

"This is a different kind of monster, Sasha. He wants to kill you, and you're his fucking blood. He's insane."

"I'm not wishing dear ole dad will pull me into his arms for a great big hug and welcome me into the family here, Gary. I know what the fuck he is." I throw my whiskey back in one gulp and stand.

"I don't want to talk about this anymore. I'm leaving. Are you coming?" I hold out my hand to him. He puts his hand in mine, and we exit the club.

Our drive back to his house is a quiet one. My blood boils in my veins at the thought of Boris Petrov being my biological father and all the times he's hurt Lilith. What other traits of his do I carry, aside from hair and eye color? Is it because of him I'm a cold-hearted bitch who can kill without a second thought?

Walking into the condo, I drop my bag on the floor. Gary comes in behind me and locks the door. I pin him against it so hard his head bounces back.

"I need to be fucked and fucked now. I don't want to think anymore." I run my tongue over his lips, and he opens for me. I take his mouth with hot desire and begin to unbutton his shirt. "I need you."

"Sasha," he sighs heavily.

My eyes spring up to his. "Please don't tell me you want to wait or some shit like that, because I need you to fuck me, *now.*"

"I wasn't going to say that." He grabs my thighs and pulls my body up, and I curl around his waist. He spins us, slamming my back into the door, and all the air rushes from my lungs.

"I was going to say you're mine tonight." His mouth crashes

over mine, and he strides to the bedroom, throwing me onto the bed.

"Strip!" he barks, and I do as I'm told.

"On your knees and hold the headboard." He mounts the bed behind me. When I look down, his head is between my knees.

"Sit" His voice is strong and demanding, and I know he means business. I lower my pussy to his face. "You know what I want, Sasha. Sit. On. My. Face."

He grabs my thighs in his huge hands and pulls me down hard and fast to his waiting tongue. He's not playing around as he licks my eager clit. Pulling it into his hungry mouth, he begins to suck. I moan with pleasure. He nibbles on my sensitive bud as I rotate my hips in wide circles and grind my pussy to his mouth.

"That's it, Baby. Just like that."

His tongue finds my center, and I'm in ecstasy. My hands grip the headboard as his strong arms circle my legs and pull me down tighter to his mouth. Fingers enter my pussy from both hands and begin moving in and out in tandem. Working my G-spot. The pressure is intense and makes me feel like I need to pee.

"Gary, I need to pee!" I yelp as I try to pull off his mouth, but he shakes his head no and continues his assault on my pussy. Flutter form in my core, telling me my orgasm is approaching.

"Oh shit! Don't stop," I cry. My body spasms with each swipe of his tongue, and a gush of fluid releases from my core.

"Gary! Shit! What the fuck!" I squeal and try to pull free from his grasp. He pulls me into his mouth, taking everything my body has to give.

"What the hell was that?" I ask.

A dark chuckle comes from Gary's chest as he says, "You squirted for me, Baby. And it was so fuckin' hot."

Embarrassment floods my senses as he pulls me down from the headboard and kisses me passionately.

"Are you okay?" he asks, smoothing my hair back out of my face.

"Yeah, I just never did that before," I say sheepishly. "I'm sorry."

"Don't you ever be fucking sorry," he growls. "That was the hottest thing ever. Think you can do it again?"

"I don't know how I did it the first time." We both laugh.

I grab for his zipper. "Are you going to fuck me or what?"

"Oh, I'm going to fuck you all right."

Standing from the bed, he removes his clothes. I lick my lips at the thought of swirling my tongue over the crown of his thick cock. I lie down on my back, with my head hanging over the side of the bed, tongue out. He knows what I want. He steps forward, placing the weeping tip of his cock on my tongue. The taste of his precum fills my mouth as he pushes his cock until it hits the back of my throat, and I gag.

He slides a hand behind my neck to support it so I'm able to open my throat wider for him. I grab the backs of his legs and hold myself steady. His rhythm grows faster, and I move one hand to his balls, rolling them in my palm. He lets out a growl and pulls his length from my mouth. He pumps his dick until hot cum shoots all over my chest, covering my tits in his seed. He runs his fingers through it, as if he's drawing a picture, and he smiles.

"What did you do?" I ask playfully, pulling my head off the edge of the bed and resting it on the pillow. I look down at my chest to see he drew a heart in his cum. "You're so silly."

"You're mine forever because I marked you with my cum." His deep blue eyes sear my soul.

"I'll always be yours," I coo.

He brings a wet washcloth from the bathroom and cleans off my chest, shuts off the lights, and climbs my body. He hovers above me, resting his weight on his forearms, and lowers his face to mine.

"Do you feel better yet?" he asks.

"I'll feel better when you bury that gigantic cock of yours inside me," I tease with a devious grin. I can be myself with Gary. I can say whatever I'm feeling, and he doesn't judge me.

I reach for his semi-hard cock and stroke it once, twice, and it twitches back to life in my hand. "Fuck me, Gary."

"Yes, ma'am." His voice is deep and low as he kneels between my legs. "I love this pussy so much." He drags a finger through my folds. "You're so needy for me," Never taking his eyes off me, he brings his finger to his mouth and sucks.

His eyes are dark with lust as I spread my legs wider for him. He notches his cock at my entrance, and I lift my legs around his hips. He's deep inside me with one hard thrust, and I don't ever want him to let me go.

I raise my hands to his shoulders and hold on tight as he drives into me again and again, just the way I like it. My hands move to his hair, and I pull. Gary moans into my mouth.

"Is this what you wanted?" *Thrust.*

"Me taking your hot pussy." *Thrust.*

"You're mine." *Thrust.*

"And I take care of what's mine." *Thrust.*

The top of my head bumps into the headboard. Without missing a beat, he moves his hand between me and it. He's taking care of me, even while he's railing into me.

"I'm almost there, Baby. Come with me."

Electricity shoots through my body as we fall into bliss together. He stays inside me as our bodies convulse and twitch. I'd warm his cock until tomorrow if he would let me.

After he pulls out, he lies beside me and pulls me over his chest the way I love. His warm hand rubs circles over my back.

"That was amazing," I say with a long sigh.

"You're amazing."

"It was exactly what I needed." I melt into his body.

He clears his throat. "We need to talk about the 'I'd like you to meet my...Gary' thing."

"I didn't know what to say. We've never discussed what we are to each other."

"I'll make it official then... Sasha Matthews, will you be my girlfriend?"

"Yes, Gary West, I'll be your girlfriend."

⌒

It's pitch black. I can't see anything, not a sliver of light. My ragged breaths fill the small space. It's hot in here. Sweat slides over my skin. I try to move, but my hands are tied behind my back with scratchy rope poking into my skin.

I kick my legs, but they hit something hard. I push up on my feet, but my head hits something too.

Panic surges through my body as I realize… I'm trapped. I kick and thrash in my restraints, as I scream at the top of my lungs, "HEEELLLLPPP!!!"

"Sasha! Sasha, Baby, wake up! You're dreaming…Sasha!" Gary yells. My eyes spring open, and he pulls me tight against his body.

"It's okay. You're okay. I got you." I grab on to him for dear life while my lungs search for air.

"Shh. It's over now," he soothes. He strokes my hair, and I begin to calm down. "What were you dreaming about?"

"The same thing I always dream about."

"Tell me."

"My hands are tied behind my back, and I'm trapped in a box. It's pitch black, and I can't get out."

"Your deepest, darkest fear," he whispers.

I nod my head. He holds me close until I fall asleep, safe in his arms.

Chapter 39
Sasha

The following morning, Gary and I are at the office with Ethan and Freddy. They heard everything over the microphones at the club, and we're here to discuss what to do about Petrov.

"Did they find out where Lilith went after she left the bar?" Gary asks.

"No. They lost her on the bridge."

"Damn it!" he barks.

I don't give anyone else a chance to speak before I blurt out, "I want your permission to kill Petrov."

"Now, hold on a minute," Ethan says, holding up his hands. "We need to think this through."

"Yeah, you can't just kill him without provocation. You'll start a fucking war," Freddy says.

"I want to set up a meeting with him," Ethan says.

"What the fuck for?" Gary barks.

"I want to find out what his intentions are toward Sasha."

"We know what his intentions are. He wants to fucking kill her," Gary snaps.

"You don't know that for sure. If he *was* watching Lilith last night, he could've taken her out and ended it all, but he didn't. Maybe he wants to meet her," Freddy says.

"Sure… he does, and fairy dust is going to shoot out my ass," Gary grumbles sarcastically, throwing his hands down and pacing the room.

"I don't want to meet him," I say. "I don't need anything from him."

"Maybe after he meets you, he'll leave you alone," Ethan interjects.

"Are you fucking delusional?" I yell. I can't believe I just raised my voice to my Don…again. He raises his chin and glares at me. "Boss, I'm sorry for being disrespectful, but he's a cold-hearted killer. He beats Lilith. He doesn't love her. He doesn't know how to love. I need to kill him before he kills me."

Freddy stands and walks over to me.

"Sasha, you'll start a war if you kill him without provocation. All the other leaders will be afraid it will happen to them, and they could start coming after us. We've turned The Organization around. The leaders in our city respect us and look to us for guidance and stability. If we assassinate a major player for no reason, other than you found out he's your father, everyone will lose confidence in our leadership. We have to be strategic about this."

I huff out a breath because I know he's right. I would never do anything to harm The Organization or the people in it who I've grown to care about. I grab my hair and pull, throwing my arms up in defeat.

"Fine. I'll follow the rules, this time. But I want to be there when you talk to him."

"You can be in the van with Daniel, listening to the conversation." Freddy looks at Ethan, and he nods in agreement.

"But you're only listening. I don't want him to know you're anywhere nearby. After we find out what he wants, then we'll decide what the next step will be."

"Fine," I concede. *I fuckin' hate to lose.*

A dinner meeting is set up with Petrov at Lowell's Steak-house, three days later. I'm in the black van around the corner with Daniel. Gary and Beckett are sitting at a table in the back of the restaurant. They have eyes on the kitchen, bathrooms, and exits. There are four more tables with our soldiers strate-gically placed around the room.

Freddy sits at a table in the center with Rosco, his second. He lifts his water glass to his lips and says under his breath, "Can everyone hear me?"

Daniel answers back for us, and Gary answers, as do some of the other men in the restaurant. It's a few brief minutes before Petrov's team strolls in.

"All right, everybody, here we go," I hear Gary say. My eyes are glued to the screen as I see Freddy hold out his hand to Petrov.

"Boris, how have you been?"

"Well, Fredrick, and you?" he asks in his thick Russian accent. I know he hates being called Fredrick, but he swallows it down, puts a softer look on his face, and chuckles.

"Good. Good. Please sit." He gestures for them to sit.

"So tell me, why did you want to meet tonight, comrade? To discuss the killing of three of my men?"

"Three of your men?" Freddy sounds confused.

"Yes, the three of my men you took out with fire and phosphorus."

"Phosphorus? Holy shit, Boris, I'm no fucking chemist."

"I thought you were bringing me here to confess," he says, crossing his arms.

"I didn't take out your men, and I don't know who did."

"Why did you bring me here, Fredrick?"

"I need to talk to you about someone."

"Who?"

"Your daughter."

There's a long silence while Petrov lowers his head. Quietly, he responds, "My daughter is dead."

"You and I both know that's not true." He raises his gaze to Freddy.

"I don't know what you are talking about."

"We both know you've been searching for her for years, and you recently obtained new information telling you she is, in fact, alive."

"So what if I did? She's no concern of yours."

"She works for The Organization, and she's very much my concern."

Petrov's face grows blank. "I want to talk to her. Where is she?" His eyes search the restaurant.

"She's not here. She doesn't want to see you. I need your word you'll leave her alone."

A loud, hearty laugh bursts from Petrov's chest.

"She's my daughter, Fredrick. I haven't seen her since she was two months old. You are *not* going to keep her from me."

"I'm not keeping her from you. I'm here to tell you that she wants nothing to do with you. She doesn't want to meet you. She doesn't want to talk to you. She wants you to stay away from her."

"My friend, I cannot do that. I need to see my daughter."

"Why?"

"Because she's mine!" His bark comes out loud, and he looks around the room. He takes a breath and leans in close. "I have a right to have my daughter by my side."

"You don't have any rights where Sasha is concerned. She's a grown-ass woman, and she makes her own decisions. You'll just have to accept it."

"I can't. I won't," he says through gritted teeth.

"I think we're done here, Boris," Freddy says. Petrov stands and drops his napkin on the table.

"I will find her, and you can't stop me."

"We'll see about that, Boris." Freddy's voice is firm and strong as he takes another drink of his whiskey. Petrov leaves the restaurant with his entourage.

I speak into the microphone. "What do I do now?"

Gary answers, "We kill him before he kills you."

Chapter 40
Sasha

It's been five days since Freddy met with Petrov, and we've heard nothing from him. We need to take the son of a bitch out, and soon. Freddy's sending Gary to LA tomorrow to take care of some business. We've spent the evening together, eating and watching movies in bed, when Gary gets a text from Freddy.

"What did Freddy want?" I ask.

"To make sure I'm still going tomorrow." He tosses his phone on the mattress.

"I know how to take care of myself. I'll be fine while you're gone."

"It's not *you* I'm worried about, Baby. It's Petrov."

"When you come home, we'll work out a plan to get rid of him *together*."

"Promise you won't do any stupid shit while I'm gone?"

"I promise. I know you want a piece of him too."

"I hate all of this."

"I know. So do I. Hopefully, it'll be over soon," I say. I have a bad feeling dear ole dad is going to try something soon, but I don't want to worry Gary. My phone rings.

"It says unknown," I whisper as if they can hear me.

Gary motions for me to put it on speaker.

"Hello," I answer confidently.

There's a dark laugh from the other side of the line. "Sasha?"

"Who is this?"

Again, with the fucking laughter. "It's your father," the deep Russian voice rumbles through the phone.

"How did you get this number?" I only talked to Lilith on a burner phone, and I destroyed it after we met.

"You have your people, and I have mine. You thought I wouldn't find out you met with Lilith at the Golden Giraffe?"

"What do you want?"

"I want you to come home, devchonka." (little girl)

Laughter flies from my mouth this time. "Home? I am home."

"I want you to come live with me. I missed your whole life because of my father. Come... take your place beside me."

"If you think I'll come be your dutiful daughter after all these years, you're crazier than I thought."

"I hoped you would come to me peacefully. But I suppose I need to be more convincing. Turn on your camera. I have something to show you." I look at Gary, and I click the button. On the screen is Lilith. Her face is bloodied and bruised.

"Lilith," I say under my breath. As the camera pans out, Boris stands beside her with a gun to her head. Her clothing is in tatters, and her hair looks like a rat's nest.

"What the hell, Boris! Let her go!"

"After all these years, she finally led me to you. I knew if I waited long enough, she would figure out a way to find you," he croaks.

Lilith's eyes are wide, and she shakes her head the best she can. "No... Sasha... I swear I didn't tell him anything about you," she begs as tears stream down her face.

"No, she didn't. That's why she looks the way she does," he says as he shakes her back and forth in frustration. "If she had just told me what she knew, this would've been so much easier."

"You found me. Now let her go!" I yell.

Lilith squirms in his grasp as she whimpers, "Please. Let me go."

"All these years, I have searched for you. I *knew* you were alive. I could *feel* it. Everyone thought I was crazy. But I was right! I'd almost given up hope until the message came through from the DNA website." Lilith cries softly and keeps shaking her head. "I knew using her would eventually lead me to you. Now that I've found you, I don't need *her* anymore."

"No! No! Give her to me," I plead.

"I can't do that. She's been my responsibility since our fathers forced us to marry when I was twenty. I loved Samantha. I never loved Lilith. She's only been good for one purpose in my life, and it's been a way to find you. Lilith was my only lifeline to you."

"Lifeline? I don't understand."

"Samantha swore the baby was Troy's, but I didn't believe her. I had to see you for myself. So when you were two months old, I broke into their house. When I saw your beautiful face, I knew you were mine."

Chapter 41
Boris

The house is dark when I enter through the side door. I watched Troy leave for work five minutes ago. I make my way to the bedroom and find Samantha propped up in bed with the baby lying on her naked breast, feeding.

"What are you doing here?" she asks softly so as not to startle the child.

"I had to see the baby. I need to know if she's mine, Samantha." She pulls the soft flannel blanket back from the baby's face. I sit on the edge of the bed and lean in for a closer look.

"Oh my God." The child's hair is jet black, just like mine. I use my finger to rub her little cheek. She unlatches from her mama's breast and looks up at me. Seeing those twinkling brown eyes looking back at me, I know she's mine.

"She is my daughter."

"Yes." She nods.

"But why? Why did you lie to me?"

"Because our fathers would never have let us be together, Boris. I told my father I loved you, but he still forced you to marry Lilith."

"We could've figured something out if I only knew the truth.

I would've killed them all to be with you, Samantha. I loved you then, and I love you now. You know my heart belongs to you and not your sister." She places her soft hand on my face.

"I know, my love. I love you too, but you know in your heart it has to be this way."

My head lowers to the baby, and I rub my nose on her cheek. I breathe in her sweet baby scent. A mixture of her mother's milk and powder. I stare at her for a long while, memorizing her every feature and burning her sweet face into my memory forever. "I love you, detyo moyo." (my child). I place a kiss on her cheek and one on the lips of my love.

"Promise me you'll tell her about me one day."

"I promise. She'll want to know her real papa someday."

"After I left Samantha that night, I wanted to burn the whole world to the ground for taking you both from me."

"What does Lilith have to do with you staying connected to me?" Sasha asks.

"Samantha would send Lilith one picture every year on your birthday." I pan the camera over to my desk, where twelve little pictures of Sasha sit in frames. I hear her gasp through the phone.

"I can't believe this. You kept *my* photos," she whispers.

"I stayed away from both of you, just like I promised. But after your twelfth birthday, I couldn't take it any longer. It was eating me alive not to have you both with me. I broke my promise and called Samantha.

"Hello."

"I cannot wait any longer, Samantha."

"Boris?"

"Sasha is old enough to know the truth."

"I don't know if I can tell her."

"You must tell her I'm her father. She needs to know me, and I want to know her."

"Will you take us away from here?" Her speech sounds slurred and tired.

"Of course, my love. Tell Troy the truth, and I'll come get you both."

"I'll do it tonight," she says. "I need help, Boris."
"I'll fix everything. Just tell them."
"I'll call you when it's done."

"It was the last time I heard my true love's voice," Boris says.

"That must've been the night Troy came to my room for the first time. She must've told him the truth, and it pushed him over the edge. He wanted to punish me for being your daughter. For taking his life away. So he...raped me."

"I didn't know he was hurting you. If I had, I would have..." In my rage, I shake Lilith wildly.

"Why didn't you come get me when my mother died?" she asks.

"I wanted to, but you didn't know anything about me. How could I take you away from the only father you ever knew?"

"Couldn't you *feel* he was hurting me?" she snarks.

"I was trying to give you time to grieve the loss of your mother."

"Grieve. I never got to grieve for my mother! The paramedics took her body away, and I never saw her again. Troy made me his whore after that!"

Fury surges through my body. If that piece of shit wasn't already dead, I would kill him myself. My grip on Lilith growing tighter. She cries out in pain.

"You weren't there to protect me, *Daddy.*" Her words echo through my head. *You weren't there to protect me. Protect me.*

"So I took care of him myself. I gutted him like a pig, burned the house down, and ran for my life." Her voice rages.

"Come to me, Sasha. Let me make this up to you."

"No! You're a monster. I know all about the empire you've built. The ruthless killer you've become. You can't change any of that, and you can't make all the hell I've lived through any better. It's too late."

"I'm not the only killer here, devochka (little girl). You've become a killer too. We're both the same."

"I get rid of men who hurt defenseless women. Like that piece of shit Tony Manillo. These women need me."

She's the one who killed Manillo? She killed three of my men?

"Maybe that's how you sleep at night, but you're no better than I am, and you know it," I snap.

"My deaths are quick. You torture and maim for pleasure," she snaps.

"I do what I have to do to get what I need."

"What do you want with me, anyway? I won't sit around and be your princess."

"I don't want you to be my princess. I want you to be my enforcer and someday take over for me. We'll work side by side and take over this town."

"Now, I know you're crazy! I'll *never* deceive The Organization. Ethan saved me when I lost everything."

"You *will* come to me."

"Let Lilith go."

I turn to look at Lilith. My burden for so many years. I never wanted her. I wanted Samantha. I've found my daughter, so I don't need her anymore. I raise the gun to the side of her head and, without another word, fire. She falls lifeless to the ground at my feet.

"No!" Sasha's scream pierces the air.

"You *will* be mine, docha' (daughter). I *will* come for you, and you *will* do my bidding."

I press the red button on my phone and toss it to the ground.

Chapter 42
Gary

After the conversation between Boris and Sasha, I know I can't go on this trip to Los Angeles anymore. She's furious and wants him dead.

I'm alone in the bedroom so I dial Freddy.

"What?" he barks.

"Boris just called Sasha from an unknown number. He killed Lilith."

"Damn it."

"I can't go to LA with all this shit going on."

"Listen, man. I know you're upset, but she's a *fucking assassin*. You're acting like she's some prissy little bitch who can't take care of herself. Sasha is a warrior. She'll be fine for a few hours."

"I know who the fuck she is, but…"

"Just say it."

"Say what?"

"That you love her."

"How do you know how I feel?"

"It's obvious to everyone how you feel, man."

"It is?

"Jesus, you're so fuckin' blind? Do you love her or not?"

"Yeah… I love her." I keep my voice quiet so Sasha can't hear.

"I hate talking about feelings and shit. Get your ass to LA, take care of business, and get the hell back here. Then we'll figure out what to do about Petrov."

"Yes, Boss."

I hear Sasha in the kitchen banging stuff around. I walk up behind her and wrap my arms around her, "What are you doing, pretty girl?"

"Well, I was trying to make pancakes, but I can't find the baking powder."

Reaching up into the cabinet beside the stove, I lower the container down to her. "Here you go."

"Why do you keep it all the way up there? How was I supposed to find it?"

"Well, until you started staying with me, I never had to worry about anyone else finding shit."

"I can go back to my house, if you want me to," she says in a teasing voice.

"No, thank you." I bury my nose in her hair and breathe her in. "Just get rid of your townhouse and move in here with me."

"But where would I put all my guns and ammo?"

"Oh! You haven't met the *ladies* yet, have you?"

"The ladies?" She raises her eyebrow at me. "I thought I was your only *lady*."

I kiss the tip of her nose.

"You *are* my only lady, but let me introduce you to the *ladies*," I say in a sultry gigolo voice.

"What the hell are you doing?" she asks as I pull her down the hall and come to a stop in front of the bookcase.

"This is where I keep *my ladies*."

"In a bookcase?"

"It's what's behind the bookcase that matters. Watch." I reach up to the top shelf and pull the second book to the right forward until it clicks. Sasha turns to me wide-eyed and watches as I pull hard on the shelf and the whole thing swings open. Her mouth falls open and she scans the walls.

"Holy shit."

I flick on the switch, and the backlighting comes to life.

"They're beautiful," she says in awe, moving around the room.

"These are *my ladies.* This is Bertha. She's a Benelli 4 shot-gun. My pistols, Roxy and Trixie. Josie is my MP7 submachine gun, and I can't forget my pride and joy, Eleanor."

"Eleanor?"

"Yes, Eleanor was my grandpa's. She's a 1916 Chiappa Triple Threat. He called her Eleanor. He left her to me when he died."

"Is this gun really over a hundred years old?" she whispers as if someone could really hear her in here.

"No. She was made in 2013. These guns are not cheap though. When he found out they were coming out with it, he saved his money and bought one of the first ones they ever made. He only got to shoot her a few times before he died."

"How old were you when he died?"

"I had just turned eighteen."

Her hand gently glides over Eleanor, and I can tell she loves her as much as I do already.

"This place is amazing. Why do they have names?"

"It makes my connection to them more personal. 'You must take care of your weapon if it is going to take care of you,' Gramps always said."

"Jerry taught me to take pride in my weapons also."

"So I take good care of them and give them places of honor on my wall."

"Classy. How many do you have?" she asks.

"I probably have seventy-five now."

"Do they all have names?"

"Well, no. That would be crazy." I chuckle awkwardly. "Just the ones most special to me. I have more in those drawers over there, and in the black cabinet in the center of the room. My sniper rifle is behind you." I know Sasha is a fan of sniper rifles. "Gramps always said you should have the right tool for the job. My tools just happen to be guns."

"You must've really respected your grandfather."

"I did. He was the first person to take the time to teach me about weapons."

She lingers around the room, inspecting each weapon.

"Where would mine go?" she asks, tapping her chin.

"I'll make room for them. Don't you worry."

"Thank you for sharing your *ladies* with me."

"Of course."

"I'm hungry. Let's go eat," Sasha urges. I pull her toward me and kiss those soft pink lips.

"I'm going to eat my breakfast right here on top of this cabinet."

"Ooh. Yes, Daddy," she coos, never missing a beat.

I lift her on top of the smooth black cabinet in the center of the room, and she lifts her ass so I can pull her sleep shorts off and lies down on the cool, smooth surface. Goose bumps cover her legs as she plants her feet at the edge. Her legs fall open for me, inviting me to feast on her sweet, sweet pussy.

"Fuck, Baby. I don't even have to touch you, and you're wet."

"Gary," she whines, and I swat the side of her leg.

"Who?"

"Daddy. Oh, Daddy," she rasps.

"That's better." My tongue glides over every delectable inch of her pussy before I slide two fingers to either side of her clit, rubbing her needy bud. When I give her a little pinch, she mewls and bucks her hips. Her wetness leaks onto the cabinet.

"My little brat likes that, doesn't she?"

"Y-Y-Yes, Daddy." Her eyes are closed, and her breathing is ragged. I move my fingers to her entrance and slide them inside as my mouth devours her clit. I work her G-spot, finding the rhythm she likes, and never let up the suction. She's lost in the sensations. When I add a third finger, her climax erupts.

Her pussy clenches around my fingers, and I don't release her clit until the sensations are too much for her to handle, and she pushes my head away.

I take a soft cloth from one of the drawers and wipe her pussy clean. I lift her from the cabinet and pull her sleep shorts up.

"Thank you," she says with an innocent smile.

"Sasha, I'm serious about you moving in with me. I like what's happening between us."

"I do too, but I'm not sure I'm ready to give up my home quite yet. I've been on my own a really long time. It's all mine. How about I bring some things over and we take it slow?"

"That sounds fair." I place a quick kiss on her forehead, and I lead her out of the room and back to the kitchen to make pancakes.

Later that afternoon, when she's been thoroughly fucked, I'm packed and ready to head to the airport.

"Stay here and shower," I suggest, pulling a key out of my coat pocket. "You can come and go as you please."

"Is there anything I need to know about the security system?" I hand her a piece of paper.

"This is the code for the alarm. Be sure to set it when you leave and reset it when you come back."

"I will," she says as she covers my mouth with kisses. "Be careful and get your ass back here. We need to take out Petrov."

"I will."

I land at LAX on time and head straight to find my mark, William Bronson. He owes Freddy a hundred grand. He ran off to LA last week to hide. People should know by now they can't hide from Freddy Acosta. He always finds his target.

Willie's been hiding in plain sight in Chinatown. I head to where our informant spotted him last, and sure enough, he's sitting in the restaurant eating lunch. I watch from the cover of the alley across the street until he exits and starts walking. Cocky son of a bitch isn't even trying to hide himself.

He crosses the street, and I fall into step behind him. My black hoodie is in place, and my knife is in my pocket, ready to slit his fucking throat. Two blocks down, there's another alley. As we approach, I grab him by the collar and thrust him inside. Slamming him against the brick wall, I pin him with my hand to his throat.

"What the fuck, man!"

"Shut up!"

"I don't have any money. Let me go!" Willie begs.

"I'm here for Freddy Acosta." His eyes grow wide, and he breaks out in a sweat.

"Freddy? How did he find me?"

"Don't you know by now you can't escape Freddy? He sent me to kill you, Willie. You should've paid your debts months ago."

"I-I-I'll pay him back, I swear!"

"Why did you run if you were going to pay up?"

"I-I-I don't know. I panicked."

"Freddy's tired of waiting." I raise my knife to his throat, and he sobs.

"Please, man, don't do this."

"I have one simple question for you. Do you have Freddy's money?"

"No."

I slice his throat from ear to ear. Gurgling sounds come from his throat as I lower him to the ground behind the dumpster. I pocket the knife and head back to the airport.

I dispose of the knife in a trash can on the way to the car. I left my duffel bag in an airport locker. I booked time in a pod to clean myself up and change my clothes. I settle in for the two-hour wait for the flight back home to Sasha.

Chapter 43
Sasha

t's late in the evening before Gary sends me a text.

GARY

I'm waiting for my return flight.
I should be boarding in twenty
minutes.

When do you land?

2:30 a.m. your time.

Wake me up when you get here.

Will you be at my house or yours?

Ours.

Can't wait to see you in our bed.

I might as well try to get a little sleep, so I put on Netflix and fall asleep watching some corny romcom with Lucy Hale in it.

I wake up at 6 a.m. and the television is still playing, but Gary's not in bed beside me.

"Gary," I yell, but there's no answer. I rise from the bed and flip on the lights. There's no sign of Gary. The office is dark. The living room is dark. The whole fucking house looks like it did when I went to bed. I pull out my phone and text Gary.

> Hey. Was your flight delayed?

I put my phone on the counter, turn on the coffeepot, and go take a hot shower.

There's no reply on my phone after my shower, so I try again.

> Did you at least land yet?

I pour my coffee and take it out on the patio and watch the sunrise, trying my best not to throw my phone out into the field behind the condo.

> Did you go see Freddy first?

I'm beyond frustrated now. I decide to get dressed for work.

> What the hell, Gary? Why won't you answer me?

I grab my bag and head to the car. I don't go to my office. Instead, I go to Freddy's. His assistant hasn't arrived yet, so I burst through his door unannounced. Freddy jumps from his desk, gun drawn.

"What the fuck, Sasha! Did you want me to blow your goddamned head off?"

"Where the fuck is Gary? Did you hear from him yet?" He

looks at me, confused. He places his gun back into his shoulder holster and picks up his phone.

"He texted me when the job was done, and again when he was waiting to board," Freddy says scrolling through his messages.

"Yeah, I got a message like that too. Did he text you when he landed?"

"Let me see, there's another message. Yeah. It was 2:27." I snatch the phone out of his hand, and he glares at me.

The message reads: Landed. Heading home to see my girl.

It makes me smile, but now I'm even more confused.

"That was almost six hours ago, Freddy. He never came home." I hand him back his phone and sit in the chair across from him. He gets Ethan on the phone. I can barely concentrate on his side of the conversation.

"Hey.

"Yeah, we might have a problem. Gary's missing.

"He texted when his plane landed, but never made it home.

"She's here with me.

"I'll keep you posted."

I need answers. My head is swimming with questions. Did he have an accident? Is he hurt or worse…dead? Oh God, did Boris take him?

"Sasha!" Freddy yells, and I snap out of it.

"Yeah."

"Ethan is sending a team to the airport to see if they can find his car first. Daniel is going to try to find him on the airport cameras. We'll find him, Sasha. I'm sure he'll come waltzing into the office any minute."

"Yeah, I hope you're right," I say softly.

An hour later, Freddy gets a call.

"What?

"Where?

"Bring it with you and get your ass back here."

"What?" I shriek, jumping out of my chair.

"Vito and Bennie found his car in the parking garage at the airport. The trunk was open, and his duffel bag was inside." He holds out his hands, knowing what I'm going to ask. "It was just dirty clothes." I let out a sigh of relief. "But there was an envelope on the seat… with your name on it."

"What the hell?"

"I told them to bring it straight here. We can open it together. I need to call Ethan."

Freddy's assistant, Lori, brings us some coffee, and I sink back down into the brown leather chair.

Within the hour, Vito enters the office.

"Here you go, Boss." He hands Freddy a large white envelope. "Bennie's driving the car back to Gary's. I gotta go pick him up."

"Good work, Vito."

"Thanks, Boss."

I wanna rip that envelope out of his hands, but I steady myself on the edge of his desk and hold on tight instead.

"What's it say?" He looks it over and then lays it on the desk in front of me.

> *I have your precious boyfriend. I'll kill him if you don't meet me at*
> *Don's Pub on Main at 6 tonight.*
> *Come alone.*
> *Papa*

"Oh my fucking God! He took Gary to get to me! You were all so worried about me doing something stupid that we didn't see this coming. I have to get the hell out of here." I take off toward the door, but Ethan walks in just as I'm reaching for the handle.

"What the hell's going on? Where do you think you're going?"

"I'm going to get Gary back, that's where the hell I'm going." I try to push past him.

"The fuck you are." He uses my shoulder to push me back into the room, but I break from his grip.

"You can't stop me!" I yell.

In a flash, he has my arms behind my back and my chest pressed on Freddy's desk, pinning me there.

"The hell I can't. Now, you're going to listen to me. Got it?" I squeeze my eyes closed, but nod my head. "Take a deep breath." I do as he says. "Good. Now, stand the fuck up." He lets me go, and I stand, smoothing down my clothes. "You need to get your fuckin' shit together. You have some time before you meet with Petrov. You need to go home and change, grab your gun, and calm your shit down." I take in more deep breaths. He's right. I can't help Gary if I'm not thinking clearly.

Ethan continues, "I spoke to Don. The place will be closed for our little get-together. I already have a team headed that way to get the microphones and cameras in place. Daniel will monitor everything from the van outside. Holden will be at headquarters, ready to dispatch whatever we need. Nico and Beckett will have soldiers stationed nearby. A spare Glock will be under your chair. You need to keep him talking. Find out what the hell he wants from you."

"I told you I was afraid he would get hurt. I told you I shouldn't let myself get close to Gary. I told you no one can *love* me." I'm in full-blown panic mode now. He pulls me into his chest and gives me a moment to break.

"Sasha…We'll get him back. He loves you so much. He'll fight until his last breath to come home to you." Ethan's voice is low and steady.

"Did he tell you he loves me?" My voice quivers.

Ethan opens his mouth to speak, but Freddy beats him to it.

"He told me." My head snaps to see Freddy bowing his head, as if he just told a secret. "He didn't know if you felt the same way he did, so he didn't want to say it yet."

"Oh my God. Oh my God. Oh my God." I'm spiraling out of control. Not because he loves me and I love him, but because he's probably hurt, and I can't help him.

"Sasha!" Ethan growls. His deep tone rumbles through my whole body but brings me back into my brain. "Calm down."

I take a deep breath and try to slow my racing heart.

"I can do this. I'll go home and change and take my bike to Don's."

Freddy hands me a box containing jewelry.

"I don't wear jewelry, Boss. And this isn't really my style." I try to hand it back to him.

"You're so goddamn stubborn. The right earring has a microphone in it, the left one has a tracker, and the necklace is a camera. Just let it hang around your neck. It'll do the rest. The earpiece is tiny, just put it in your ear as far as it will go."

"Oh," I say hesitantly. "Daniel's really bringing the spy shit now, isn't he?"

"Only the best for our girl," Ethan says with a smile.

"Thank you. You're the closest thing to brothers I've ever had."

"Yeah, well, don't let word of all this hugging and shit get out. I have an image to uphold," Ethan says.

"I won't. Thanks, Boss."

Chapter 44
Sasha

After going home and changing into my black jeans, long-sleeved black Henley, biker boots, and leather jacket, I head for my gun cabinet. Boy, this is a downgrade from Gary's *room,* but it'll do. I tuck a knife into each boot, a Glock into the back of my jeans, and my Beretta in my jacket.

I pull my hair back into a low pony and put my helmet on. I take a deep cleansing breath before I start my bike.

When I'm a block away from Don's, I stop the bike and push the flesh-colored earpiece a little farther into my ear and test my high-tech jewelry.

"I'm here. Can anybody hear me?" I ask, waiting for a response.

"I gotcha, Sasha," Daniel confirms.

"Are the tracker and camera working?"

"Yes. It's all working properly."

"Who's inside?"

"Chris and Johnny are in the kitchen. Phil is around back, and Max is across the street in the alley," he answers. I see the black service van decorated with a plumbing company logo parked up the street. "There's a goon at the door. He'll probably search you."

"We're all listening, Sasha," Freddy says in my ear. "You can do this."

"On it, Boss," I give my bike some throttle and head for the bar.

Stepping inside the door to Don's, I'm immediately confronted by the goon at the door. I pull out my guns and lay them on the counter. He searches me, just like Daniel said he would.

"Anything else?" he says with a smirk.

I huff out a breath and reach into each boot and pull out my knives.

"That's it, I swear," I say. He tilts his head toward the room, and I walk inside. I scan the place, and it's empty, except for Petrov sitting at a table in the center. He stands and holds his hand out for me to come forward.

"Petrov." My voice is unfazed and dismissive.

"Please, can't you call me Papa?"

"Like hell I will," I snap.

"Boris then?"

"Fine, Boris." The word comes out of my mouth like vinegar. "Where is he?"

"Please sit. Would you like a drink?" He raises his hand to wave for Don.

"No, thank you. Where is he?" I clench my teeth. I don't have fucking time for his bullshit games.

"Fine," he says, waving off a relieved Don and pulling out his phone. He holds it out so I can see the screen. I gasp when I see Gary. He's in what looks to be a dungeon. The walls and floor are painted black, and there's a silver drain in the center of the room. I don't want to think about what it's used for.

The handcuffs are digging into his wrists, and there's blood dripping from the cuts. The cuffs are attached to chains that hold his arms above his head. They have his body pulled taut; his toes barely touch the blood-soaked floor.

I scan the rest of the room. There's a cart beside him with some sort of machine on it. Little white pads with wires sticking out of them are taped to his torso. He's blindfolded, and there's a black ball-gag in his mouth. Spit and snot are leaking down his chin onto his chest. There's blood everywhere. So much blood.

"Let him go. You want me, not him."

"I had to do something to get your attention." I look into his black eyes, and all I see is evil.

"Let's get this over with, Boris. What do you want me to do?"

"Easy. Kill Rocco Martinelli, and I'll give you back your boyfriend."

"Have you lost your fucking mind!" I laugh out loud.

"Well then, I see it's going to take a little more convincing to get you to come around." He presses a button on the phone, and shock waves surge through Gary's body. He screams around the ball stuffed into his mouth, his eyes grow unnaturally wide, and his body becomes rigid.

"STOP IT! STOP IT!" I scream. Boris does as I ask, and the shocks cease. Gary's head slumps forward, and I can only hope he's passed out. I hear Freddy in my ear.

"Tell him you'll do it. Tell him you'll kill Ethan. We'll figure it out."

I try to drag in a breath before I can speak. My voice is shaky. "Fine. I'll do it. When and where?"

"You're the assassin here, Sasha. Those are your decisions."

"Do you want it public?" I ask.

"Yes. The more, the merrier."

"How can I be sure Gary will be safe?"

"I rarely make promises detyo moyo, (my child), but for you, I think I can promise I won't kill him… yet."

"I want to see you take him down on the camera. Now!" My eyes are glued to the screen. There are cuts on his chest and blood dripping down his legs. It looks like he has all of his fingers and toes. That's a good sign. They must've beaten the shit out of him because bruises are forming on his ribs and stomach.

"Do it!" I scream.

Boris stares deep into my eyes and pushes a button on his phone. Then he says, "Take him down."

I watch as two men in masks come into view and use the chains to lower Gary down to the floor. They remove one cuff, pull both arms behind his back, and cuff him again. They drag his naked body to the corner of the room and drop him onto the concrete.

"Take the ball-gag and the blindfold off," I demand. Boris's eyes pinch tightly. I glare back at him and bat my eyelashes.

"Please...Papa," I say sweetly. A light flickers in the depths of his black soul, and he barks into the phone again in Russian this time. The men return and do as they're told. I see Gary's chest rise and fall as he pulls in a deep breath when he's free of the gag. He coughs and sputters, but seems to be breathing all right.

"Thank you," I say genuinely.

"You'd better figure it out fast, because he will lie there until you kill Rocco Martinelli."

I jump from my seat and stride out of the bar.

When I'm out of earshot of Boris, I say under my breath, "What the hell are we going to do?"

Freddy's voice comes through my earpiece. "I'm sure you're being watched. Look for a tail and go to Gary's house. Lock yourself in. I'll come to you."

I fly down the highway to our house. I let myself in, lock the door behind me, and reset the alarm. I close all the curtains and start pacing the room. A million different scenarios float around my head when I hear a noise come from the hallway. I pull my Glock from my waistband and aim it toward the sound.

Slowly, I start down the hallway toward the weapons room. The bookcase door is cracked, and light shines into the hall. Who the hell would know about the weapons room? All at once, it pushes open, and there stands Freddy.

"Holy shit! I could've blown your fucking head off!" I yell, the gun pointing at his head. Freddy reaches out and pushes the gun down.

"Now, we're even."

"How did you get in there?"

"Gary showed me the *ladies* a long time ago. I have a key to the back door and know how to disarm the alarm."

"You'd better promise to never let yourself in while we're home."

"Only in an emergency, promise."

"I sure hope you have a plan."

Chapter 45
Sasha

It's been almost twenty-four hours since I watched Petrov electrocute Gary on the phone at Don's. I'm in our bathroom putting the finishing touches on my makeup, trying my best not to think about the business I need to take care of tonight.

I'm wearing a blond bob wig, long fake eyelashes, dark red lipstick, red mini skirt, six-inch heels, and an off-the-shoulder black shirt with my boobs shoved up as high as they'll go. I look like I just stepped out of the hooker's fashion catalog.

I want to look like the other woman scorned to the people in the restaurant. Pulling on a gray trench coat and tucking the gun Freddy left for me into the pocket, I climb into my beat-up Ford Escape and head for Mariah's. Ethan and Lola are celebrating their first night out since the baby was born.

Parking in the lot next door, I exit the vehicle and remove my coat and tuck the gun into the back of my skirt. Thankfully, it stays where I put it, and my shirt covers it.

I walk into the restaurant and see Petrov seated at the bar. He has a front-row seat to all the action, just like he wanted. He nods his head in approval, and I scan the room. The entryway opens into an elaborate space, filled with crystal chandeliers and gold accents. Not the kind of place I would ever be caught dead in.

Lola and Ethan are dressed to the nines. He has on one of his signature Tom Ford suits, and she's wearing a floor-length burgundy gown. They're huddled into one another in a booth on the right side of the room.

"Miss, may I help you?" the maître d' asks quietly.

"Oh no, I see my party sitting right over there," I reply with a thick Southern drawl and a curt nod of my head. I stride across the room toward Ethan. My hips sway back and forth, calling everyone's attention. His eyes look up and meet mine, and they grow wide. As I reach behind my back and pull out the gun, Lola's head turns to follow Ethan's eyes. He pushes her down under the table. I train the gun on his chest, and without hesitation, pull the trigger. I walk past the table and into the kitchen.

People are screaming and running, but I just keep walking. Never looking back. I hear Lola's blood-curdling scream, and the need to throw up consumes me.

My breathing is ragged as I make my way to my car. I reach for the door handle, and someone grabs my hand. I'm thrown against the car, and a large hand covers my mouth. Our eyes connect, and I stop struggling when I see it's Petrov. He removes his hand and takes a step back.

"What do you want?" I spit in disgust.

"You were amazing in there. Cold and calculating, just like your papa." His gaze sends chills down my spine.

"I'm nothing like you."

"You are more like me than you wish to admit, Sasha."

"I did what you asked. Now let Gary go."

"You must really love this man." His breath smells of whiskey and cigars as he leans into me. "I think I'll keep him a little while longer."

"No! Dammit! I did what you asked. We had a deal." I try to keep my composure, but panic is surging through me.

"Don't you know you can't deal with the devil, docha (daughter)?" "What the fuck do you want from me?"

"I already told you. I want you to come work with me."

"And if I refuse?"

"Then I guess your fuck boy will die with you by his side."

"So I was right. I mean nothing to you. You just want to use me to kill for you. You don't love me."

"I haven't loved since the day I had to give up your mother."

"That wasn't my fault. I wasn't even born yet."

"It was because of *you* that Samantha pushed me away. It was because of *you* she was forced to marry Troy. It was because of *you* I could never be with her. It was because of *YOU* I lost the only woman I ever loved!" he growls behind gritted teeth and clenched fists. He's blaming his whole life on me. I need to get out of here and regroup. To come up with a plan to get Gary away from this maniac. In the distance, we hear sirens.

"You have twenty-four hours to make a choice." He leaves me as fast as he came.

I jump in my car and get the hell out of there. Driving to the condo, visions of Gary fill my mind, and the pain he must be going through. If Petrov holds to what he said, Gary's had no food, water, or medical attention in more than a day, and it will be another day until I hear from him again.

I enter the garage, put down the door, and reset the alarm. Ripping off my wig, I make a beeline for the bedroom. When I flip on the light, my heart stops. On the bed lies Gary fast asleep, and Freddy sits in a chair by his side.

"Fuck, Sasha. You could warn a guy before you turn the lights on," Freddy whisper-shouts. I can't speak. My brain isn't working. I walk over to the bed in a daze. Freddy stands, and I take his spot in the chair. After I take Gary's hand, my head falls to the bed.

"How?"

"I told you we would get him back." He flashes his crooked smile, one he rarely lets show.

"How?!"

"Calm down, Ruck says he needs to rest for the next few

days." Freddy pulls over another chair and sits down beside me. "Remember when you were meeting with Petrov at Don's, and he pulled Gary up on the live feed?"

"Yeah."

"Holden was tracing it. Luckily, you kept him connected long enough for him to find the location. While you were *pretending* to take out Ethan, my team rescued Gary. They took out five of Petrov's men getting him out of there. Ruck met us here and gave him a thorough check. He has a few cracked ribs and deep cuts across his body. His wrists were cut up pretty badly from the cuffs, and he's dehydrated."

"What about the shocks?"

"Ruck said the electric shocks can make him weak. He may also experience some pain and tingling in his extremities. He did a few tests here and doesn't think there's any nerve damage, but we'll have to wait and see."

"What happened after I left the restaurant?"

"Our paramedics would've taken Ethan and Lola to the hospital."

"I heard her screaming when I ducked out the back."

"She thought the love of her life had just been killed in front of her eyes. Of course, she was distraught. It had to look real to Petrov. The coroner will make the death announcement in a few hours, and then we'll smuggle him out of the hospital and back to the mansion." At times like this, it helps to have people in your pocket. Makes these little details so much easier to handle.

"Petrov came to me in the parking lot. He said he had other jobs for me to do, and he wasn't fulfilling his part of the deal and returning Gary to me. He'll be furious when he finds out you stole him back. But I'm so glad you did. Thank you, Freddy. Thank you for everything."

"I told you…We got you."

"Thank you."

"There's a list on the counter of the medication he needs to take and when to give them to him. A nurse will be here tomorrow morning at eight to check his dressings and the IV. Try to get some rest. Ruck said he'd be asleep for hours. Let me know when Petrov contacts you."

"I will."

I walk Freddy to the door, set the alarm, take a shower, and eat a quick sandwich. Carefully, I climb into bed beside Gary and wait for him to wake up. I'm afraid to go to sleep. I don't want to have a nightmare and hurt him, so I lie beside him all night and stare at him. I'll do anything to keep him safe.

The nurse comes promptly at eight, just like Freddy said she would. She's an older lady, around sixty. Her name is Nellie. She's the grandmotherly type. She explains everything she's doing and shows me how to check his bandages and the IV. She takes his vitals and prepares his medication. Gary's eyes open wide, and he gasps for air when she removes the dressing on his wrist.

"It's okay, Baby. I got you." I try to comfort him, but it's killing me to see him in pain, all because of me. I kneel beside him on the bed.

"Sasha," he murmurs, his voice hoarse and unrecognizable. He's heavily medicated, so I'm not sure if he even sees my face.

"Shh… You're okay. Freddy got you out." I carefully lift his hand to my cheek and pepper his palm with kisses. He cups my face.

"I love you," he says weakly.

"I love you too." Gary falls back into a deep sleep as the nurse pushes the plunger on his meds.

"You two are so sweet," Nellie gushes.

I'm not sure I wanted the first time Gary told me he loved me to be in front of the nurse, but I'll take it just the same.

Twenty-four hours after I showed up at Mariah's to kill Ethan, my cell phone rings.

"Hello," I say sweetly.

"Have you made your decision yet?" Petrov demands.

"Yeah, you can go to hell."

A dark, haunting laugh comes from the other side of the phone. "You may have gotten your boyfriend back, but you just signed your death warrant, Sasha. I'm coming for you, you little bitch."

"Bring it on, asshole." The phone goes dead. I pray I didn't just make a mistake.

Chapter 46
Sasha

Two days have gone by, and I'm not sure what's happening. I thought for sure Petrov would come for me immediately. Maybe he's building the suspense to drive me crazy, but it's not going to work. I have the house booby-trapped, and guns are hidden everywhere, thanks to Gary's *ladies*. This place is a goddamn fortress, and he'll have a fight on his hands if he comes here.

I talk to Ethan every day. He's going stir-crazy in the mansion, but he's determined to stick with the plan. Lola is livid at me for what I did, even though Ethan tried to explain it all to her. She's fake planning a funeral for next week. We need to finish this soon, or he'll have to go through with that also.

Gary sleeps a lot. He's not awake very long before she fills him full of sleeping medication again. Nellie has been coming twice a day.

"When is he going to wake up for more than ten minutes?" I ask.

"Recovery time is different for everyone, my dear," Nellie says, saccharin-sweet.

"Do you think we can pull back on the pain meds now? Let him decide if he needs them or not."

"Maybe tomorrow, dear."

"You said that yesterday."

Gary's eyes flicker open. "Sasha."

"I'm here. I'm right here." I take his hand in mine. "How do you feel?"

"Like I was hit by a Mack truck."

"You went through a lot at the hands of Petrov. Do you remember anything he said?"

"Everything is foggy." I look to my left, and Nellie is readying a shot to go into Gary's IV again.

"Can we hold off on the medication for just a few more minutes, please?" I ask, pointing at her.

"Yes, but I have more patients to see. I can't stay too long." She replaces the lid to the syringe and sets it on the dresser. "I'll go use the restroom and be right back."

"Thank you."

I lean over and place soft kisses on his split lip. He winces, but pulls me back for more.

"I'm sorry," he says.

"What are you sorry for? This is all my fault. He took you because of me."

"I wasn't paying attention when I got off the plane and started through the airport. All I wanted to do was get back to you, to keep you safe. I wasn't thinking about myself. When I got to the parking lot, I remember opening the trunk, and then everything went dark."

"Holden found the camera footage. A white van pulled up alongside you, and three guys with masks and hoodies jumped out and grabbed you. They injected you with something, threw you in the van, and you were gone. Holden lost them in the tunnel."

"I woke up naked in his basement of horrors, hanging from the ceiling."

"Did Petrov say anything?"

"Oh, he said a lot of things. How he wasn't going to let me stand in the way of you becoming his enforcer. How he was going to teach you everything he knows, and how he would teach you to take over for him someday."

"Why the electric shocks?"

"He wants Ethan's investments." Gary winces at the word shocks. "He didn't believe I didn't know anything about the financial part of the business, so he started torturing me. Cutting me and watching the blood flow over my skin. When I still wouldn't talk, the shocking started."

"I'm so sorry."

"Stop being sorry. I'm sorry he used me to get to you. What did you have to do for him?

"He wanted me to kill Ethan."

"You didn't do that, so what happened?" I stare into his eyes. I can't tell him the truth. He has to believe Ethan is dead like the rest of the town. If Petrov comes back, it'll be safer for him that way.

"Sasha…What did you do?" he pleads with me. My firm stare tells him all he needs to know. His pupils are blown, and he cries out in pain when he tries to sit up. Our loyalty to The Organization has been unwavering. I know this is killing him.

"I had to do it. I had to do whatever he wanted me to do to get you back. I killed Ethan at Mariah's three nights ago." His face goes chalk white, and his mouth hangs open.

"Gary," I say quietly. "Gary, look at me… Please…" He turns his head to look at me, and his eyes could bore holes straight through me.

"You're not the woman I thought you were. How could you? He saved you."

"I had to save you. Don't you see? I would've done anything to get you back. Shooting Ethan was the hardest thing I've ever had to do." How can I lie to him like this? He hates me.

"I'd like to be alone."

"Gary—"

"Leave, Sasha. Go back to *your* house. I'll be fine." Nellie steps into the room.

"Can I administer the shot now?" she huffs. I look at Gary, and he looks to Nellie.

"Yes," he answers. I know he's trying to escape what I just

told him, as Nellie pushes the plunger down.

"I'll call Freddy, so he can come take my place." With that, Gary's eyes go closed.

I pack a bag, and when Freddy arrives, I fill him in on what happened.

"I know you're upset, Sasha, but when Petrov is dead, we can tell him the truth. He'll understand it was all a ruse, and the two of you will be okay."

"I hope you are right."

I stop and pick up Chinese food on my way home and barricade myself in. I wish I had a high-tech security system like Gary's. I eat dinner and climb into bed with my Glock under my pillow. I text Freddy to check on Gary one last time for the night.

You up?

FREDDY
Yeah.

How's he doing?

Still sleeping

I forgot to tell you.

What?

Try to get Nellie to stop sedating him when she comes the next time. Maybe she'll listen to you.

Who the hell is Nellie?

The nurse you hired.

Our nurse's name is Paula.

What the fuck?

Chapter 47
Sasha

need to sleep, but I can't stop thinking about who the fuck Nellie is. Freddy said he would check with Ruck and see if he sent someone new to fill in for Paula. He'll see her face when she arrives at eight in the morning, so maybe she'll look familiar. The last time I looked at the clock, it was around two.

It's pitch black. I can feel the movement of the road beneath me. I'm lying on my side with my hands tied behind my back. The ropes are digging into my skin. Trying to sit up on my elbow, I hit my head on something.

"Ouch. Damn it."

I try to stretch my legs out, but there's a wall below.

"Fuck."

I use my feet to push up on the wall until my head bumps into another wall.

"Am I in a box?" I tell myself it's just the same nightmare I always have, take a few deep breaths and fall back to sleep.

I wake up again. This time, I'm lying on cold concrete in my pajamas. My arms and legs are tied outstretched like a starfish

on the beach. I'm shivering from the cold seeping through my thin clothes. Where am I? This is the worst nightmare I've ever had...

There's a bright light illuminated above my head, and I realize this isn't a dream. I'm awake and tied to the floor in a solid black room.

"What the fuck!" I try to yell, but my throat feels like I swallowed glass.

"I see the sedative finally wore off," a woman's voice says. I try to lift my head to see who's speaking, but I can't. I'm groggy and weak.

"You did an outstanding job, Nellie," Petrov praises. Nellie? For fuck's sake. She's his spy?

"Where's Paula?" I spit out.

"Dead, of course. Do you think we would keep her alive for some reason?" Petrov questions, and they both laugh. Sick fucks. They killed an innocent woman so that Nellie could infiltrate my home. Our home. Oh my God, Gary.

"Where's Gary?"

"I don't know. The son of a bitch was gone when Nellie went to kill him," Petrov says.

I let out a sigh of relief. Freddy must've figured out Nellie was a fake and got Gary the hell out of there.

Chapter 48
Gary

"We have to go get her, dammit!" I yell as I double over in pain as my ribs scream. Since Nellie is not around to drug me anymore, I'm alert and hobbling around the room.

"Would you sit the fuck down? You're making my sides hurt just looking at you," Ethan grumbles.

"We think they're holding her at the same place we found you, but we're not positive yet. I sent Vito and Roscoe to do some recon. We'll know more soon," Freddy explains. I slump back in the leather chair in front of Ethan's desk and wince. I run my hand through my hair and try to get my memories in order. My gaze hovers on Ethan.

"I thought you were dead. I told her to get out… because I thought she killed you."

"We had to make it look like I was dead."

"You see how that worked out, didn't ya? She could've told me."

"No, she couldn't. She had to stick to the plan. It's a good thing she didn't tell you now, since your nurse was a spy."

"I still can't believe that sweet old lady was working for

him," I say, rubbing my hand down my face.

"You know by now looks can be deceiving."

"She was keeping me so out of it, I never would've been able to defend myself. Why didn't she just kill me?"

"I'm glad she didn't. We need you," Freddy says as his phone rings. He puts it on speaker.

"Yeah."

"Fredrick, my friend. It's good to hear your voice." That thick, boastful Russian accent comes across the line.

"I'm not your friend, asshole. Where's Sasha?"

"Ah, my daughter is indisposed at the moment."

"She doesn't want anything to do with you. Why don't you fucking understand that?"

"Now you know I cannot do that, comrade. She's still of some use to me and my men." His dark laugh seeps through the phone, and I feel like I'm going to explode. Freddy's eyes focus on mine, and he puts his finger to his lips, telling me to be silent. My jaw clenches.

"Just tell me what the hell you want."

"I want all the assets from The Organization."

"You're out of your fucking mind." Freddy laughs. "They were all under Ethan's name, and you had Sasha kill him. What else?"

"I want *you* dead."

"You don't scare me, motherfucker. Try again."

"I should scare you, comrade, because I have your lovely lady in my dungeon right now." Freddy's brows clench with confusion.

"Sasha's not my lady."

"Oh, not Sasha...Amelia?"

"You're lying," Freddy dismisses.

"No, I'm not. Here. Listen."

"Freddy?" Amelia whimpers softly.

"Amelia, Sweetheart, are you all right? Did he hurt you?" Freddy's eyes glare into mine.

"I-I-I..." She's so upset that she can't speak.

"You son of a bitch. I'll fucking kill you!" Freddy's voice booms into the phone, while he clutches the corner of his desk.

Amelia is naïve about The Organization. Freddy has done his best to keep her out of the line of fire, until now. Amelia was Lola's assistant during her time working for Kingsley and Masters. When Lola left and started the shelter, Amelia came with her. She's her best friend and right-hand woman. She's the youngest of the six of us. She's a free spirit who's always happy and smiling. He has obviously traumatized her by the way she sounds.

"Hold on, Amelia. I'll find you."

"All this mushy shit makes me sick," Petrov spits.

"Fuck you!" Freddy snarls.

"You have two hours to bring one million dollars to the train station, or I'll kill her."

"That's not enough time to…"

"Bullshit! Leave it in locker 547 and walk away. I'll contact you with further instructions."

"You'll let her go. That's what you're gonna do!" He demands.

"We'll see. Be there. Two hours! If you want to see your pretty little girlfriend alive again."

"Goddammit!!" he shouts, launching the phone across the room. He picks up the receiver on his desk phone and calls Daniel.

"I need a million dollars within the hour.

"I don't care!

"Just get it!" His voice blares into the phone before he slams it down.

"We'll get them back." Ethan's voice is controlled and unforgiving.

"We'd better because she's the best thing in my life, man. If he kills her, he may as well kill me too."

Ethan, Freddy, and I are monitoring the coms for Vito and Roscoe.

"Boss, can you hear me?" Vito says into my ear.

"Copy, Vito. Go," Ethan responds.

"We're outside the house. We can hear sounds coming from the basement, but I can't confirm it's Sasha."

"Could it be Amelia?" Freddy questions calmly.

"Amelia?"

"He's got her too."

"Damn…"

There's rustling on the line when Vito speaks again. "I can't be sure, Boss. They're…"

"They're fuckin' what, Vito?"

"Crying."

Freddy takes the earpiece out of his ear. He sends it flying across the room to join his phone and walks out.

"We're out of time. I want you to breach the structure and get them out." Ethan takes over.

"Copy." We don't have cameras on them, so we have to rely on our imagination for a picture of what's happening.

We hear them moving around the space. Footsteps on a wood floor. A door creaks open. Then footsteps on metal stairs. There's gunfire, and all at once, everything stops.

"What the fuck's happening?" Ethan barks.

"Boss, it's not Sasha *or* Amelia."

"Who the fuck is it, then?"

"There are about twenty women in cells down here. What do we do?"

"Fuck! Daniel, do you copy?"

"Yes, Boss."

"Get a truck and a team and get those women out of there. Petrov must be into sex trafficking in addition to all his other fucked-up shit," Ethan orders.

"On it," Daniel confirms.

"Vito."

"Yes, Boss."

"Take out anyone you see and get those women the hell out of there."

"Copy that."

Ethan calls Lola on the phone and tells her about the women they found. She insists they bring them to the shelter, and she'll call Ruck to meet them there with his medical team.

We listen as Vito and Roscoe try to calm the women. They try to explain to them that they are there to help them, and they can take them somewhere safe. We hear metal clanking as the cell doors are released.

Roscoe tells us of the injuries he can see, and we relay it to Ruck so he can prepare for their arrival. Roscoe carries a young, unconscious girl with the most injuries as Vito leads the women out. By the time they all make it upstairs, the truck is there.

"How many soldiers did you take out, Vito?" Freddy asks, back on comms now.

"Five. That was all we came in contact with."

"Get the women to the shelter. We'll meet you there." Quick on his heels, he turns and heads for the door.

"I'm going with you," Ethan says.

"No! You have to stay hidden," Freddy grits out.

"I'll hide in the back of the SUV. I need to do something to help. I can't be in this fuckin' house any longer. At least there, I can be with Lola."

"Fine," Freddy concedes.

"I'm going too," I say, standing with grinding teeth.

"Goddammit! Has everyone lost their fucking minds!"

"Maybe one of them has seen her. Maybe they have answers. You'll need help talking to them all. There are too many. And you're running out of time to get the money delivered."

"Whatever. Get in the fuckin' car."

We arrive at the shelter just as the women are being unloaded. Lola gives them her little speech about safety, food, phones to use to call home, and more. Some are hurt. They're all traumatized, but before she shows them to their rooms to shower and rest, I get a chance to address them.

"My name is Gary, and this is Freddy," I say calmly.

Freddy is a big man. He has fifty pounds of muscle on all of us. You would never know that Freddy is a big, scary Mafia boss right now by the distraught look on his face.

"We're looking for our girlfriends. Their names are Amelia and Sasha. Amelia has long blond hair and stands about this tall. Sasha has long black hair and is about this tall," I describe, using my hand to show their height. "Did any of you see them? Or talk to them?"

These young women are traumatized and scared to death and I feel badly about asking them too many questions but we have very little time to find the girls before they harm them. I'm sure they are afraid to breathe, let alone speak to two big, scary men. When no one replies, I thank them, and we turn to leave the room.

There's a tap on my back, and I turn to see a petite young girl, probably fourteen or fifteen, standing behind me.

"I think I saw the one with the black hair." Excitement claws at my insides.

"When. Where?" I try to stay calm. I don't want to spook her.

"At the house. They brought me in after the others. They had…" The look on her face is heartbreaking.

"It's okay. You don't have to say it, I understand." She sniffs and wipes a tear away.

"They were going to take me down the stairs to the basement, but we had to wait while they carried out a girl with long black hair. I remember it because it was dragging on the ground." My jaw tightens at her words.

"Was she awake? Did you hear her say anything?

"No. She was unconscious. There was rope around her wrists, and the big man they called Bruce was carrying her over his shoulder. They said something about going to the country."

"The country? Thank you so much for your help. What's your name?"

"Veronica," she replies quietly.

"Thank you, Veronica." She smiles, and Marissa leads her to the medical clinic. I turn and look at Freddy.

"I guess that's as good a start as any. I'll have Holden start searching for a building in the country belonging to Petrov or the Ravens." Marco comes in behind us, carrying a black satchel, and hands it to Freddy.

"Now let's get you to the train station to deliver the money," I say.

I wait at the curb in the Escalade. I lose sight of Freddy when he enters the train station with the duffel full of cash. Five minutes later, he emerges empty-handed and climbs into the car.

"Now what?" he asks.

"I heard on the radio that the mayor is giving a speech tonight." We look at one another.

"I think we need to attend."

Chapter 49
Sasha

The door to the room swings open, and they shove Amelia inside.

"Amelia? What the hell! She's got nothing to do with this, you psycho!"

"Haven't you figured out by now, devochka (little girl)? I always get what I want, and I don't care who I hurt in the process."

"Freddy's going to fucking kill you!" Amelia yells. I've never seen Amelia remotely close to being mad before. I didn't know the kid had it in her. The goon who's tying her down to the floor smacks her across the face. She spits blood from her mouth. It looks like she has a cut on her lip. Tears are filling her eyes, but she stuffs them down and raises her chin.

"Don't hurt her. I'll do whatever you want." I turn my gaze up to Petrov.

"I want you to kill the mayor—sniper style." My stomach falls. He wants me to kill the mayor.

"Why would I do that?"

"To save your little friend here."

"You don't have a good track record with keeping your promises to me, Boris."

"There's no guarantee I will keep this one either, but what choice do you have?"

He walks closer to Amelia and pulls out a Beretta Fusion. This weapon is magnificent. Laser engraved and hand fitted. It would be an honor to have a gun of this quality and craftsmanship. Any other day I would complement someone on a weapon of this caliber, but not today. He clicks off the safety and points it at her head.

"You will agree to kill the mayor, or I will kill her right here, right now." Amelia's eyes are as big as saucers when she turns her head to look at me.

"Fine! I'll do it. Now leave her alone." That maniacal laugh of his echoes off the concrete walls, as he puts the safety on and returns it to his holster.

"I thought you might agree to do things my way." How the hell am I going to get out of this one? I can't kill an *innocent* man. Maybe when he takes me out of his hole, I can figure out a way to send a message to Gary to warn the mayor.

"I'll need some clothes, boots, and a sniper rifle." I think of Gary's ladies. Francesa is the name of his sniper rifle, if I remember correctly.

"Oh, you'll get everything you need soon enough. The mayor is making a speech tonight in the square, and you're going to be there." He walks out and closes the door behind him.

Goonie Man ties Amelia down. She's spread out across the floor like I am. He leans over her and licks her face, and her entire body shudders.

"I'll be back for you later, Sunshine. Petrov promised me your sweet cunt first." When he opens the door, I can hear noise coming from the hallway. It's Petrov. He's screaming and throwing shit. He pushes past Goonie Man and stands above me. Rage boils out of him as he lowers his face to mine. Droplets of sweat fall on my face.

"You fucking bitch!"

"What did I do? I'm just lying here?" Now is not the time for the smart-ass in me to come out and play.

He slaps me across the face, and my head whips to the right. I open my mouth to speak, and he slaps me again, my head whipping left. My vision blurs, and this time, I keep my mouth shut. I stare at him, waiting for him to tell me what the hell set him off. His breathing is ragged, and his chest heaves and shudders.

"Freddy took my girls!" he bellows.

"Girls? What girls?"

"The girls I was going to trade to my brothers in Russia," he grunts as he kicks me in the side. I lose my breath and cough.

"He'll pay for this with *your* blood!" He kicks me again. I hear something pop this time, and I'm not sure if it was a rib or something internally, because the pain is too sharp to tell. I can't shield myself in any way because of how I'm tied to the floor. I have to lie here and take every blow.

Petrov lets out a huff and throws down his hands in frustration. I guess he prefers to do the dirty work himself when it comes to me. He leaves me bloodied and bruised. Pushing Goonie Man out of his way as he stomps from the room.

"Sasha. Sasha, are you okay? Oh my God. Please say something. Are you alive? Sasha," Amelia pleads.

"Shh... I'm here," I choke out the words.

"Oh, thank God."

I feel snot or blood running from my nose. My eyes are blurry, and I hurt everywhere. How am I supposed to shoot a rifle like this? I have to get it together so I can get us the hell out of here.

"Are you okay?" she asks.

"Yea...Yeah. I'll be okay." I cough.

"I'm sorry," she says quietly.

"Why the fuck are you sorry? It's that crazy bastard's fault. He wants to take out The Organization, and he took you to get to Freddy." Now is not the time for I told you so.

"Freddy told me I needed to be more careful since Petrov was sniffing around, and I didn't listen. I wasn't paying attention when I walked out of the shop on Main Street. They grabbed me and threw me in a car. It happened so fast."

"I was in my bed asleep, *Amelia*. If they want you, they're going to get you."

"The big man said he gets me first. Does he mean...?" Amelia's voice quivers. She knows what it means. Her tears start to come now.

"Hey. Amelia. Hey! He won't hurt you if I have anything to say about it. You can't help yourself if you're all blubbery. Freddy needs you to be strong and fight." I hear her sniffling and taking deep breaths.

"You're right."

"You really like Freddy, don't you?" I ask.

"Yeah." Her voice sounds all dreamy, even tied to the cold, hard floor.

"He's always so grouchy," I say.

"He's not like that with me. Unless I want him to be." A naughty giggle escapes her throat.

"Doesn't it bother you that he's so much older than you? What is it like, twenty years difference or something?"

"No. He's only twelve years older than me. When we're together, age doesn't matter."

"Have you said I love you yet?"

"No. Not yet. He had a bad time growing up, and I think it's hard for him to say it."

"Doesn't it bother you?" I ask.

"What?"

"That he doesn't tell you he loves you?"

"No. He'll say it when he's ready."

"How about you and Gary? Have you said the L-word yet?"

"Kinda," I say timidly.

"How do you kinda say I love you?"

"Well, after they saved him from Petrov's basement and he regained consciousness for the first time, we said it. But I'm not sure if he remembers."

"Do you love him?" Amelia asks.

"Yes. I'm just... scared," I say in just above a whisper.

"What are you afraid of?"

"He'll stop loving me. He'll leave me, or someone will take him from me again."

"I can understand your worry, but...are you going to stop living your life because you're afraid something *might* happen?"

"I-I don't know."

"Are you going to miss out on one of the greatest feelings in the world because you're afraid?"

"I don't know, Amelia." I can't think straight anymore. "Let's take a nap, okay? My head really hurts."

"Okay," she concedes.

I know what Amelia is trying to say. I used to think I was afraid to allow myself to be happy. I haven't had a lot of happiness in my life, and I thought maybe I just didn't know what it felt like. But when I'm with Gary, he makes me laugh, and it's never awkward. We just settled into one another so easily. I didn't even see it coming.

I do want to be happy. I just never thought love would be an option for me. I'm a cold-blooded killer. And I'm fucking good at it. But I guess we understand each other and the job we have to do for The Organization.

I want to be in love and live my life with Gary. But I gotta get out of this mess first before I can think about anything else.

I notice Amelia has stopped talking. I hope she's getting some rest because this day isn't over yet, by any means.

I fell asleep for a little while, but I was jolted awake by a man's voice.

"Hey, Sunshine," Goonie Man says. My eyes shoot open, and I see him stalking toward Amelia. He licks his lips, as if he were getting ready to eat a plate of chicken wings or something. His eyes are glued to her. She's shaking her head, and her breathing increases as she starts to panic. I have to do something.

"Hey, dumbass," I croak. His head snaps to me, and his eyes are glaring. "Keep your slimy hands off her." He changes direction and comes toward me instead.

"I've about had enough of you, bitch." He reaches down, taking my sleep shirt in his fist. He lifts my torso off the floor as much as he can, straining my already aching arms. The door opens, and Petrov comes inside.

"Bruce! What the fuck are you doing? I said you could have the other girl. Now you can get the fuck out!"

Bruce stares at me like I just took his last piece of gum. He drops me back to the floor with a thud and stomps out of the room.

"Thank you," I say softly to Petrov, but he doesn't acknowledge me. He unties the ropes holding me down and offers me a hand to stand. Hesitantly, I place mine in his and wince as he helps to lift me from the cold concrete. I rub my wrists, and now I can see all the blood on my body.

"You need to get ready," he commands.

"Please don't let him touch her while I'm gone." His eyes meet mine. He doesn't say a word, but nods his head once. I can only pray, for Amelia's sake, that he can control his monster.

Petrov leads me to a bathroom. There are clothes and toiletries on the counter.

"Take a shower and get dressed. We leave in one hour." He closes the door and locks it from the other side. There's no window, no vent, no way out. I resign myself to the fact that I won't be escaping from here. I catch a glimpse of myself in the mirror. I don't know who the person is looking back at me. My cheeks are puffy and have the outline of a hand on them. Lifting my finger to my lip, I flinch at the sting from the cut. I remove my bloody clothes and survey the rest of the damage dear ole dad inflicted on my body in his tirade.

My ribs are black and blue, but I don't think they're broken. It's uncomfortable when I breathe in deeply though. I take a hot shower and get dressed. I'm pulling my hair back into a low braid when Petrov unlocks the door and lets himself in.

"I'm going to need to see the gun." My voice is dark and serious.

"You can't." My eyes move to his in the mirror.

"How do you expect me to take someone out in one shot with a weapon I've never even seen before?"

"You can't see it because it's not here. It's at the location already. Besides, you're perfectly capable of doing this job with your eyes shut."

"Oh," I say quietly. And I can take it apart and put it back together with my eyes closed, but I won't tell him that. Thanks, Jerry.

"Let's go." He grasps my upper arm and ushers me out of the house to a waiting car. I memorize my surroundings as we exit the house. He pushes me into the SUV, and before I can take in too many details, he places a blindfold over my eyes.

"Really?" I huff out a breath. This will be a little harder, but I can do it. Jerry used to blindfold me and take me on drives. I memorized each turn we took. When we arrived at our destination, he would put me behind the wheel and tell me to find my way back. I got pretty good at it, but it's been a while.

By the time we pull into the parking garage downtown, we've made three left turns, two rights, driven for about ten minutes before pulling onto an off-ramp of some kind, and merging to the right. It felt like three red lights, then a right into the parking garage. I'm saying it over and over in my head as he removes the blindfold.

"Here's what's going to happen," he explains, making me turn in my seat to face him. "Larry up there is going to escort you to the office building across the street. The room has a clear shot of the stage. There will be a pair of black gloves on top of the gun case. Put them on. The rifle is a Barrett M82. You'll have five minutes to get acquainted with your weapon before the celebration begins, and the mayor approaches the podium. Five minutes after his speech begins, a bell will sound, and you'll take your shot. One shot. Put down your weapon and leave the same way you came in. We'll meet back at the car and return to the house together."

"Where will you be while I'm killing the mayor?" I ask.

"I have to make an appearance near the podium, so my alibi

is rock solid. Let's go, the clock is ticking." Larry exits the driver's side and comes to open my door. Not allowing me a chance to run, he puts his death grip on my left bicep, and he leads me to the building across the street. Larry's not as big as Goonie Man, but he's still six feet tall and maybe two hundred pounds. He's younger too. Early twenties. Not knowing who might be waiting in the room, I hold off on making my move for now.

We enter the big black building and head for the elevator. He presses the button for the tenth floor, and we stand in silence while he continues to hold my arm so tightly, I'm sure he will leave bruises. We take a right off the elevator, and three doors down on the left, he pulls out a key card and lets us in. Scanning the room, I don't see anyone else. I can't believe it's just me and Larry boy here. This will be a piece of cake. His phone vibrates, and he pulls it from his pocket.

"Geez, he won't let me do anything without checking on me," Larry grumbles under his breath. I watch him text a message to Petrov, then lay his phone down on the coffee table. The rifle is in its case near the window, just like he said it would be, and black gloves are sitting on top of it. He shoves me into the room.

"Get to it, bitch."

I pull on the gloves and start assembling the rifle. I look down at the crowd from the window and see that no one is on the stage yet. I still have time to get my hands on his phone.

"I need to check it out to make sure it's a clear shot," I tell him. He nods, so I use this moment to look through the scope to see if I can see Petrov or anyone from The Organization.

"Hurry up," he barks. I have no intention of shooting the mayor, but I have to play the part. I see Petrov approaching the stage. He's talking to some people and laughing. I spot Gary and Freddy in the crowd. They're coming around the other side of the stage. Now is my chance. In one quick movement, I used the butt of the gun to hit Larry on the forehead. He lets out an oof sound. I don't give him a chance to regroup. I use all my strength and continue to hit him again and again. His eyes roll back into his head, and he falls to the ground. Dead. His phone uses facial recognition, so I hold it up to his bloody face, and it unlocks. I text Gary.

> Francesca has eyes on the mayor at six o'clock.

I see him look down at his phone and then up at the building. I wave the curtains, and he punches Freddy.

> Warn him to play dead.

Again, he looks at his phone, then in my direction, and nods. He types frantically into his cell.

Moments later, the mayor steps onto the stage to a roaring crowd. Five minutes into his speech, a bell goes off in the room. I squeeze the trigger. Like clockwork, the mayor drops to the stage and plays dead. I drop the gun beside Larry's dead body and get the hell out of the room.

Chapter 50
Sasha

I run down the ten flights of stairs as fast as I can. Slowly, I open the door to the vestibule, and there's chaos everywhere. People are yelling and pointing, pushing and shoving. Through the window, I can see Gary standing across the street. I swipe a baseball hat off some man's head as he runs past me, and I move through the crowd to the area where I last saw Gary. When I get there, he's gone.

I know I have to keep moving, so I start walking south as casually as possible. I only get to the corner before I feel an arm snake around my waist.

"Don't look at me, just keep walking." My shoulders relax when I hear his voice. He leads me around the corner, and we pile into the Escalade. Beckett is driving, and Freddy is shotgun. Gary and I are in the back. As soon as we're locked inside, Gary pulls me into his arms.

"How the fuck did you get away?" he asks.

"I killed the guy Petrov left babysitting me and ran like hell."

"Where the fuck is Amelia!" yells Freddy.

"She's back at the house."

"Tell Beckett how to get there."

"I can't. You're going to have to let me drive."

"Why?"

"I can't really explain how I do it, but let me drive." With grumbles and a huff, Freddy opens his door, and we all do a Chinese fire drill and change seats. This time, I'm driving with Gary in the passenger seat. Beckett and Freddy sit uncomfortably in the back.

"Look, I know you have a million questions, so do I, but you have to let me think. So everybody just shut up," I say as I adjust the seat.

"Gary, you need to talk to your girlfriend about the way she's been talking to me when this is over," Freddy says. I look at him in the rearview mirror. He has one eyebrow lifted and a smirk on his face.

They do as I ask, and we sit in silence while my mind plays back where I came from backward. When I'm confident we're almost there, I take Gary's hand and squeeze it tightly. Freddy's phone rings, and he picks it up on speakerphone.

"Hello," he says with a smile.

"What the hell did you do with her?" Petrov's voice booms over the phone.

"I'm sorry, I don't know what you're talking about, *comrade*." His voice comes out almost...sassy.

"Sasha. You took her from me, you bastard!"

"It seems to me you can't keep control of your captives. Besides, I didn't take her from you. She found *us*."

Cutting in, I say, "I did what you asked, Boris. I shot the mayor. Now I want my freedom." I pull off the road and park in the bushes.

"Fu..." Freddy hangs up on him. "Oops, I think we had a bad connection." The weight of the situation lifts for a moment, and we all laugh.

"The house is just up this driveway. Amelia's in the basement. She's tied to the floor, like a starfish." Freddy's face is back to the scowl he always wears. "You'll need a knife or something to cut her free."

"There are weapons in the back," Gary says. "How many guards are there?"

"I don't know. I was tied up in the basement most of the time. There is this big guy named Bruce though." Gary's head snaps to Freddy.

"Veronica," they say in unison.

"Who the *hell* is Veronica?"

"It's a long story, but Petrov has been doing a little sex trafficking on the side. Vito and Roscoe stumbled upon twenty women in cages in his basement while searching for you. Veronica is a teenage girl. She came forward and told us she thought she saw Bruce carrying you out of the basement over his shoulder. She alluded to the fact that Bruce had raped her."

"Be sure to kill Bruce for Veronica," I say flatly.

Freddy goes to the back of the car and opens a hidden compartment. There are enough guns and knives in there for an army. We load up and start for the house. We stick to the trees as we work our way closer. A silver Land Rover flies up the drive, and we all hide.

"That has to be Petrov," I say. We watch as the car comes to a stop on the gravel and slides a few feet. He jumps out and runs into the house.

"We gotta go before he takes all this out on Amelia," Freddy says. He stays low and starts running in the direction of the house. We all follow.

When we get close, he motions for Beckett to go around the back of the house. Gary moves to the left, I go to the right, and Freddy goes in the front. When I crouch down and peer into the screen door, it's a laundry room. I quietly slip inside and move to the next door.

I can hear Petrov screaming at someone. Glass shatters against the door I have my ear pressed against, and I jerk away. I hear footsteps heading in my direction, so I plaster my body to the wall behind the door as a tall man with dark hair walks into the room. He leans down to pick something up off the floor. Before he can stand upright, I hit him across the back of his head with the butt of my gun, and he falls to his knees, catching himself.

"What the hell?" That's all he can say before I grab his head from behind, yank it back, and slice his throat from ear to ear. I ease him to the floor and listen at the door once more. I hear the creaking of a door opening and the heavy footsteps descending metal stairs.

I poke my head out the door and slowly enter the kitchen. The crunching of glass under my feet causes me to stop. With no one in sight, I start to move forward when Goonie Man, I mean Bruce, comes around the corner and stops in front of me.

Now that I'm not looking up at him from the floor, I can tell how huge he really is. Probably six foot seven. His biceps are as big as my thighs. His catlike reflexes reach out to grip my throat before I can even flinch.

My pistol falls to the ground as I instinctively grab his hand at my throat. His cold, dark eyes stare into mine as I reach out and try to scratch his eyes, but his long arms keep me too far from his face. My feet leave the floor, and he holds me up like he's inspecting a piece of meat. My kicks bounce off his tight muscles as black dots begin to fill my vision, and I gasp for air that doesn't come. Before I lose consciousness, I see the shadow of a man come around from the left and hit Bruce with something. I'm dropped to the floor in a gasping heap when I see Freddy.

Bruce turns his attention to him instead, and they begin to fight. They exchange jabs before Bruce lunges forward and tries to get Freddy in a headlock. Freddy backs out of his grasp and hits him in the back of the leg. Bruce almost goes down, but pushes him away. They square off again. This time, Freddy moves first. Using the heel of his hand to drive Bruce's chin up and back, Freddy pelts his chest with hammer fists and forearm shots.

A knee comes up from Bruce and catches Freddy in the gut, and he doubles over briefly. Bruce sucker punches him in the ribs, but Freddy comes back with an uppercut with his left and a cross to his jaw with his right.

Gary comes into view as he watches the fight, but I haven't spotted Beckett yet.

Bruce backs away from the fight. I'm sure it's to try to catch his breath.

"Is the bitch downstairs yours?" His breaths are heavy.

"Did you fuckin' touch her?" Freddy grunts.

"Petrov promised her pretty cunt to me first."

"First? She has nothing to do with any of this."

"Too bad. I can't wait to taste her sweet little cunt." That's the last straw. Freddy grabs him by the shoulders and drives his knee into his chest. Throwing him to the ground, he slams his fists into his face over and over. His rage explodes over every inch of Bruce's head.

Gary walks forward and taps Freddy on the shoulder. "Boss. Boss! BOSS!" Freddy halts, his fists midair. "I think he gets the point."

Freddy leans back, and Bruce groans. Freddy nods at Gary, and he stands above Bruce. Taking his gun out, he's ready to administer the kill shot.

"This is for Veronica."

Bang.

Gary steps toward me and holds out his hand. He pulls me off the floor and into him. We get a quick embrace.

"Where is everyone?" I ask.

"I took out four," Freddy answers, catching his breath.

"I took out five," Gary says.

Behind me comes another voice. One I had almost forgotten was there.

"I took out seven because you fuckers left me," Beckett mutters.

"We knew you had it covered," Freddy says.

I toss him the keys to the car. "Go get the car, so once we get Amelia, we can get the hell out of here," I say. He looks at Freddy.

"You heard her. Get moving."

"Yes, Boss," he says and takes off running.

All of a sudden, the air is filled with an ear-piercing scream, and Freddy flies through the door to the basement. Falling in line, we follow him.

Approaching the bottom of the stairs, we can hear Amelia crying. Freddy jumps down the last four steps and takes off running. He throws the door open, and there stands Petrov, holding Amelia in front of him by a fistful of her long blond hair. The barrel of his gun is pointed at her temple.

"Don't take another step or I'll blow her brains all over the wall."

Freddy knows what kind of man Boris is. He has no remorse. Killing her would be nothing to him. We have to get her away from him.

"Let her go, Boris," I yell. His black eyes flash to mine.

"You bitch!"

"You don't want Amelia. You want me. Let her go, and I'll do whatever you want." Boris pulls back harder on her hair, and she cries out. Tears stream down her face.

"Put your guns down...Now!" he bellows. We all look at one another and lower our weapons to the floor.

"Kick them away!" he shouts. We each use a foot to kick them out of the way.

"There. See... We did what you asked. Now let her go and take me instead."

Gary leans forward into me, and he slides a switchblade into my back pocket.

"This is family business," Boris spits out and pushes Amelia in Freddy's direction. She stumbles forward, and he lunges to catch her.

"Take your bitch and get the hell out of here. Don't ever come back."

Freddy looks between Gary and me. I know he doesn't want to leave. But Amelia can't be here for this.

"Get her out of here, Boss." Gary points at the door. Freddy doesn't take the time to argue. He pulls Amelia out the door and up the stairs. Boris moves his gun to Gary.

"You. Get the fuck out too." He waves his gun at the door.

"No, I don't think so," Gary refuses. I shake my head at him. "I'm not leaving without Sasha."

"Didn't you get enough while you were hanging naked in my basement?"

"I'm not going to let you hurt her," Gary says in a deep, gravelly voice.

"Do you want to be her knight in shining armor and save the day?" Petrov croons.

As Gary keeps his attention, I slowly move in the direction of the gun on the floor. I also move the switchblade from my back pocket to my front pocket.

"Maybe she deserves a knight. You sure weren't a father to her."

"Shut up!"

"You know I'm right."

"I did what I had to do." Just as I begin to lower my hand to the floor to pick up the gun, Petrov swings his gun and points it at me.

"Get the fuck over here." I let out a sigh in defeat and move to him.

He pulls me into his body with his big hairy arm across my chest and points the gun at my temple.

"Sasha, tell your boyfriend it's time to go."

"Gary, Honey, you need to leave. I'll be okay. I need to do this. He's won."

"No, you can't stay with him."

"I have to," I plead.

"I said... Get the fuck out, or I'll kill her!" His booming voice fills the room.

"Okay... Okay... I'm going." Gary surrenders, holding up his hands.

"I love you," he says.

Tears pierce my eyes as I reply, "I love you." *Again, not the way I wanted to hear those words.* With all his attention on Gary backing out of the room, I pull the switchblade from my pocket and stab Petrov in the stomach. His eyes grow wide, and his grip on the gun falters. I knock it away with my other arm and pull the knife out of his gut with a sucking sound, just to plunge it back in. He falls to the ground.

"You son of a bitch!" I scream and push him onto his back. I climb onto his bleeding body, and I stab him over and over and over. Thoughts flash through my mind. Troy raping me. My mother's cold, dead body. Killing Troy. Burning the house down. All the degrading things I did for drugs just so I didn't have to feel anything. I stab and stab and stab.

Gary clutches my shoulder. "Sasha. I think he's dead, Baby."

I stop and look at Boris Petrov, my father. He's covered in blood. It's on the walls and the ceiling. The pool beneath him slowly growing. I drop the knife with a clang to the concrete floor and stare at my hands. They're covered in the blood of a maniacal killer. A man who tortured innocent women and men for his own gain. Killed my aunt right before my eyes and would've killed me too when he was done with me.

"It's over, Baby. You did it. He's dead." He pulls me off Boris's dead body and surrounds me with his warmth.

Beckett saunters into the room and stands beside us. Looking down at Petrov, he whistles.

"Remind me to never piss you off. Come on, let's get the hell out of here. The cleaners are on the way, and the Boss wants to get Amelia home," he says as he heads for the door.

Chapter 51
Gary

Beckett drops us at the condo. We enter through the garage; both covered in Boris's blood. Sasha hasn't said two words since we left Petrov's lair.

"Let me run you a bath and get you cleaned up. You'll feel better." She nods.

I take her by the hand, lead her to the bathroom, and have her sit on the counter while I get everything ready. I go to the kitchen and bring back two bottles of water and a black trash bag.

"Drink some of this, and I'll get you some food when you get out. How long has it been since you've eaten?" She shrugs as she lifts the bottle to her lips. I grab two clean towels from the cabinet and hang them on the hooks beside the tub. Her eyes look up at me, but it's like she's in a daze.

"It's okay, Baby. I got you." I take her hands and lift her to stand. I remove her blood-soaked clothes and throw them in the trash bag. After checking the water temperature, I help her to stand in the tub.

"Aren't you getting in with me?" she asks.

"Do you want me to?" She nods. I remove my clothes and step in beside her.

"Let me wash you off first, and then we can soak." I pull the curtain and direct the shower spray over her black locks. I let the water soak in before using her berry shampoo and massaging her scalp. When the water runs clear, I plug the tub and lower myself into the hot water. I pull her down to sit between my legs, and she leans her head on my chest.

"Are you okay?" I ask, running the loofah over her skin. "I'm worried about you."

"Did you mean it?" Her voice is so faint I almost don't hear it.

"Mean what, Baby?"

"When you said you love me."

"Of course I did."

"Nobody's ever loved me before." My heart sinks in my chest. I wrap both arms over her and hold her firmly. "I mean, I think my mom loved me. I'm sure she said it, right? I just can't remember."

"Of course she did. She was your mom. Moms love their kids no matter what."

"My life is so fucked up. I mean... I killed my father."

"He was never a father to you."

"I know, but what kind of person am I if I can kill my own father?"

I slide her head to the side and make her really look at me. "Sasha, he was going to kill you. You had to do it. Fuck, I would've done it, but you asked me not to." I snuggle her back into my chest. "I know it probably wasn't the greatest time to tell you I love you for the first time, but I had to tell you."

"You don't remember saying it before?" she asks.

"I said it before?"

"I knew you were too out of it to remember." Her body slumps a little in my arms.

"When did I say it before?"

"When they rescued you from Petrov. I came home, and you were lying in our bed. The first time you regained consciousness, you told me you loved me."

"I'm sorry, I don't remember." There's a long pause, and I add cautiously, "Did you say it back?"

This time, her whole body turns in the water. Placing her legs over mine, she takes my face in her hands.

"Of course I did. I love you."

I lean forward and kiss her lips, careful not to hurt her more. "I love you, Sasha, so much." I lean my forehead to hers. A smile lights up her beautiful face. "We're going to be all right."

Chapter 52
Gary

Three weeks have passed since the shit show that was Boris Petrov came into our lives. Ethan is alive in the world again. Lola has forgiven Sasha for pretending to kill him. Freddy has ramped up security around Amelia, and life is returning to whatever you can call normal in The Organization. Actually, everything has been kind of quiet since Petrov's death, until today when Freddy called me to his office.

"Listen, I have a job for you, but it's out of town. Do you think you'll be able to *not* tell Sasha where you're going? It's a very delicate situation."

"She knows what I do for a living. She'll understand."

"Good, then pack your shit and get to the airport. See Lori on your way out. She has your flight arrangements."

I go home and pack a quick bag, then leave Sasha a note and head for the private jet.

Chapter 53
Sasha

"**B**oss. Don't do this to me again. This is bullshit, and you know it!" I whine, throwing my hands in the air.

"You need to get away, Sasha. All this shit with Petrov has taken its toll on all of us. But it's affected you the most."

"But things have calmed down now. I feel fine." I stand a little straighter.

"That's the whole reason I want you to go now. Just get the hell out of here and relax."

"Relax! Relax! That's the same shit you and Lola said the last time you sent me away," I bellow.

"Did I hear my name?" Lola says as she walks into Ethan's office.

I point my finger at her. "You! You're the one doing this to me! Ethan was never this soft before you came along! Now he's all about *feelings* and getting enough rest and shit!"

"Oh, you told her already." She pauses. "Hey! Why is it always my fault?"

"Because you start shit," I snap.

Ethan doesn't say a word. He just lets the two of us get it out. After a few minutes of arguing, he intervenes.

"Sasha, one week. Now get out." He points at the door.

"Fuck!"

"This time, you're taking the private jet," Lola singsongs with a little wave.

When I get home, there's a note on the counter from Gary.

> Sasha,
> I have some business to take care of for Freddy.
> I'll be back next week. I'll text you when I
> get there.
> Love you,
> Gary

Digging my suitcase out of the closet, I throw some clothes inside and head out the door. An hour later, I'm sitting on the private jet all alone, remembering riding on the airplanes to the Caribbean. All the tap, tap, tapping sounds Gary made make me smile. I dig through my bag and pull out the book I started to read on my last vacation. Still fuming from the fact I'm being forced to leave again; I turn toward the window and bury my nose in the book.

I hear someone clear their throat, and I look up.

"Is this seat taken?" he asks with a smile. I lower my book and can't believe my eyes.

"No."

Gary stows his bag and sits down beside me. We're both grinning from ear to ear.

"Taking care of business, huh?" I ask with a smirk.

"Freddy said I had a job to do and not to tell you until I got there. How did he get you here?"

"Ethan used all the same old bullshit about me needing to get away and *rest.*" We both laugh. The flight attendant comes to take our drink order.

"Are you traveling for business or pleasure today?" We look at each other and smile.

I say, "We're on a forced vacation."

THE END

If you liked this book...

Please leave a review on Amazon or Goodreads.

Follow me on...

Tik Tok: @authormkmanson
Instagram: authormkmanson1
Facebook: authormkmanson

Also by M.K. Manson...

Until Then
Tell Me

Coming Soon in 2025...

Come Back – The story of Freddy and Amelia

Acknowledgments

Thank you to my husband for sharing this experience me. I couldn't do any of this without your strong arms and calming voice. Thank you for putting up with my late nights tap, tap, tapping on the computer, and for being there to support me when I left the job, I loved so much to do this. You are my everything.

Thank you to Frank for all of the hours you spent on cover designs, logos, and 3D printing those key chains you love so much. We still have some more of that mountain to climb. I hope you're ready.

Thank you to Katie for helping me talk through scenes. For helping me see a different perspective and making my brain work overtime. Thank you for becoming my assistant. We make a great team and who better to share this ride with than my daughter.

Thank you to Frank and Austin for fielding all the questions about weapons and motorcycles.

Thank you to Deanna, Taylor, Kathy, Elizabeth, and Allison for always giving me the little push I needed when the self-doubt snuck in. For not letting me quit on my dream. You are a strong group of women, and I am so very proud to call you my friends.

Thank you to Christy Jones for always being up for my crazy ideas. Thank you for your patience to let me work through them until they match my vision. Thank you for the photo shoots and all the time you spent creating promotional materials. Thank you for always showing up for me. I know you always have my back, and know I have yours. You are an amazing business woman and roll model. My boudoir sessions have become a defining moment in my life. They opened something inside of me that I didn't know was there. It gave me the confidence I needed to go for what I wanted and not look back.

Thank you to my Beta readers, Shae, Beth and Christy M. Thank you for telling it to me straight. You helped me so much more than you could ever know. You all asked for Sasha's book after you read book one. Well, we made it. I hope I did her justice.

Thank you to all the readers out there who took a chance on a new indie author. I hope you love The Organization as much as I have enjoyed writing it.

The fourth book is on its way, and it follows Freddy and Amelia's story. I think it will tug on your heartstrings a little more than the other books have, but all your questions will be answered as The Organization Series comes to an end.

About the Author

M.K. Manson began a journey of self-discovery on her 58th birthday. It started her on a path to become a dark romance author. She has been a lover of smut for years. Whether listening to audiobooks or poring over paperbacks, she reads all genres and loves a dark and twisty story. Give her a spicy why-choose romance any day of the week, and she's a happy girl.

With four dark mafia romance books self-publishing in 2025, she is on her way to her life's goal of being a best-selling author. For more information on M.K. and her books, follow her online on TikTok and Facebook at authormkmanson. And on Instagram @authormkmanson1